LOVE OF THE GAME

BY
ROGER HARDNOCK

CambridgeLane
publishing

Copyright © 2017 by Roger Hardnock

Inquiries should be addressed to:

contact@rogerhardnock.com

http://www.rogerhardnock.com/love-of-the-game

ISBN 978-0-9989371-0-6

Cover and interior design by Roger Hardnock
Author photo by Emilie Hardnock

Printed in the United States of America

For Emilie and Ryan

When I was a child
I caught a fleeting glimpse
Out of the corner of my eye
I turned to look but it was gone
I cannot put my finger on it now
The child is grown
The dream is gone

—*Pink Floyd*

1
THE OLD MAN ON THE PORCH

ehind closed eyes, Edgar Howard stood silent and alone at the threshold of his most sacred place, gazing with familiar wonder at the giant stars surrounding the deep indigo sky, illuminating the vast field of green before him with an aged vibrancy that had once bordered on surreal. In his mind's eye he had visited here countless times over the years, over the decades in fact, most often in that quiet space between the final out and calling it a night, when the radio voices spoke of things that no longer mattered. It was not about just resting his eyes, as he had so often claimed. Nor was it a pointless reprieve from his long, yet otherwise unextraordinary life. No, he stood there with purpose—for something honorable—a commitment to a promise he had made to someone very special— nearly a lifetime ago.

§

Edgar's eyes opened abruptly as something undefined pulled him back to where his body was. With his mind still groggy in that in-between space, he re-settled himself in the folding metal lawn chair, which creaked irritably under his shifting weight, and forced himself back into the present. His small antique radio sat silently at his side; the baseball game was over, as was the season—much too soon. From beyond the tattered screens of his small front porch, disconnected sounds of the night echoed up and down Hawthorne Street. Somewhere to his left a dog was crying to be let in, while something unknown rustled in the nearby bushes. He shivered as a cool October breeze blew across his face, and he wondered (quite seriously) if he could make it through another harsh Michigan winter, to spring and a brand new season of hope. He expected no answer, and none came. Instead, that indistinct rumble caught his attention once again, a vibration deep in the frequency of sound, felt more than heard. It approached as a stirring from somewhere high in the night sky.

Leaning forward to get a better view, of what exactly he didn't know, Edgar pressed his face to the screen and looked out. Partially obscured by the barren fall branches, a faint greenish glow pulsated from within a small cluster of low-hanging clouds. *Is that lightning?* But there was no storm predicted; Channel 4 and their *Doppler* radar said so, as did his radio. At most, some isolated drizzle, which was now tapping softly on the aluminum roof overhead. Before he could surmise anything else, a crackling formation of light erupted from the clouds and pierced down through the atmosphere. It appeared to strike somewhere out of sight, back behind the neighboring houses just down the street. *Yes, just lightning—but that was close.* The stalk remained in place though, holding its position longer than lightning typically would. Edgar rubbed his tired old eyes as a small, bulbous protrusion of more intense light pulsated within the stalk, descending through it rapidly. A piercing screech cut through the deeper rumble, and before he could get his hands to his ears, the spot of light had already fallen. A faint metallic sound, a pop, came from that same direction. *Just some kids fooling around back there, throwing rocks at garbage cans. Or, maybe it was a meteorite.* Edgar chuckled at the thought. *That's ridiculous; things like that just don't happen in small towns like Wayne, Michigan.*

Edgar paused as the strange lightning evaporated back up into the clouds. The rumbling faded as well, leaving only a subtle, high-pitched buzzing, which he couldn't place as inside or outside his head. He attempted to rub it away, while listening for movement from within the house. Satisfied that Wilma was undisturbed by the unexpected commotion, hopefully asleep by this late hour, he breathed a sigh of relief and settled back into his chair.

After a brief reprieve, the light returned—without the spectacle—and not from the clouds above. Inorganic chartreuse in color, it glowed out from between two houses down the street to Edgar's left. *That's probably from a car in the alley out back, or someone driving along the next street over.* Despite lacking a definitive source, the light slithered out into the surrounding lawns. Appearing to be more *in* the grass, glowing from the roots up, than a reflection over the wet surface, it bumped up against the hard edge of the street and faded. Seconds later it reappeared on the other side, spreading across more yards before dissolving into the denseness of the night. On Edgar's side of the street, the iridescence reached his own yard, appearing as if burrowing animals were carrying powerful flashlights. Smaller branches broke off and worked their way between the houses, with a segment moving toward his own back yard. *That's peculiar.* He looked again for the source, but saw nothing that could reasonably justify what his eyes were witnessing—or more likely—imagining.

Inside the porch, a separate climatic occurrence began to storm. A turbulence of warm air concentrated near the corner where Edgar sat. As if sensing his presence, it hovered over the surface of his body, tingling like a low-voltage electrical current, painless but disconcerting. It was a sensation that he could only describe as organic and alive—breathing the wind. The invisible examination moved around, pressing randomly at spots over his sweater and exposed skin with unseen fingers. The rational part of his mind pleaded with his body to rise and retreat indoors, but it refused to comply. With only his head willing to cooperate, Edgar glanced down. The comforter resting in his lap rippled in gentle waves. He wondered if the *something* that had inserted itself between his mind and his muscles was related to what was happening in his lap, and out beyond the porch, and presumed it was. He uttered, squeaky and soft, "Wilma?" But his voice had no chance of penetrating the wall of the house and reaching his intended recipient. *What could she do anyway? Nothing.*

And there's no sense in both of us getting all worked up. This is nothing but an anomaly in the weather, an unexpected surge of atmospheric phenomenon, an imbalance in air pressure—probably due to global warming. That's how the Channel 4 newsman would describe it.

As if realizing there was still more to Edgar, the invisible touch moved up toward his head. Through the tingling in his ears he heard the faint melody of piano music and the metallic creaking of a screen door. He glanced instinctively to his right. The old wooden front door, glowing in the dirty yellow of the porch light, was closed. *But that wasn't the sound of a wood door, and there hasn't been a metal screen there since before the porch was enclosed; that was over 40 years ago.* As his eyes began to drift, he caught a movement—a fleeting glimpse—a mirage—or perhaps to tired old Edgar, another hallucination. It shimmered briefly in the opposite corner and then faded through the outer porch door and disappeared. The sweet smell of gardenias followed, and Edgar found himself remembering his mother.

Certain that his imagination was getting the better of him, Edgar closed his eyes, hoping to get his head back on straight. It didn't work. On his inner screen there appeared rapid snapshots, firing one after another: baseball and his beloved *Detroit Tigers*, old Briggs Stadium, the scent of freshly cut summer grass, the buttery taste of popcorn. Salivating, his imaginary arm reached for a cold drink that wasn't there. *Why am I thinking these things?* His lovely Wilma emerged as the cute girl with the sparkling blue eyes—his bride, fifty years of marriage, hopes for a family that never was. Their small home on Hawthorne Street, once vibrant and colorful, now old and gray. Jimmy, his childhood friend. The small antique radio, still at his side after so many years—well cared for—the result of a promise he had made, and kept. Other images came and went. Most were quickly discarded. Some were held and examined with greater curiosity. A few returned, like they were being re-considered for some grand prize—the most defining moment in Edgar's uneventful life; the version that was never meant to be.

Perhaps unsatisfied, or just searching for more, it worked its way down, as if seeking something more profound—possibly a dire secret—buried deep. His father's long-ago voice spoke, clear as day, callous and harsh: *real men get jobs and work for a living.* Edgar cowered down, his heartbeat escalating in anticipation. *Foolish dreams don't pay the bills.* Those ancient and devastating beliefs slashed again at Edgar's heart, as they had done so long ago, scarring the soul of an impressionable young boy who (all alone) fought the best he could. But the cruel hand of fate had won, as it has a way of doing, and that boy became the essence of his father—instead of what could have been.

Edgar wondered within a pause, what the purpose was of this turbulent stroll down memory lane. Was it latent self- judgment, or timely self-reflection? Maybe it was just depression needing comfort—his *Tigers*, now done for the season. That always made him sad, but had never escalated in such a cryptic manner. He quivered at the thought of Saint Peter waiting for him at the Pearly Gates, poised to decide his eternal fate.

Without warning, the silhouette of a man appeared in the blackness behind Edgar's eyes, clouded in the pungent aroma of tobacco. Instead of tensing in fear, Edgar's muscles involuntarily relaxed. The sensation of a long-forgotten fondness welled up from deep within, carrying with it a distinct texture of love and understanding— like he had not felt in an eternity. Although he couldn't see the man's face, he felt his unmistakable essence, like time had never separated them, and he knew—it was his grandfather. Tears flowed down Edgar's physical cheeks, but he took no notice. Instead of moving forward in his mind and embracing the figure, he retracted in shame, of the disappointment he had surely caused—that other promise—the one he had failed to fulfill.

In an instant, the veil of inner darkness pulled away, and the presence of his grandfather disappeared as quickly as it had arrived—as *he* had done so many years before, leaving Edgar alone once again, and without answers. His mind silent, save for his own disjointed thoughts, he wondered if this was another moment of reprieve, a sensing of his despair and an ensuing act of compassion. Or perhaps his final judgment really was at hand. He took a deep breath as his eyes opened freely. Raising his arms, also back in his control, he rubbed his face and looked around. His world appeared normal again, but only for a moment.

Before he could rise and call it a night, and sleep all this nonsense off, a subtle movement in the yard caught his attention, causing him to flinch in his seat. *What now?* In the darkness was a figure, standing on his part of the sidewalk down near the street. As Edgar's hands clenched the armrests, he reasoned that no person with good intentions would be standing out there on such a damp, chilly night. Leaning forward, being cautious not to warn the intruder of his presence, he tried unsuccessfully to squint his old eyes into focus. His left hand felt for the rim of his eyeglasses, sitting on the old wooden crate next to his radio, and he slid them on. Yes, it was a figure—not a man though, but a boy. He was thin, wearing a light colored shirt and tattered shorts; he couldn't have been more than 12 or 13 years old. A baseball cap was pulled over his head, and covering one hand was a baseball glove. Next to him in the grass was a bicycle. There was also something peculiar about the boy, beyond Edgar's ability to rationalize. He rubbed his eyes under his glasses, but the sight did not improve. *I'm just imagining this; it can't be. It's dark and rainy; I'm just seeing a reflection, or an illusion caused by this unexpected weather.* He squinted once again, but the image refused his plea to become normal. The boy on the sidewalk was translucent; Edgar could see right through him. And so was the bike.

As the ghostly boy's gaze came to rest in Edgar's direction, he appeared startled himself, as if he had not anticipated someone sitting there (on his own porch) so late at night. He seemed to be looking less *at* Edgar and more *into* him, inquisitively searching for an explanation as to whom the stranger was and why he was there. Edgar himself sensed something familiar—a curious sense of déjà vu—an inexplicable feeling that the boy was not wrong to be standing there. The boy's face shifted into the expression of a question, and his lips moved, but Edgar heard no words. The boy rubbed his eyes as his attention shifted to his outstretched arms, and then up into the night sky. He appeared surprised at the rain. Looking down toward his feet, he moved one aside, then shook his arms and wiped each one across his shirt. He pulled something from one of the pockets in his shorts and put it into his mouth. He pulled another object from his shirt pocket and stared at it. The boy then knelt down next to the bike; his attention focused on something near the rear wheel. He fiddle around back there before grabbing his glove and ball and standing back up. He looked around, perhaps lost and unsure which direction was home, then turned and started across the street. After a few steps he broke into a run, heading toward the old alley.

"You left your bike," Edgar creaked, but to no avail.

Halfway down the block the boy faded into the darkness. When Edgar turned back toward his own yard, the bike was gone, too. In that instant, so briefly that his mind barely registered it, he felt the faintest hint of joy—for that strange boy.

The joy quickly faded to apprehension, of what might still be to come. Edgar gazed around the inside of the porch, and then out beyond the screens. There was no movement anywhere; the night had calmed; the only sounds were the wind through the trees and that faint buzzing. Even the rain had stopped, clearing the sky all the way to the stars. He took the opportunity to try and make sense of what had happened. Was any of it real, or just the delusions of an old man? *No, the lightning was just lightning; the weather channel is not always right, you know. That green light in the yard, well, that was caused by headlights out of my line of sight, shining across the grass. The boy was just some kid from the neighborhood. He was familiar because I've seen him before; I just don't remember. Of course he was there, so was his bike; don't be ridiculous, Edgar. One of his friends just came and got the bike when I was looking the other way—simple as that.* Edgar allowed his mind to unravel further. *All those memories rushing through my head though—what could those possibly mean? Did they have anything to do with the boy in the yard, or was that just a coincidence?* He folded the comforter in his lap, took off his glasses and sat them next to the radio. *This is all from just too much caffeine;*

that extra cup of coffee I had earlier, during the game. Wilma warned me about having another cup so late at night, but it was cold and I didn't listen. That's it; I fell asleep and the caffeine got inside my head.

Not completely convinced, but exhausted from the ordeal, Edgar reluctantly allowed his eyes to close for a moment of rest before calling it a night. As he did, he couldn't help but wonder what might still be to come.

2
BEST FRIENDS

June 12th in the year of 1948 was a typical spring day in suburban Detroit. By late morning, the temperature had risen to a comfortable 73 degrees. Hawthorne Street was in full bloom, especially at the Howard's house, where annuals and perennials were blossoming in an explosion of visual and aromatic delight. Twelve-year old Edgar Howard stood on the front lawn, awaiting the arrival of the family's first real guests in ages. His hands picked at his dirt stained pants while his eyes focused at his feet, which were twisting and digging into the grass. Sitting on the porch bench, with a beer in one hand and a folded up newspaper in the other, was his father. Their rusty old Model A sat motionless in the driveway up near the gate. Standing by Edgar's side, fiddling with the small bouquet of flowers she had just picked, and chattering on about how long it had been since she'd last seen her parents, was Edgar's mother. "You were young at the time," she said, "so you probably don't remember them."

Edgar learned that his grandparents lived in North Carolina. His grandmother spent the summer months in her own garden, and his grandfather was retired from some place called the *American Tobacco Company*. For over 50 years, he had worked selling cigarettes and doing other things. He was a big *Detroit Tigers* fan, so Edgar was warned that there would be plenty of baseball talk. As an unfamiliar looking car approached from the right, Edgar wondered just how boring the next three weeks of his precious summer vacation were going to be.

§

Thick whitewall tires crackled over the gravel as the dusty blue car pulled slowly into the driveway. Across the front of the hood was the word: *PLYMOUTH*. To Edgar, the car looked new, except for the dirt and the remains of insects scattered across the front end. He watched his reflection in one of the chrome hubcaps as the car rolled to a stop; a faint cloud of dust hovered low as the car's engine went silent. Then, both doors swung open dramatically, as if the grandparents had pre-rehearsed their grand entrance. Howling with delight, even before their feet touched the ground, Jacob and Eloise Rick popped out and converged upon their daughter and grandson. Edgar stood frozen as his grandmother threw her arms around him and kissed him multiple times across the face. She smelled like a whole gardens worth of flowers, sprinkled with a dusting from the ashtray. Trapped within her ample bosom, he blushed uncomfortably.

Separating herself from Edgar, his grandmother cried out, "Oh my, I haven't seen you since you were just a little boy! Look how you've grown!"

After Edgar was released, and his grandmother had moved over to her next victim, his grandfather appeared before him. He was a big, burly man with thick white hair, a close-cut beard and a large welcoming smile. He lunged forward and engulfed Edgar in his massive arms. Edgar held his hands at his sides, noticing the smell of tobacco, but without the flowers. After a powerful hug, his grandfather released his hold and stepped back. In a booming voice he said, "Look how tall you are, Edgar. I bet you're a pitcher, right? Pitchers are always tall like you."

Edgar had never thought about being a pitcher, or even a baseball player for that matter, but he smiled anyway. "I'm not really good at baseball or pitching," he said, before adding hesitantly,

"Grandpa."

His grandfather chuckled, coughed and patted Edgar on the shoulders. "You will be when I'm done with you."

§

The small house on Hawthorne Street vibrated with a rare combination of happiness and festivity. Edgar's mother had few visitors, mostly the ladies from the neighborhood who came by to look at her flowers, have a quick chat about the weather or how the vegetables were doing in the garden. Every so often, his father's chums from work would come over and play cards in the basement, drink beer and smoke cigars. Edgar's job was to fetch drinks and food from the icebox. They asked him to play once, but then laughed at him when he didn't know what cards to put down. After that, he decided it was best to stay away from the house when strange cars were parked in the driveway.

As directed, Edgar retrieved the old metal lawn furniture from the back yard. He placed the four chairs and small table in the grass near the flower bed that lined the front of the house. After the grandparents' things were set up in the sewing room, temporarily converted into a guest room, everyone moved back out front to relax and catch up. His mother brought out iced tea and a tray of sandwiches. She placed them on the table as his grandmother handed bottles of beer to the men. During lunch, the ladies talked of gardening and flowers while Edgar ate quietly by himself on the corner of the porch.

"You should really put a screen around this porch, Earl," Edgar's grandfather said to his father. "Maybe with one of those fancy metal roofs. It would be nice protection, when it's hot or raining out."

Edgar's father responded in moderate agreement, but added that the cost for such an addition would be outrageous. And who had the money for that?

After lunch, the women cleared the dishes as Edgar's father left for an afternoon shift at the factory. His mother switched on the family radio that sat just inside the open front window. She increased the volume until baseball talk could be heard out front.

§

Edgar sat restlessly on the porch, considering his next move. It was the beginning of summer vacation and he had yet to acclimate to so much free time. With his grandparents visiting, he didn't know if it would be okay to go over to his best friend Jimmy Schmidt's house and play. He was caught between asking, and getting in trouble for asking, or just going and not asking, and getting in trouble for that. As he considered his options, a shadow passed over him. He looked up to see his grandfather blocking the sun.

"I just love the *Tigers*," he said as the pre-game broadcast radiated out through the screens. "I don't get to hear them much down south, only when they're playing the Senators. Sometimes I can find an article in one of the papers, and of course I always check the box scores, but there's nothing like listening to a live game. Baseball is the greatest game ever invented, don't you agree?"

Edgar didn't have much of an opinion on which game was the greatest ever. He occasionally listened to parts of the *Tigers* games, but it was a bit difficult to follow what was going on. He played football once, in the snow during the previous winter, with some of the kids in the neighborhood. But they played rough and kept knocking him down, and it hurt. He liked to toss basketballs in the gym at school, but he wasn't very good at that either. Running through the other sports in his mind he decided that, at least for the moment, baseball could be his favorite. "Yeah, Grandpa, I like baseball."

His grandfather sat down next to him on the porch and continued. "That man talking on the radio is Harry Heilmann. I remember when he played for the *Tigers* back in the teens and through the twenties. Played for them for 17 years—now he's an announcer. He was one of the best to ever wear the old English D. Did you know that?"

"No, Grandpa, I didn't know that."

"Did you also know that I got my love of baseball from my father—your great grandfather? You never met him. Way back before I was born, he lived in New York State, just outside of Lansingburgh. Worked for the railroads for a while, then decided to form a baseball team. That must have been around 1860 or so, if I recall correctly. They were called the *Union of Lansingburgh*."

"That's a strange name," Edgar said.

"Their nickname was the *Troy Haymakers*," his grandfather added, "and then later they were called the *Trojans*. They ran out of money in the early 1870's, so my father had to find work again. He decided to move to Detroit with my mother, and went back to work on the railroads. He never lost his love of baseball though. They bought a house just a few blocks from old Bennett Park and started a family. Bennett Park was were the *Tigers* played before Briggs Stadium was built. I was born in 1880 and my sisters came a few years later. They had no interest in baseball, so it was just me and my father going to games together. What a great time we had."

Edgar thought about his own father; they had never gone to a baseball game together. His father had never taken him anywhere special, except to the carnival that one time when he was five. Listening to his grandfather talk about his own father that way made him feel angry, or sad, or something he had no words to describe.

"We went to games all the time," his grandfather continued, "and I got to know many of the players. I even played some baseball myself. I started young, playing with my friends in the street, at the park or anywhere we could find a game. By the time I was in high school, all I could think about was playing baseball. When I turned 18, I had saved up enough money to move away, so off I went, looking for a league to play in. I spent some time in Grand Rapids, and from there I moved to Dayton and then to Toledo. I was getting pretty good, too, maybe even good enough to make it to the big leagues. I started thinking about moving south, so I could play ball year 'round, convinced that that was all I needed to make it. Then one day, just before I was about to move, we were playing a game against Youngstown. I was coming home to score, running as hard as I could. The catcher was this big guy, and he was blocking the plate. My foot got twisted up with his and I went down hard. Tore up my ankle and knee real bad. And that was the end of my baseball career. It took me almost two years before I could walk right, and I never could run the same."

"What did you do after that, Grandpa?"

"I moved back to Detroit to be near my folks. My sisters were married by then, and with my father being sick and all, I stayed around and helped my mother take care of him until he passed. I worked odd jobs for several years, and even sold peanuts at the ballpark on game days. I knew that even if I couldn't play, I wanted to be close to the game. That's when I met a man who offered me a real job. That was around 1908. His name was J. B. Duke, but he liked to be called Buck. He was a very rich man, traveling through Detroit on business, and decided to stop and see a ball game. He stood under a nearby lamppost and watched me. 'You're a natural salesman,' he finally said. 'How would you like a job selling cigarettes?' I listened as he told me about the job. It sounded great, so I accepted his offer right there on the spot. I moved down to North Carolina, and that's where I met your grandmother."

Edgar's grandfather was about to tell the story of his greatest job ever when the radio announcer proclaimed that it was time to play ball. As the play-by-play began, the conversation diminished. Edgar relaxed in the warm sun and tried his best to follow along. He glanced over at his grandfather and noticed that his eyes were closed. Worried that he was missing the game, Edgar whispered, "Grandpa, are you asleep?"

A few seconds later, his grandfather opened his eyes and smiled. "Hey, pal. You know what I like to do while I'm listening to a game? I like to close my eyes and feel myself there at the ballpark. I imagine it so hard that I can actually see the game in my head, playing like a movie on the inside of my eyes."

Edgar thought about that, but had nothing good to add. It was like being in school when his teacher asked the class a question, and there was nothing but silence. In those moments he wanted so badly to have the right answer, so everyone would look at him and wonder how he could be so smart. In the real world though, the one with his eyes open, he was just another kid sitting there with a dumb look on his face.

Unaware of Edgar's internal dialog, his grandfather said, "Come on, pal, you try it. Just close your eyes lightly and listen to the radio. Relax and let your mind focus in on what you hear. Imagine you are there. It's like dreaming into a far away place. At first you might not see much, or anything at all, but if you keep at it, you will."

Edgar did as he was directed, feeling a bit silly at first, sitting there on the porch with his eyes closed in the middle of the afternoon. If anyone walked by, they might think he was sleeping. If Stupid Sally Morgan rode by on her bike and saw him doing that, she would blab about it forever. As his grandfather talked in his gentle, calming voice, describing the game, what the ballpark looked like and what the players were doing, Edgar could feel himself sinking into it. He could not actually *see* anything yet, but it felt good.

"Someone once told me, Edgar," his grandfather said, "that magic lives behind closed eyes."

Edgar smiled and waited for it to happen.

§

Early the next day, Edgar wandered out onto the front porch. The lawn furniture from the day before was put away and his father's car was gone, which meant he was at work. In the driveway, the previously bug-covered Plymouth had been transformed into a shiny blue sedan with sparkling chrome and crystal clear glass. A large metal bucket sat in the grass, with several rags draped over the side. A green garden hose twisted like a snake back toward the side of the house. Leaning over the front bumper and polishing the hood with a clean white rag was his grandfather. When the screen door closed with a thump, he looked up and saw Edgar.

"Hey, pal, you missed all the fun."

"What fun, Grandpa?" Edgar asked, rubbing his morning eyes.

"Cleaning the car," his grandfather replied. "Take good care of your things, and they will take good care of you."

Edgar jumped off the porch and moved in for a closer look. "That sure is a nice car."

"Thanks, pal. Got less than 10,000 miles on her, even after driving all the way up from North Carolina. Of course, I haven't driven much these last few years, being retired and all. But I always keep her in the garage and clean her once a week, even in the winters, which ain't so bad down south."

Edgar wondered why he referred to the car as a *she*, but didn't want to feel stupid for asking a dumb question. His father called their car an old piece of crap, and that he understood perfectly.

Together they put the hose and bucket away, then returned to the front porch.

"What a beautiful day," his grandfather said, looking toward the sky. "Let's say we go for a walk, before it gets too hot out."

"Sure," Edgar replied hesitantly. He had never *gone for a walk* before. That was something mothers with baby carriages did, and old people. It seemed boring and senseless to just walk around for no good reason. He walked to the bus stop for school because he had to, and to Jimmy's house, but that was just three houses down. If he wanted to go anywhere else in the neighborhood, he would ride his bike.

Across the street and several houses down on the left, a narrow alley connected Hawthorne Street to Arlington Street the next block over. Rusty chain link fences and overgrown weeds separated the path from the houses on either side. The two exited the alley where, just across the street, the local park spread out before them. Straight ahead, parts of the grass were worn down to bare dirt, indicating the shape and look of a makeshift baseball diamond. Several teenage boys were playing catch in the outfield area while two others were swinging bats and talking over a piece of worn plywood, roughly cut into the shape of a home plate. From the left, more boys with bats and gloves were approaching. And much to Edgar's relief, his grandfather guided their walk to the right, away from the older boys and toward the other side of the park.

"This is a nice park," his grandfather said.

Edgar responded in agreement as he kept a cautious eye on the boys getting ready for their game.

They continued past a patch of large oak trees and a children's playground area. Several little kids were playing in the sand while their mothers gossiped on one of the nearby benches. They settled themselves at an open picnic table in the shade and looked back toward the baseball field. Relaxed in the safety of distance, Edgar watched as his grandfather pulled a small brown paper bag from his pocket and laid it on the table. Unshelled peanuts spilled out.

"Can't watch baseball without peanuts; it's un-American!" his grandfather proclaimed in his thundering voice, followed by a smile and then a burst of coughing.

Edgar looked around to see if anyone had heard. With nobody looking, he picked up one of the nuts. "How do you get the peanut out?"

"Never had peanuts before?" his grandfather asked.

Not sure whether he should be embarrassed or not, Edgar replied, "Not like these—just the kind in the *Planters* jar."

His grandfather waved his hands wildly and shook his head in exaggerated disbelief. "No, son, that's not how you eat peanuts!"

Edgar held his breath, afraid that he had said something offensive. He then realized from his grandfather's grin that he was being teased.

"Like this." His grandfather placed a nut on the table and thumped it with the palm of his hand. Pieces of peanut debris flew out the sides. He raised his hand to survey the damage, picked out the nuts and wiped away the shell residue. "It's as easy as that," he said. "Be careful you don't hit it too hard though. You don't want to hurt your hand for a peanut; a walnut maybe, but never for a peanut."

Edgar chuckled, but didn't get the joke. He placed a peanut on the table and hit it softly with the base of his clenched fist. He could feel the shell give under his hand, but it remained intact. He expected to be reprimanded, but his grandfather just watched, and then said, "That's okay, pal. It takes a few tries to get it right. Try again."

The second attempt did the trick. The shell cracked enough to gain access to the contents. Edgar's hand hurt a little, but he kept that to himself.

They de-shelled peanuts and watched as teams of six players each formed across the park. Even before the first pitch, the boys began shouting insults and vulgarities back and forth. Although Edgar had heard every word in the book, he was surprised (and impressed) at the creative use of the vernacular—and made a point to remember some of his favorite phrases—to try out later on Jimmy. A bit embarrassed in that moment though, he glanced over at his grandfather, wondering what he was thinking.

Seemingly oblivious to it all, his grandfather began speaking in the voice of a make-believe radio announcer getting ready to call the game. "Chubby McGee coming to the plate, stretching his pants at the seams and waiting on the first pitch from Bird Beak Williams."

Edgar was again caught off-guard by his grandfather's antics. He was not used to adults having such a sense of humor. After laughing themselves out, the play-by-play evolved into a session on the strategies of the game. From Edgar's observation, the game was simple; some kid on the mound threw the ball toward somebody holding a bat, who then tried to hit it as far as he could. If he hit the ball, he got to run the bases and mow down anyone in his way—or not—depending on how big the other kid was. Throw in some insults regarding family members, especially mothers and sisters, and an occasional punch here and there, and you've got a baseball game. Edgar never realized that baseball could be so dangerous, but he was having fun watching—from afar.

At the end of the third inning, his grandfather changed subjects without warning. "Hey, pal, why don't you go over and ask them if you can play?"

A chill ran from Edgar's neck, down his spine and nearly to

his toes. His heart thundered in his chest. Never, not even in the deepest depths of his imagination, could he have conceived of such a preposterous idea. His body trembled faintly as his mind sought out a reply that wouldn't make him sound like a scaredy-cat. After several terrifying seconds, the excuse he needed came to him—like a gift from God Himself—the perfect and indisputable answer. He replied in a voice that was only barely crackling, "Oh, I don't have a glove, Grandpa."

"Oh?" his grandfather asked. "I think there's one in the garage; I saw it in there this morning when I was looking for a screwdriver to tighten one of the mirrors on the Plymouth."

A new layer of fear began to settle over Edgar. It was not an immediate threat, but more of a longer-term dread, a sense that he may have to continue dodging this bullet for the next few weeks. He wondered if his grandfather was going to be one of those adults who were always trying to get kids to do things they didn't want to do. He thought of Jimmy, sitting alone on his porch, happily reading his comic books. Jimmy was afraid of everything, and would never propose something as ridiculous as walking up to a bunch of older kids and asking if he could play baseball with them. If he didn't get beat up just for opening his mouth, he would surely be picked on and teased as the world's worst ball player.

The question lingered in the air like one of Jimmy's toxic farts. Edgar needed another excuse, and fast. Fortunately, the divine presence returned a second time, whispering in his ear and demanding that the subject be dropped for good. "Oh, that's my dad's old glove," he said. "It's too big for me, and he doesn't like me using his things. Plus, it fits on the wrong hand." Perfect! Not because it was an excuse or a lie, but because it was the honest to God's truth.

As his grandfather reached an arm around him, Edgar instinctively tensed.

"Well then," his grandfather said, "today we just watch."

Edgar silently thanked God, or whomever it was that had been listening.

As the game continued along, Edgar asked questions as his

grandfather drew out a baseball diamond in the dirt and explained the intricacies of the game with an (adult) enthusiasm that was as foreign to Edgar as the stars that filled the night sky. He didn't understand all of it, but was drawn in by his grandfather's contagious passion.

"You sure know a lot about baseball, Grandpa."

"Well, I've been around the game my whole life so, yes, I guess I know just about everything there is to know. Boy, I could tell you some stories. But right now I think we need something cold to drink. What do you say? Is there a market nearby?"

"Yeah, the next block over," Edgar replied, "on the other side of the baseball field."

They headed slowly in that direction, and with Edgar's subtle nudging, maintained a safe distance from the field. He hoped that the boys wouldn't tease him with an adult around. Regardless, he wanted to get past them as quickly as possible. As they reached the far sidewalk without incident, Edgar noticed that his grandfather was sweating and coughing more than usual. Edgar slowed their pace, which did not go unnoticed. "I'm getting old, Edgar. Us older folks need to rest a lot." He smiled, pulled a handkerchief from his pocket and wiped the sweat from his face. After a few more pauses along the way, they arrived at Jake's Market.

Inside the front door was a green cooler with *7-UP* printed on the door. On top, a refrigerator unit hummed softly. "What do you say about a couple of *7-UPs*?" his grandfather asked. "That's my favorite."

"Sure," Edgar replied.

The bottles were placed next to the register. Edgar looked for the opener while his grandfather reached into one of the boxes on the counter and pulled out at least a dozen packs of baseball cards. "We'll take these, too," he said, handing half of the packs to Edgar.

They found a rickety wooden bench sitting in the weeded half-lot next door and settled there. After a long gulp of pop, Edgar sat his bottle down and glanced at the unopened cards in his lap.

"I've been buying baseball cards most of my life," his grandfather said. "Actually, anything at all having to do with baseball, I collect. My father got me started on it. He loved clipping articles and saving just about everything he could get his hands on: tickets, programs, cards and even baseballs. He was actually one of the very first people to make baseball cards. Did I tell you that?" Without waiting for a response, he continued. "He had them done for his own team back in New York, called the *Union of Lansingburgh*. I told you about them, right? Sometimes I can't remember so well. Before he passed away, my father gave all of his things to me, and I've been adding to it ever since. I guess it's just something in my blood—in our blood. I even have a journal that I use to keep track of everything: where it came from, who gave it to me, the date, everything. Sounds crazy, huh?"

Edgar smiled. He had never heard of such a thing. He had a few really old cards that Jimmy had given him, but he'd never paid much attention to them. They just clipped them to their bikes and let them snap in the wheel spokes, pretending they were riding motorcycles instead.

"Yup, that's about all I do now that I'm retired, except for a little bit of woodworking." His grandfather paused with an introspective smile on his face. "I spend a lot of time in the basement making boxes—lots of little boxes." Looking at his own unopened cards, he continued. "They just started printing baseball cards again. Did you know that?"

Edgar shook his head.

"Because of the war, the big companies stopped making them, like most everything else. That was back in '41. Seven years it's been. So, let's see, counting these cards here, I've now got—" He thought for a moment, counting in his head while doing invisible addition with his fingers in the air. "9,442 baseball cards, and counting."

"Wow," Edgar replied, trying to imagine such an inconceivable number of cards. "I've only got these, and a few more old ones at home."

"Well, that's a start," his grandfather said. "You know, everything starts at one."

Edgar thought about that for a moment, chuckled and then opened his first pack of cards.

"Hey, Grandpa, look! I've got a Tiger!"

"That's Hal Newhouser. That's a good card, Edgar. It looks like that kid might have another great year. He won the MVP here two years in a row—44 and 45."

"What's an MVP?" Edgar asked.

"Most Valuable Player. That means he was the best player in baseball."

"Oh, did he hit a lot of home runs?"

"Well, no, he's a pitcher you see. They don't play every game, so they don't hit a lot of home runs. And pitchers are not always the best hitters. Because they don't play every day, they don't get as much practice."

"Oh," Edgar said again, trying to understand. "So how could he be the best player if he doesn't hit very good or hit a lot of home runs?"

"Well, that's an excellent question, pal."

Edgar smiled. Nobody had ever said he asked an excellent question before.

His grandfather continued. "Batting is not always the most important part of the game; there's more to winning and losing than hitting the ball. Actually, the pitcher can be the most important player on the field because it's his job to keep the other team from hitting the ball and scoring runs. The pitcher helps the team win by not allowing them to lose. If he can do that, then he can be the most valuable player. And pitching is what Hal Newhouser does very well."

"Oh, I see." Edgar got it, but he didn't. He would think about it later, and maybe then it would make more sense. He drank his pop and watched as his grandfather began the strangest ritual of opening baseball cards. With the pile of unopened packs sitting neatly to his side, he gently lifted the top pack and laid it on his lap, upside down, with the folded side facing up. Like a doctor preparing for a dangerous surgery, he delicately peeled back the flaps of the wrapper, one side at a time, until the covering was completely opened out flat and the cards piled neatly in the center. After wiping his hands on his pant legs, he lifted the small pile of cards out by the edges and, with the utmost care, placed them face up in his open hand.

Noticing that he was being examined, his grandfather looked over at Edgar, smiled and said, "Take good care of your things, and they will take good care of you." He chuckled, which turned into a new fit of coughing. He sat the cards down carefully, took a few sips of pop, and then continued as if nothing had happened. "If you handle your things with care, they will last a long time," he said. "Not only that, they will look their best and you will be proud to own them. My cards make me happy, so I take good care of them. My father taught me that, and now I'm teaching you. See, you want to hold your cards gently by the edges, like this. Also, you never want to shuffle or bend baseball cards; that will damage them and they won't look as nice. Now, nobody else probably cares about such things, but I do."

"Yeah, I like that, too," Edgar replied. Until that moment he had no real thought on the subject, but since his grandfather liked it that way, he did as well. "Take good care of your things, and they will take good care of you," Edgar repeated. "What does that mean, Grandpa, that they will take good care of you?"

"Well, pal, it's a bit different for everything. Let me use my car as an example. I keep it clean so it looks nice, and that makes me happy. I use clean rags and lots of water when I'm washing it, so I don't scratch the paint. I change the oil regularly, so that the engine lasts a long time and the car doesn't break down on me. That's what I mean by take good care of your things, and they will take good care of you. And I suppose that also means taking care of the one's we love, which is really the best thing of all. Don't you think? Does that make sense?"

"Yeah," Edgar replied. "But how can *baseball cards* take good care of you?"

"Well, I'll tell you what my father told me when I asked a question like that. He said, Jacob, we don't always know how things will play out, but if we stick to what we believe in, everything will be taken care of—maybe in ways we can't even imagine. How does that sound?"

Edgar thought about it. It was still kind of confusing, but he didn't want his grandfather to think he was dumb, so he decided it was best to just believe. "Yeah, Grandpa, that sounds good."

"Good. Did you know, Edgar, that I have my very own baseball cards?"

"Really! With your picture on it?"

"Well, no, not exactly like that," his grandfather replied. "I mean that I had a job once where I was responsible for having baseball cards *made*. The cards were for real baseball players, not me. My job was to get them produced; it was the greatest job ever."

Edgar had never heard of such a job. He only knew of people who worked hard in the factories, like his father, making important things that people needed. And then there were the lazy pencil pushers who worked in offices and got paid too much for doing a lot of nothing but sitting around on their cans all day.

"Yes, sir," his grandfather continued. "I did them long ago, for the company I worked for before I retired. It was called the *American Tobacco Company*. Did I tell you about that?"

"Yeah, but I thought they sold cigarettes."

"Yes, we made and sold cigarettes."

"And they made baseball cards, too?" Edgar asked, confused again.

"Another good question," his grandfather said. "I'll get to that part of the story shortly. First, I learned about making baseball cards from my father. He had cards made for his baseball team back in New York. I told you about them, right?"

"Yeah," Edgar replied. "The union of something."

"The *Union of Lansingburgh*," his grandfather said.

Edgar listened intently, now curious as to how cigarettes and baseball cards were going to come together and become the greatest job ever.

"He thought the cards would help to promote the team, to get some sponsors and money to buy uniforms and equipment, and to allow them to travel around to different towns throughout the league. So the cards helped them that way. I still have those cards, too. My father gave them to me when I was just a young boy, even younger than you are now. I put them in a special tin box so they would be protected. I guess I started taking good care of my things way back then. Would you believe those cards are now almost ninety years old?"

"Wow, that's old, Grandpa," Edgar replied.

"Sure is. So shortly after I moved down to North Carolina to take that job, I got the idea of putting baseball cards in cigarette packages. I was at a local ballpark one afternoon, smoking a cigarette and enjoying the game. I had my ticket, and you know me, I keep everything. It was raining a bit and, without thinking, I slid it into my cigarette pack. It was just the right size, you see, and that got me to thinking. I figured that if we could print up some cards, put them into our cigarette packs and then sell them at the games, well, people would really like that. Fans would buy our cigarettes and get a card of their favorite player. My boss didn't seem to like the idea too much at first; he thought it crazy, I suppose. Then, a few weeks later, he came up to me and said, 'Let's try putting those cards in our cigarette packs; I bet we could sell more product that way.' He said it just like it was his own idea, which made me a bit mad. But I got a new job out of it, and a promotion as well, so I kept my mouth shut. For a few years then, that's what I did for the company; I made baseball cards."

"What's a promotion, Grandpa?" Edgar asked.

"It's when you get a better job and more money. Not a lot of money, but more."

"Oh."

"Once I started, my job was to go around and visit each team and sign up as many players as I could, both in the big leagues and the minors; we wanted everyone. We needed to get their permission, and have them sign a form our lawyers wrote up. Once they signed up, we took their picture. I had a photographer who traveled with me. The photographer would set up space wherever he could, with this white backdrop and fancy lights, and then snap the pictures. We sent the negatives back to the office, to the art department, so they could prepare the illustrations and the color lithograph plates. Yeah, that was fun work, but it didn't last long. Ended in 1911, if I recall. We did over 500 different cards in total, more if you count the ones we never actually put in the packs. Some were just mistakes, or already printed by the time we were told not to use them. After the sheets were trimmed down to size, we just threw the rejects away. Of course, I kept a few for myself, even those we didn't use. Nobody cared, but it made my collection a little more special. When you come out to visit, I'll show you."

"Okay," Edgar replied excitedly, mostly at the thought of a trip to somewhere outside of Michigan.

"Oh, then there was this Wagner fellah," his grandfather said. "He was a big-shot player that got me into some hot water."

"What did he do, Grandpa?"

"Well, he decided he didn't want his cards in the cigarettes after all, after he told me to my face that we could print them. He even signed the form. He had some lawyer put up a stink, and they demanded that all the cards be pulled and destroyed."

"Why did he change his mind?"

"Said he didn't agree with cigarettes and never wanted his picture going out in our product. Well, he let us take his picture. Why would he do that if he didn't want us to use it?"

Edgar shrugged.

"We were right in the middle of production when all this happened, and some got through before we could stop them. The boss was mad at me. I thought I was going to lose my job, but it all worked out. A couple of years later, I ran into that guy again. Baseball cards were very popular by that time, and all the players loved them; they loved looking at themselves, I suppose. He asked me if I had any of his cards left; said he wanted one. He talked to me like we were best pals; the nerve of that guy. After all the trouble he caused me, and he acted like it never happened. I told him no, but of course I did. If I had a hundred of them, I wouldn't have given him one. But that will be our little secret, okay?

"Okay, Grandpa. I won't tell anyone." Edgar didn't know who he would tell anyway, but he liked having a secret to keep.

"By the teens," his grandfather continued, "everyone was making cards: Cracker Jacks, sports magazines, department stores, bakeries. Baseball cards were everywhere. I traveled a lot in those days, so I guess I got to see and buy more of them than most folks. Candy companies made them; I bought theirs, too. I was even heavier back then," he said, patting at his belly. "I guess I liked the treats as much as I liked the cards. It was all great fun; what a job I had. One of these days you'll come out to visit your grandma and me in North Carolina, and I'll show you all my baseball treasures. You've never seen so much baseball stuff."

"9,442 and counting," Edgar added with a chuckle.

"That's right, pal." He put his arm around Edgar's shoulders and pulled him in tight. Edgar didn't flinch.

§

By the time they returned home, it was past one o'clock and they were both tired and hungry. After lunch was served, grandfather and grandson retreated to the living room. The windows were open and a small rickety fan produced a surprisingly comfortable breeze. They each fell into a chair as the radio station was changed from music to the *Tigers* pre-game broadcast. As Edgar reached into his shirt pocket and pulled out his cards, the announcer listed the starting lineups for each team. With great care, he sorted through the stack until he found the card he wanted—Hal Newhouser. The card showed the pitcher holding out a baseball in front of a bright yellow background. Along the bottom was a red band with the name *HAL NEWHOUSER* printed in bold, knockout type. Edgar turned it over and read through the statistics on the back. He didn't know what it all meant, and the snoring coming from the next chair over told him that he would have to wait until later to ask. After kicking off his shoes, Edgar laid back, closed his eyes and listened as the game got underway. By the second inning, they were both sleeping.

3
HERE WE GO AGAIN

Wilma Howard sat in her chair in the corner of the living room. Skeins of navy blue, orange and white yarn sat atop the nearby basket, with a strand of blue passing through her knitting needles and into the partial scarf draped across her lap. In less than three months it would become one of Edgar's Christmas presents. From the porch beyond, she could hear the faint creaking of Edgar in his chair, and a dog barking somewhere down the street. She yawned and glanced toward the clock on the mantle. By this late hour, his game, and the baseball season for that matter, were most likely over.

Done for the night, Wilma put the scarf and yarn away. In the small wooden box that Edgar had given her years before, she placed her needles. She turned off the floor lamp, leaving the room in a dim monotone, highlighted only by the night-light glowing out from the kitchen. As her mind relaxed, she thought of Edgar, who had been grumbling for days now about the untimely end of the *Tigers* baseball season. She enjoyed baseball, too, but never as much he did, and not in the same way. She rooted for the *Tigers*, but mostly for her own reasons. What she had learned, over the past 50 years of living with Edgar, was that winter life was much better for *her* after his team had a good year. Even if they didn't win the World Series, but had a winning season, the ensuing winter would be mostly pleasant. Edgar would talk about how they just missed it, and if they improved only a little bit, a new player here or some better pitching there, the next year could be the one. But after a bad season, he would mope around the house under a cloud of unmanageable dreariness that often lasted until spring training.

Since Edgar's retirement, she had tried everything to keep him happy and occupied through the long off-seasons. She bought him puzzles, games and model kits. He would be content for a while, but would lose interest and become restless again. Whenever she tried to buy him baseball books or magazines, he would have her return them, reminding her that he could read at the library—for free. One year she suggested that he look for a part time job, just to keep occupied and have some new people to talk to. That idea was not well received by a man who had spent 40 years in a tiny office managing the bus schedules for the local school district. She had even tried to get him more involved in the church, but that didn't work either; Edgar's spirituality was somewhere else.

Wilma knew in her heart that the source of Edgar's restlessness went beyond merely waiting for the next season to begin. It was something buried deep, hidden and well protected behind his resting eyes; a remnant of his childhood perhaps. He never acknowledged it, but every so often it would seep to the surface and expose itself, often carrying with it a sensation of guilt, as if he felt somehow responsible for the fate of his *Detroit Tigers*. He once said, "I should have been there," after a particularly rough season. She thought it was an odd thing to say, and that it probably meant being at the ballpark, as in rooting the team on. But Edgar had always refused to go to a live baseball game; he claimed to be content just listening to his radio on the porch. She asked him to explain what it meant, but he just pulled away, almost embarrassed or ashamed, and replied, "Oh, nothing, hon. Nothing at all."

§

From around the edges of the curtains covering the front windows, a faint glow of light flashed out onto the walls. Since the Six O'clock

News had said nothing about a storm, just the possibility of some light rain, Wilma presumed it was the headlights of a car stopped somewhere out on the street. She got up, wrapped her shawl tightly around her shoulders and moved toward the front door. She placed one hand on the door and the other on the doorknob. As her hands touched the unexpectedly warm surfaces, there was an immediate sensation that she could not quite define. Magnetic in quality, it tingled across her skin. In her mind, she became caught between two thoughts, or places, at once. Edgar was calling her faintly from out on the porch, while a more distant and unfamiliar voice was calling Edgar—from back near the kitchen. There was a hint of piano music and the stomping of feet over a wooden floor. She felt something move past her—through her. It was not a physical move-ment, but rather an energy of some kind. That was followed by the metallic creaking of a door opening. Without consciously realizing it, she rested her head against the door and let her eyes close. As she did, a flurry of impressions flooded into her mind—random images and memories from her life. Edgar appeared there, but it was not her husband of today. It was Edgar from long ago—that day they first met. A smile came over her face as she let the image draw her into a time long since passed.

§

She fell in love with the skinny boy who, like such a young gentle-man, had helped her up after she had fallen. Of course, he was the one who knocked her down to begin with. She had just turned eleven and was new to the neighborhood in 1948. Her father had been transferred from Cincinnati to Wayne, Michigan, to work in the booming post-war auto industry. She was walking down the sidewalk with Sally Morgan, her new best friend, wearing the sum-mer dress her mother had just made for her. It was only to be worn for church, or for special occasions, but she wanted to show it off; she needed to feel special in her strange new world.

Down near the alley, she stepped sideways to avoid a crack in the sidewalk. *Step on a crack; break your mother's back.* Without warning she was hit in the shoulder from behind. Twisted around, she lost her footing and fell into the grass by the street. Behind her, Sally started yelling at whomever it was that had bumped into her, using words that were so inappropriate for a young lady. When she looked up, she saw the cutest boy stumbling around and almost falling on top of her. She bit her lip to keep from laughing. The baseball he was holding fell into the grass next to her. Once he had gathered himself, he turned back her way. There was an unexpected expression on his face, as if he thought *she* was to blame for what *he* had done. She was certain that he was going to yell at her, but as their eyes met, his face changed—softened. He looked at the ball lying in the grass, and then back at her. Without a word, he turned and looked down the alley, where she noticed some other boys playing baseball at the park. She knew that he was trying to decide what to do. In her mind, it was a simple courtesy to apologize, or rude not to. But the decision for him seemed to be far greater than that. Instead of picking up the ball, as she had expected him to do, he reached out his hand to hers and, when they touched, she was in love.

"Sorry about that," Edgar said.

They held that pose for what seemed like forever, until he spoke again. "My name is Edgar. Edgar Howard."

"I'm Wilma Richardson," she said, flashing her most girlish smile. Her heart was dancing nervously in her chest; her face felt hot and flushed. It was the first time she had felt that way about a boy.

"Are you okay?" he asked, gently helping her to her feet.

"I think so," she replied.

She liked his hand touching hers, and didn't want him to let go. But he had a game to get to, and she felt fine, really. Still, she couldn't help herself. She took a half step, and then faked a limp. "Oh, that hurts," she cried out in her most dramatic voice.

With Edgar still holding her hand, she looked down at her dress. There was a barely noticeable grass stain on the side where she had landed. "My mother is going to kill me," she said. "This is my new dress and she told me not to get it dirty."

"It's all my fault," Edgar said. "I'll help you home, and you can tell your mother that it was all my fault. I was just thinking about... uh...not paying attention to where I was going."

"You don't have to do that," she said halfheartedly. "You're probably in a hurry—to get to your baseball game."

"No, It's not important; they'll never let me pit—" He stopped himself again. "I want to make sure you get home; that's the right thing to do."

Meanwhile, poor Sally was doing her best to save her from Edgar. "Come on, Wilma," she said, "let's go. I'll help you home. We don't need Edgar here to cause any more trouble."

"Shut up, Sally!" Edgar blurted out.

Wilma took a few steps, secured in Edgar's arm, then turned toward Sally and winked.

"Well!" Sally replied in a huff. "I'll just see you later then, Wilma," and strutted off in the opposite direction.

As they walked down Hawthorne Street, Edgar held her arm as she continued to feign a limp. It was all very unnecessary, of course, but she couldn't resist the attention. She was walking fine by the time they got to her house, but Edgar didn't seem to notice her miraculous recovery.

"What happened?" her mother asked through the screen door, looking at the stain on her dress.

"It's my fault, ma'am," Edgar said. "I knocked her down by mistake. I'll do chores to pay for her dress."

Her mother looked at Edgar, sizing him up. "Oh, that's very noble of you young man. What is your name?"

"Edgar Howard. I live just down Hawthorne Street, past the next corner."

Edgar stayed with her for a while that day; the two of them sitting together on her porch, talking. He never did have to perform any chores; her mother got the stain out easily. She had expected him to call on her after that, to at least come back and see how she was recovering, but he didn't. Her mother told her that she was too young to be seeing a boy anyway; it was not a proper thing for a girl to do until she was at least 15. It wasn't until years later, just before high school, that they actually became a couple. On her 15th birthday, they rode their bikes all the way to town for ice cream. She had Rocky Road and Edgar had chocolate chip. He surprised her with a candle he had brought along. He put it in her ice cream and sang Happy Birthday, right there in the ice cream shop. It was one of her sweetest memories of Edgar.

They went to their proms together, and after high school she was eager to get married. But Edgar wanted to settle into a good, steady job first—to support her properly. Looking back now, she thought that his words sounded more like a reflection of his father: *real men get jobs and work for a living; A man's responsibility is to put a roof over his family's head; Foolish dreams don't pay the bills.* Edgar refuted it all, but she knew. As much as he denied it, his father's words had most certainly influenced a lifetime of choices and beliefs—and she suspected also—his dreams. She wondered what his father might have dreamed of when he was a little boy, what he had aspired to become, and then what influences altered his life and made him the man he became—the person who believed that real men were judged by how hard they worked, and not by how they dreamed or loved.

Wilma's mind drifted forward, toward their early years of marriage. She and Edgar both worked then, though neither made much money. But they were able to save enough to buy the house from Edgar's parents when they became too old to take care of it, or themselves. There was talk of children; they both envisioned a home filled with purpose and laughter. They had tried for years, and it almost worked out once. But God had other plans for that sweet little soul—who came into the world way too early—and left it much too soon. They were encouraged to give up, and that dream was put away.

Always preferring the simple life, Wilma never had grand expectations for herself. Even when she couldn't understand why things happened as they did, she trusted that God was watching over her life—in His mysterious way. Growing up, her father worked while her mother took care of the home. It was how things were done, and that's what she imagined her life to be—settling down in their little home and taking care of what family she was given. Her part-time work outside of the house stopped a few years before Edgar retired. At that time she turned her attention to her work at the church and the charities that were deeply important to her, most of which focused on the needs of sick children. Never able to make a difference financially, as she'd always dreamed of, she instead gave willingly of her time. She spent many hours volunteering at the children's hospital, and even served on several fundraising committees that did raise money.

The one dream she allowed herself to indulge in, however unrealistic, was taking a luxury cruise. The idea came to her while she was getting her hair done years earlier. Someone at the salon before her had left a magazine, and curiously she picked it up. It was filled with pictures and stories of the things that rich and famous people did. There was an article about cruising around the world for months on a magnificent ocean liner, visiting the world's most exotic ports. There were photos of people dressed in the finest fabrics and wearing the most gorgeous jewelry, dining on unimaginable delicacies using polished silver, fine Oriental china and European crystal. She slid the magazine into her purse, and had since kept it hidden in the bottom of her knitting basket, bringing it out now and again. As wonderful as such a trip seemed to her, she knew that even in her fantasy, Edgar would never agree to such an extravagance. She imagined instead of taking her girlfriends along, and they would lounge around in luxury as the seas passed them by. And best of all, there would be no dishes to clean or laundry to fold.

§

Wilma's eyes opened. She found herself leaning against the front door, disoriented, her arms dangling at her sides. *I must have drifted off.* The faintest recollection of pleasant memories lingered in her head, but like most of her dreams, the details quickly evaporated.

She stepped back, staring at the front door, and then remembered that she had come to check on Edgar. She reached a hand out toward the door, but something caused her to pause. Her senses told her that he was fine. She was tired, and it was well past her bedtime. Edgar would come in when he was ready—when he was done resting his eyes.

4
A SPECIAL GIFT

After several minutes of rustling on top of the sheets, Edgar crawled out of bed, pulled on the crumbled up pants he had exited the night before and wandered out into the kitchen. On the yellow Formica table was a slice of dry toast and a small glass of orange juice; it was the breakfast his mother had waiting for him every morning. By the time he got to it, the toast was cold, but that's the way he liked it. Sitting next to his breakfast was the *Detroit Free Press,* opened to the sports page. The headline read: *Hit Happy Tigers Wallop Nats Twice, 9-3, 9-2.* His mother, standing at the sink, clipping flowers and humming softly, said without turning, "Your grandfather left that for you. He said you might want to read it."

Edgar wondered how she knew what he was thinking, but decided it was probably better not to know. He had never read the newspaper before, except for the comics. His favorites were *Dick Tracy* and *Moon Mullins.* The rest of the paper was just boring grown up stuff and advertisements. He sat down, grabbed his toast and chewed off a small bite. He pulled the paper in closer and began browsing as crumbs fell from his mouth.

"Edgar, would you like some preserves on your toast?" his mother asked. "Grandma brought some home-made strawberry preserves; they're really good."

"No, thanks," Edgar replied.

He looked up as the back door opened and his grandmother

appeared with a small basket of fresh vegetables. Between trying to read the paper and the activities in the kitchen, something occurred to him. He asked, to whomever might have the answer, "Where's Grandpa?"

"He had to go out, dear," his grandmother replied. "He'll be back later."

"But we were supposed to go to the park," Edgar said, pushing the newspaper aside; his mind now focused on where his grandfather might have gone, and why he wasn't invited.

His mother replied in her *it's all right* voice, "Honey, I'm sure he'll go to the park with you when he gets back."

Edgar gulped down the last of his orange juice, got up and stormed out the back door.

§

Most of the back yard was off-limits to Edgar, as his mother's precious gardens consumed a large portion of the small lot. Her flowers ran across the backside of the house and along the side of the garage. The vegetables took up the area to the left and along most of the back fence. Between the back of the garage and the alley was a small space where nothing was planted, and Edgar was free to play there. Lying in the gravel next to the back gate were his toy airplanes. He settled there in the dirt, and for a while unenthusiastically shot down *Zeros* and *Messerschmitts*, depending on which continent he happened to be flying over. Distracted, he put his planes aside, leaned against the fence and closed his eyes, feeling the sun on his face. When the heat became too much, he made his way back to the house. It was quiet there, except for the soft murmur of voices coming from the front porch. He peeked out from the corner of the front window and saw his mother and grandmother sitting on the bench, talking. The driveway was still empty—another reminder of his suspiciously missing grandfather. He moped through the house, ending up in his bedroom. Falling onto his bed, he grabbed his Superboy comic from the nightstand and read a few pages, but soon lost interest. Being abandoned by his grandfather had made him sad, while the heat of the day made him sleepy. He closed his eyes and drifted off.

§

A knock on the bedroom door startled Edgar from his sleep. Through half-opened eyes he saw his grandfather standing in the doorway, smiling; his hands folded behind his back.

"Hey, pal, can I come in?"

"Sure," Edgar said. He sat up and rubbed his eyes.

"I've got a surprise for you."

"What is it?" Edgar replied. His curiosity was piqued, as he rarely heard such a phrase. Sometimes Jimmy's mother would ask him if he wanted a surprise, which was usually a cookie. A surprise here though—he didn't know what to think. Surely it wasn't a cookie—maybe a brownie. As Edgar wondered, his grandfather lumbered into the room and stopped at the side of the bed. From behind his back he pulled out an oddly shaped bundle wrapped in newspaper and placed it in Edgar's lap.

"I wanted to wrap it up proper," his grandfather said, "but this was the best I could find."

Edgar turned the mysterious gift over in his hands while his grandfather sat down next to him. "Go ahead, pal, open it, open it."

Edgar picked at the paper. At first he thought it was clothes, as it felt somewhat soft to the touch. Soon, a spot of brown leather appeared and, anxiously, he ripped the rest of the paper off and tossed it aside.

"What do you think?" his grandfather asked.

"Wow," Edgar uttered in barely a whisper.

It was a brand new baseball glove, and inside was a perfect white baseball. On the top strap of the glove, in red lettering over a black patch, was embroidered, *Rawlings*, and below that, *St. Louis*. Edgar sat the ball on the bed next to him and turned the glove over in his hands, observing every detail. He had no experience in receiving such a spontaneous gift, and didn't know how to respond.

"I had to drive all the way to Dearborn to get it," his grandfather said. "It's the best glove they carry—a *Rawlings*. It cost $6.00. I got to the store and they asked me if I needed a right-handed or a left-handed glove. Well, I remembered that we were talking about that yesterday and you said your father's glove didn't fit because it was backwards. Well, I didn't know if that meant you were right-handed or left-handed. Then I remembered you drawing with your left hand, so I figured you were a lefty."

"Yeah," Edgar replied, unable to take his eyes off the glove.

"Well, as it turns out, the first store I visited didn't carry a left-handed glove in that size, so I had to find another store. I wanted it to be a surprise, so when you got up this morning I could give it to you. But things took a little longer than I had planned."

"Wow," Edgar said again, "thanks, Grandpa."

"Come on, pal," his grandfather said. "I smell something good coming from the kitchen. I think your grandmother is making grilled cheese sandwiches and tomato soup. Let's get some lunch and then go to the park and have a catch. What do you say? My glove is in the car; I brought it along, hoping to have a catch with my favorite grandson."

As they walked toward the kitchen, his grandfather added, "Your mother said I'm going to spoil you with presents. You know what I told her?"

"No," Edgar said, smiling.

"I said, good!"

§

In the kitchen, the ladies were talking over the stove. Without excusing himself, Edgar said, "Look what Grandpa bought for me! It's a Rawlings—the best glove they make!"

"Oh, that is a nice glove," his grandmother said. "Are you boys going to try out for the *Tigers*?"

Edgar had never been asked such a crazy question before, but he couldn't help but smile at the thought of it.

After lunch, Edgar put the dishes in the sink while his grandfather went to retrieve his own baseball glove. A few moments later he reappeared. "Are you ready to have a catch?"

"Yeah," Edgar replied. Then, just as the words left his mouth, he recalled something from the day before, the reason that he couldn't play baseball with the other kids—because he didn't have a glove. As he glanced down at the new one covering his hand, he knew that he was going to need another excuse. He looked at the clock, which showed the time as half past noon. With all his might, he prayed that the boys had already gone home for lunch. For the moment at least, it was the best he could hope for.

§

They walked slowly, allowing their lunches to digest, and talked about how to properly care for a glove, and how to hold it in various defensive scenarios. As they entered the alley, Edgar could see the boys still on the field, and his heart sank. But at least they looked tired and sweaty, as if they had been there for a while, and might soon be taking a break. Still, Edgar had not felt so nervous since he had to stand up in front of his class at school and give a talk on the effects of the war. But at least then he wasn't afraid of getting beat up for stating his historical facts inaccurately. He took the lead and guided his grandfather off to the right, sweeping far around the baseball field and back toward where they were the day before. His grandfather just talked on, and much to Edgar's delight, seemed to have completely forgotten about his ridiculous suggestion from the previous day.

After finding a spot between some large oaks, far from the field and relatively safe from disruption, Edgar was ready. Standing barely ten feet away, he nervously tossed the ball toward his awaiting grandfather, who caught it after a slight shift to his right. Edgar dropped the return throw, forgetting how he was supposed to hold the glove. Back and forth the ball went. Most of Edgar's throws were low and in the grass or off to the side, but his grandfather retrieved each one with patience and a smile, like there was nothing in the world he would rather be doing.

"Step into your throws like this," his grandfather said as he took a forward stepping motion and released the ball. "You use your body that way. That's why pitchers wind up before throwing."

Edgar didn't know exactly what that meant, but he already felt embarrassed for throwing like a girl, so he just nodded and pretended to understand.

After a while, the lesson returned to how to hold the glove properly. "Look here, pal," his grandfather said. "If the ball is rolling toward you on the ground, you turn your glove over like this, with your fingers facing down. If the ball is in the air, you turn your glove the other way, facing upward. You don't want a fly ball to pop out of your glove and hit you in the face. It's also important to use both hands; the glove stops the ball and your hand secures it. Got it?"

"Yeah, Grandpa," Edgar replied. "I just need to practice. I'll get better."

"You're doing great, pal. You'll be a pro in no time. And remember, even the pros need to practice."

Time slipped by quickly and, before they knew it, the game across the way had finished and the older boys were gone. The only sounds remaining were the birds chirping and a light breeze blowing through the summer leaves. Edgar felt good, not only because he was with his grandfather, learning how to play baseball and starting to do a little better, but mostly because the other kids had left, and the fear of being pushed into that horror was gone—at least for today.

"Are you ready to call it a day?" his grandfather asked.

"Sure, Grandpa." Edgar didn't really want to go, but his grandfather looked tired, and he didn't want to push it. On their way back toward the alley, they cut straight across the park in the direction of the now empty baseball field. Edgar wandered onto the pitcher's mound, which was little more than compressed weeds growing out of a pile of dirt and rocks, and looked around. It felt odd standing there above the rest of the field, in the middle of everything. He wasn't sure what to think, other than how uncomfortable it must be for a pitcher—to be the center of attention. But it sparked a little something in him as well, like glimpsing a dormant inner desire that he never knew existed. In a way it complemented how his grandfather had made him feel the last few days—special.

"Pitch me a few."

Edgar looked up to see his grandfather standing behind home plate. "But there's no batter, Grandpa."

"Pretend, Edgar. Use your imagination."

Edgar did his best to imagine a batter standing there. At first it was one of the bullies from the park, but that actually made him nervous. Deciding that he wasn't going to allow himself to be intimidated by an invisible batter, he replaced the bully with Jimmy. The thought of his friend standing there at the plate with a bat in his hands almost made Edgar laugh out loud.

Waiting patiently, his grandfather held his glove in the middle of the strike zone and punched it a few times. "Just hit the target."

Edgar focused on the glove, trying to ignore Jimmy. He performed a clumsy wind-up and threw the ball. To his surprise, it was actually over the plate, and maybe even good enough for a batter to hit. Not Jimmy, but someone who actually knew how to swing a bat. It was a seemingly insignificant accomplishment, but for the first time in his life he could imagine himself as something more than a dumb kid—a baseball player—a pitcher.

§

The hot summer day had turned into a comfortably warm evening. The lawn furniture was arranged nicely in the back yard when Edgar appeared there. The small outdoor table was set with his mother's nicest glassware. A pitcher of iced tea with floating lemon slices sat next to a huge bouquet of flowers. Edgar plopped himself into the open chair next to his mother and directly across from his grandfather. He looked around at the adults, minus his father, who was working a double shift, and thought of how nice it was to be with people who were happy. It seemed to him that everyone there *wanted* to be happy, and so they were. That made him wonder. Did people make themselves the way they were, or was there some invisible force, like a Buck Rogers ray beam, piercing through their brains and controlling them, forcing them to feel and behave in certain ways? His imagination circled that thought until a burst of laughter, and his grandfather's coughing, brought him back into the moment.

"Hey, pal," his grandfather said, wiping his mouth with a hand-kerchief, "I thought you had left us there for a moment."

Edgar looked around; they were all staring at him, and he could feel his face flush from the attention. "No, I was just resting my eyes for a minute, that's all."

"Ah, that's all right," his grandfather said. "I do that all the time, except I usually fall asleep. Even if it's the middle of the day, I can drift right off."

His grandfather took a long drink of tea, then looked at Edgar with a sly smile and said, "Edgar, I've got something else for you."

"For me?" Edgar replied, noticing that he was still the center of attention. "What is it?"

"Close your eyes and hold out your hand."

Edgar closed his eyes tightly and held out his hand as directed. Something small and very light was placed in it. It was something made of paper, and a part of him felt a tinge of disappointment. He had just received a brand new baseball glove and ball, and this was just a piece of paper, maybe a newspaper clipping or a photograph. He silently scolded himself, knowing that whatever it was he had to at least pretend to like it.

"Okay," his grandfather said, "you can open 'em."

Edgar opened his eyes and looked around as he brought his hand back in. Worried that he might not be able to fake liking whatever it was, like getting a greeting card for his birthday and nothing else, he gazed down at the small, plain white envelope in his hand. On the front, written in a jagged handwriting was: *Edgar*. He rubbed his fingers across the surface, feeling the texture of the paper.

"Go ahead, open it!" his grandfather said. He was now sitting on the edge of his seat, his hands tapping on his knees.

"Oh, okay. Sorry."

The flap of the envelope was not sealed, so Edgar was able to just slide his finger in and spread it open. Inside were two small, rectangular pieces of paper. He pulled them out and knew immediately what they were. He felt his eyes beginning to water, and blinked several times. He sniffled and wiped his sleeve across his face, then focused in on the two tickets in his hand. On the front of each was printed: *Cleveland Indians at Detroit Tigers at Briggs Stadium. July 1st, 1948. 2:00 pm.*

"We'll want to leave at twelve sharp!" his grandfather said, beaming.

Edgar looked toward his grandfather. "Is this for a *real* baseball game?"

"You bet, pal!" his grandfather exclaimed. "Just you and me, kiddo. I picked them up at the box office this morning. I wasn't even thinking about it, but I was buying you that glove and it occurred to me—why not see a game with my favorite grandson? It's two weeks from Thursday, and who knows, maybe Hal Newhouser will be pitching."

Edgar hardly knew what to say. First, there was the new glove and ball, and now tickets to a real baseball game, and for no good reason. It wasn't Christmas or even his birthday. Even with everyone staring at him, he rose from his chair and gave his grandfather the biggest hug; he couldn't help himself. "Thanks, Grandpa."

§

As the evening sky faded to night, the grandparents headed off to bed. Edgar sat out back with his mother, something they rarely did since he had gotten older. He was eager to go find Jimmy before bedtime and show him his new glove and baseball, and especially the tickets. Jimmy liked to brag whenever he got something new, like a comic book, or even when his mother made him his favorite dish. Now it was time for some payback. But before he was able to ask permission to go, his mother put down her glass of tea. Her expression had changed from her earlier joy to what he perceived as something closer to sadness, which he struggled to understand. She began talking, as if her mind was packed with too many thoughts and she needed to release some of them. She told him that her parents didn't have much money, but her father wanted to spend time with him and spoil him a little, as grandparents like to do. They couldn't really afford to drive all the way to Michigan, but he insisted.

"Your grandfather is not feeling all that well, Edgar," she added, turning away and looking across the yard toward her flowers, or maybe nothing at all. "Don't expect too much from him, okay?"

Edgar didn't know what was behind her sudden change of mood, and he was afraid to ask. Instead, he replied, "I won't, Ma. I'm just really glad he's here."

"Me too, honey," his mother said. "Me, too."

5
PUTTING AWAY AN OLD FRIEND

Awakened by a sudden jerk of his body, Edgar opened his eyes and looked around. He wondered how long he had been sleeping—if he had been sleeping at all. His porch and the yard beyond looked and felt normal again. There was no crazy lightning or strangers running around, and he wondered if the boy made it home safely. Except for the buzzing in his ears, he felt like his old self, just tired and saddened by another disappointing baseball season. He unplugged the radio from the extension cord, lifted it carefully into his arms and retreated to the relative warmth of the house.

With the hands of a well-seasoned curator, he placed the radio gently on the sofa, as if it were made of the most delicate blown glass and might shatter by thought alone. He opened the coat closet and pulled the light chain until it clicked. Retrieving the radio, he sat it carefully on the top shelf where, for decades now, it had been safely stored through the long winter months. When retrieving coats or boots or umbrellas, he would notice it up there and it would bring a smile to his face. No matter the month or outside temperature, it reminded him of those enthusiastic voices that brought every pitch and every play to life. But today was over, and tomorrow would be the longest day of the year, regardless of what the calendar said—an eternity until the next new season of hope.

Edgar maneuvered the radio until the dial faced the back of the closet, so it would not be damaged. Of course, Wilma knew that nothing else was allowed up there. But still, he couldn't take the chance. With one last look, he sighed and pulled the light string. As he grabbed the door to close it, something caught his eye. It was a subtle white glow, illuminating a spot on the wall behind the radio. He reached up and around until the small patch of light reflected on his hand. *That's strange.* He pulled the radio back down and checked to make sure the power switch was off. It was. *What would cause the light to stay on?* Edgar knew nothing about electricity, but he had heard that electrical appliances could hold a charge even after they were unplugged. *But nothing like this has ever happened before.* He made a mental note to have it checked in the spring, when he would take the radio to Montgomery's Appliance & Repair in town for its annual tune-up. As he ran his hand gently over the surface, the dial light faded to black.

Momentarily satisfied, Edgar returned the radio to the top shelf and closed the door. As he did, something else came over him. It wasn't a reoccurrence of the earlier strangeness out on the porch, nor was it the sadness that typically hit him at the end of all too many baseball seasons. It was something deeper, a perception perhaps, that he wouldn't have to remember to tell Mr. Montgomery about the dial light that stayed on even after the radio was unplugged, or remind him to polish up the Bakelite finish and check the tubes and wires. It was a sense that such things no longer mattered. This unexpected awareness came with a curious hint of joy, but a layer of sadness as well. It included an unexplainable knowing that he would never again sit on his porch and listen to the *Detroit Tigers* games on his beloved radio.

Shuddering at the thought, Edgar turned off the lights and lowered the thermostat to 63 degrees. Who had the money to keep the lights on and the furnace running all night? That's what the flashlights and the extra blankets were for. He continued toward his room, then stopped at Wilma's door and whispered, "Goodnight, hon," as he did every night. As expected, there was no reply; she was well into her own dreams by now. Shuffling into his room across the hall, Edgar undressed and got into bed. Pulling the covers up tightly to his chin, he stared at the dark ceiling and tried to further separate himself from the events of the evening. Whether real or imaginary, he had already decided to keep all that nonsense to himself. Old men shouldn't speak of such things, or find themselves unwillingly escorted to fine institutions with sterile gray walls and locked doorways, sharing their days with neighbors in matching gowns—who also claim to see and hear things that normal people don't. He turned onto his side and was out within minutes, with not a single dream to disrupt his sleep.

6
GAME DAY

When Edgar awoke on the morning of July 1, 1948, his room was bright and filled with sunshine. The first thought in his head was that it was game day, which caused an excited smile to form across his face. Distant sounds of talking came from the other side of the house, along with the unpleasant aroma of coffee. He twisted around and slid his feet over the side of the bed. Laying there, thinking of the upcoming game, feeling the warm breeze coming through his open window and listening to the songbirds singing, he drifted back to sleep.

§

An uncomfortable feeling startled Edgar from his sleep. It was a sensation like being lost, or misplacing something very important. He rolled over and looked across the room at the small white alarm clock on his dresser, which showed the time to be 12:05. He listened for the voices coming from the other side of the house, but all that returned was silence. "Oh, crud." *Where is everyone? They would wake me up, right? They wouldn't let me sleep through the game, would they? Weren't we supposed to leave at noon?* Before more fearful thoughts could creep into Edgar's mind, he hopped out of bed and hurried down the hall. "Ma?" He glanced into the kitchen, which was eerily empty. Across the living room, the front door was closed and the curtains were drawn, like what responsible parents would do before leaving the house, say for an afternoon at the baseball game. He ran forward, grabbed the doorknob and turned. It was locked; of course it was. They had left and locked the house up behind them. Sliding the chain off, Edgar twisted the latch and frantically opened the door. His heart seemed to stop dead in his chest as he observed the empty porch and the cars missing from the driveway. Tears began forming in his eyes. He blinked rapidly in an attempt to hold them back. "Where is everyone?" he cried out softly.

Up and down the block Edgar looked, but there was no shinny blue Plymouth anywhere. He tried to compose himself, but couldn't keep the tears from coming. "No, no, no," his trembling voice uttered. "Ma? Grandpa?" Across the living room he shot, through the empty kitchen and toward the back door. He opened it and lunged out into the back yard, stumbling down the steps and into the grass. His watery, unfocused eyes stared at the ground in front of him. "No, no," he whispered. A swarm of thoughts crashed through his mind. What did he do wrong? He thought he was being good. He wasn't in trouble for anything, was he? Did his grandfather leave without him because he was asleep, and decided to take everyone else instead, and just leave him home alone?

Kneeling in the grass, Edgar fought to calm himself down. He wiped at his eyes with his shirtsleeves and was finally able to stop the tears. As his vision returned, he stood up and looked out over the yard. In the back of the garden, facing away from him, was his mother and grandmother, fully absorbed in tending to the crops, completely unaware of his presence. To his right, parked in front of the open garage door was the shiny Plymouth. The hood was open, and through the small crack between the bottom edge of the hood and the windshield cowl, Edgar could see movement. He watched as the big burly figure appeared from behind the hood and headed into the shadows of the garage. "What a fathead." Edgar wiped the tears from his face; he would not let his grandfather see him cry. After a few slow steps toward the car, a new horror drifted into in his mind. *What's wrong with the car? Why is it parked in front of the garage with the hood up?* When his father's car was there, it meant trouble. It might sit for days as his father waited for a new part to arrive. *How will we get to the game if the car is broken?* His father was at work and there were no other cars.

His grandfather emerged from the garage with a silver colored wrench in one hand and an old rag in the other. He glanced over at Edgar. "Hey, pal. Great morning, isn't it?"

"Yeah," Edgar replied, his eyes never leaving the open hood as he moved in closer. He could not understand how his grandfather could be so happy at a time like this, when their whole plans were in ruins because of the stupid car.

"Why the long face?" his grandfather asked.

Edgar took a deep, jittery breath and blurted out, "What's wrong with the car? Is it broken? Are we still going to the game?"

"No problems at all, pal. Just doing a little maintenance. Take good care of your things, and they will take good care of you." He smiled, leaned under the hood and pulled out a long wire, looked at it carefully and then slid the dirty rag along it. "Clean as a whistle."

Edgar leaned up against the fender and asked, "What's that?"

"Oh, I just changed the oil," his grandfather replied. "You should always change the oil after a long drive; keeps the engine running a long time."

Edgar barely heard his grandfather's words, mostly because they did not include anything like *we won't be able to make the game* or *maybe some other time.*

"Come on, pal, let's get ready to go. What do you say? We have a big day ahead of us. I'll clean up my mess here and meet you inside."

Back in the kitchen, Edgar fell into his regular chair with a deep sigh of relief. On the table in front of him was his breakfast. He grabbed his toast and started nibbling around the edges. The back door opened and his grandfather lumbered through, wiping his hands on a rag that looked dirtier than they did. He tossed it on the counter near the sink and grabbed a cup out of the overhead cupboard, poured some coffee from the percolator and looked back toward Edgar. "Dry toast?"

"Mm, hmm," Edgar replied.

"Your grandmother made some sausage and eggs. There's some more in the oven staying warm. Would you like me to fix you a plate? A growing boy like you needs a good breakfast."

"No thanks, Grandpa. I just like my toast."

"At least put some strawberry preserves on it; there's some in the ice box. Your grandmother brought them along; they're delicious."

"No thanks. I just like my toast like this."

"Okay, pal, you enjoy. We'll leave right at noon, okay?" He tousled Edgar's hair and left to get cleaned up.

Edgar sipped his juice and smiled. Through the back door came his mother with a bundle of flowers. He noticed her observing him disapprovingly.

"Edgar, you need to hurry up and get ready for your big day with Grandpa," she said. "I want you to look your best. Your nice clothes are hanging in your closet; I want you to wear them."

"Why can't I wear this?" Edgar asked.

She gave him a motherly look and said, "Edgar, please, look at yourself and answer your own question."

His shirt was ripped and stained, and his pants were frayed at both legs. They were the same clothes he had been wearing all week, which seemed perfectly acceptable to him. The idea of dressing up for a baseball game made no sense, but he had already dodged a few bullets that morning and wanted nothing else to go wrong, like being grounded for talking back. "Fine," he mumbled.

§

After a quick bath, and leaving a ring of noxious dirt around the tub, Edgar hurried to put on the clothes his mother had told him to wear. He was feeling anxious again, and wanted to stay close to his grandfather until it was time to leave. Buttoning his shirt, he noticed that his alarm clock was still showing the time as 12:05. He picked it up off of the dresser and shook it gently. "What a fathead."

He took it into the kitchen to check the time on the electric clock on the wall. He twisted the setting knob on the back until the time was correct at 11:57. After winding it up tight and returning it to the dresser, Edgar brushed his teeth and combed his hair. He was ready to go.

7
CHANGING SEASONS

The first measurable snowfall of the season came at the beginning of December, later than usual for Southeastern Michigan. Edgar awoke to a bright blue sky outside his window and small fields of white below, each separated by a chain link fence. By the end of winter, the sight of snow would be dreadful at best. But that first clean sheet of whiteness was at least an improvement over the dormant and colorless vegetation that preceded it. Staring out the window, he thought about the previous baseball season. It had been two months since the *Tigers* finished in the bottom half of the division and, to make matters worse, his least favorite team had won the World Series.

On his nightstand was a glass of water and several pills; Wilma always had them waiting for him in the morning. The blue ones were the most important, as they eased his arthritis pain, which was worse on these cold days. Wilma often suggested that they turn the furnace up, at least in the mornings. But he would have no part of it. Who had the money to run the furnace frivolously like that? No, he was fine taking the extra pill—the one *Medicare* paid for. The doctor said it was okay, and he could use his cane until his joints loosen up.

After gobbling down his pills, Edgar headed toward the kitchen. The house was empty and silent, as he had expected. Wilma had plans to leave early and have breakfast with her girlfriends. After that it was off to buy Christmas cards and look for holiday specials. Edgar eased himself into his chair at the kitchen table and unfolded the sports section. Two slices of cold, dry toast and a glass of orange juice sat nearby.

There was little worth reading in the sports section at that time of the year, with baseball still months away. He finished with a few of the comics and then pushed the paper aside. In the quiet of the house, his attention shifted to the buzzing sound in his ears. It seemed more prevalent in his left ear, but there was some in the right as well. He rubbed them, as he'd done a thousand times since that night on the porch back in October when it all started. But as always, it didn't help. Along with the other strange happenings that night, Edgar kept the ear thing to himself. There was no sense in worrying Wilma, and how serious could a little buzzing in the ears be? It was no more than a mild annoyance. Still, he did have a regularly scheduled doctor's appointment coming up in a few days. He would bring it up then, even though he knew exactly what the doctor would say—it's just part of getting old.

§

Wilma was not feeling well the morning of Edgar's doctor's appointment, and with a fresh covering of snow on the roads, even emergency driving was out of the question. Around the time of Edgar's hip surgery a few years prior, Wilma had started limiting his driving to daylight hours only, and absolutely no driving in bad weather. After the surgery, and a few close calls, she decided that enough was enough, and took away his keys for good. For Edgar, emasculating or not, it was a welcome relief; driving had become too stressful. Why was everyone in such a hurry? And nobody's eyes were on the road anymore.

Edgar lifted the phone receiver off the hook and dialed the number for the local taxi service. After the arrangements were made, he dropped a tea bag and a dollop of honey into a mug of hot water and delivered it to Wilma in bed, assuring her that he could handle a simple trip to the doctor by himself. He nodded in agreement to all the questions she wanted him to ask, and took the list she had prepared, just in case he forgot. He kissed her on the cheek and went to wait for the taxi.

After an uneventful ride, and a ridiculous term served in the waiting room, Edgar found himself sitting on the exam table, waiting for the doctor. He was noticing how old his body had become when a nurse appeared.

"Hello, Mr. Howard," she said. "How are you feeling today?"

"Oh, fine I suppose," Edgar said. "All the usual things; the aches and pains of getting old. My knees and hands ache mostly, from the arthritis."

"You be careful now, Mr. Howard," she said, "going up and down the stairs."

"Oh, I don't use the stairs anymore," Edgar replied. "Except for the outside steps, the only ones we have go down into the basement, and I haven't been down there in ages."

"That's good," she said, then checked his pulse, blood pressure, temperature and weight. She recorded the results on the computer that sat on the desk in the back corner of the room. "The doctor will be with you shortly," she said politely, and then slipped out the door.

Dr. Slawoski appeared soon after. He was close to 70, but showed no signs of slowing down. He was a short, soft looking man with bronze skin, as if he had spent time recently in a more tropical climate. His head was covered with pure white hair, and he had a bushy mustache to match. Below, a broad smile displayed a mouth of shiny white teeth—very white. He re-checked Edgar's essentials himself while inquiring about his medications and how each was working, and if there were any changes in how he was feeling.

"Well, doc," Edgar said. "I've been having this buzzing sound in my ears—mostly in the left one, but a bit in the right one, too. It started a couple of months ago, while I was sitting out on the porch listening to the ball game on my radio. There was this peculiar storm and a loud noise—but it wasn't thunder." Edgar considered the other crazy happenings from that night, but decided that this particular doctor didn't need to know. There were other specialists that dealt with the kinds of things no reasonable person would believe.

"Let's take a look, Mr. Howard." The doctor checked his left ear, and then the right. "There's no visual ear damage or infection, Mr. Howard. I think what you're experiencing is a mild case of Tinnitus. It's not uncommon to hear ringing in the ears, especially as we get older. It can be a little disturbing at first, but there are ways to manage it. It's just one of those things we learn to live with as we age. You are starting to get older, Mr. Howard."

"I've been getting older for decades, doc," Edgar replied.

"Can you hear it now, Mr. Howard?"

"Yes."

"How much does it bother you?"

"Not so much, I suppose." Edgar paused. "Lately though, it sounds like it's getting closer."

The doctor looked up curiously and asked, "Getting closer, or getting louder, Mr. Howard?"

Edgar considered his response carefully. In some inexplicable way, it seemed to be getting closer. He knew that was not logical, but it was how it felt, and honestly, it didn't sound all that crazy to him. Considering the look on Dr. Slawoski's face though, he decided to change course. "Oh, yes, louder. What did I say?"

Seemingly satisfied, the good doctor moved over to the computer and started typing. "Let's wait and keep an eye on this, Mr. Howard. Sometimes the ringing can be a symptom of other problems, but I don't think that's the case here. If it gets worse or starts to bother you, I can refer you to an ear specialist for some additional tests."

§

A different yellow taxi dropped Edgar off at the house just before noon, which was perfect; he was starving. After putting his coat, hat and gloves in the closet, and offering a quick glance at his beloved radio, he returned to the kitchen and settled himself at the table. He stared at the flowered Formica top and matching yellow vinyl chairs. Except for the seat covers, which were replaced back in the 1970s, they were the same chairs he sat on as a young boy growing up. His parents had left the dining set when they moved out, and since they made quality products back then, he and Wilma decided to keep it. A few scratches and tears, but otherwise the set was fine. And who had the money to be buying new furniture?

His attention drifted to Wilma, who was nowhere to be seen. *Is she still in bed?* He scolded himself for not checking on her before sitting down. He started to get up, and then noticed the handwritten note on top of his newspaper. It was from Wilma, who claimed to be feeling much better and had gone out for tea. She expected to be home in time to make dinner. Edgar noted that during the winter months, while he was hunkering down in the house day and night, Wilma's "going out for tea" had become more frequent—and sometimes lasting for hours. He wondered how it could take those ladies so long to drink a simple cup of tea. According to the note, she had left some soup for him in a large mug in the refrigerator, and all he had to do was heat it in the microwave. After fumbling through the process, Edgar was back at the table, thinking how much better food tasted when someone else made it for you.

As the winter wind rattled the kitchen window, the ringing in Edgar's ears intensified briefly, before subsiding to its now normal frequency. The surge was not painful, just unexpected. As Edgar rubbed his ears, a faint creaking sound came from off to his right. He looked over and noticed that the basement door was slightly ajar. His body crackled as he leaned over and pushed it closed.

After eating his lunch, and cleaning up as Wilma required, Edgar settled himself in the living room, to watch his game shows on television. At the first break he hit the mute button on the remote control, to save himself from the annoying commercials. In the silence he heard a sound that may have been the winter wind rattling the kitchen window again, or perhaps it was Wilma returning home. "Hon?" No reply. He hit the mute button again and watched the host enthusiastically introduce the next amazing prize. Before discovering whom the lucky winner was, Edgar drifted off to sleep.

§

Hours later, as the daylight was coming to an end, Edgar awoke. He got himself up and made his way back to the kitchen, to get his afternoon pills, the big ones that needed water to get down. The clock on the stove said it was 4:15 pm, which meant that Wilma should have been home by now. He wasn't worried, yet, but it did look icy outside, and with all the people heading home from work, the traffic would be bad. To his relief, a beam of light flashed through the living room curtains, and with it the faint sound of a car pulling into the driveway. Before going to greet Wilma, he noticed that the basement door was open again. He stared at it curiously, and then grabbed the doorknob and pushed it firmly shut. Satisfied, he went to unlock the front door.

§

"Mornin, hon," Edgar said as his slippers sloshed across the kitchen floor.

"Good morning, dear," she replied without turning from the pot of coffee she was preparing.

Before Edgar had a chance to sit down, read his paper and eat his toast, the basement door, open yet again, caught his attention. He stared at it perplexedly, and then asked Wilma if she had opened it.

"No, dear," she said. "I haven't been down in the basement for quite some time. In fact, I don't even remember the last time I was down there."

Edgar moved over and pushed it closed. He then pulled firmly on the knob to check the latch, which appeared to be securely set. With his hand resting there, his attention became fixated on something else; the doorknob was unexpectedly warm. Curious, he opened the door himself and was greeted by an equally warm breeze coming up from the basement. "Hon, there's a draft here; I can feel air coming up from the basement. We may have a broken window or something down there."

Edgar closed the door again and sat down to eat. While nibbling on his toast, he pondered the basement situation and considered his options. If nothing else, he was momentarily relieved from the tedium of the long winter, and invigorated by the prospect of a new project to tackle.

After breakfast, Edgar grabbed his glasses and proceeded to the basement door. The same warm breeze greeted him as he squinted to see down the bare wooden stairs, which descended at an eerily steep angle into the darkness below. In the upper right corner of the stairwell, dangling from a tired old light fixture, was a string ending in a rusted ringlet. Edgar pulled it, bringing to life a single 25-watt bulb that struggled to illuminate more than the first few steps. He surveyed the stairs and gave a firm tug on the handrail.

"What are you doing, Edgar?" Wilma asked as she returned to the kitchen.

"I want to see what's causing that draft," he replied.

"Edgar, dear, should you be going down those stairs? Why don't we call someone to come out and take a look?"

To Edgar, having someone "take a look" meant shelling out at least a hundred dollars for some stranger to do what he could just as easily do himself—for free. He was old, yes, but not entirely feeble. Anyway, he just wanted to see what the problem was firsthand; there was no harm in that. "Don't worry, hon. I'll be careful," he said. "I just want to take a look. I'm sure it's an easy fix, and paying all that money for nothing doesn't make sense."

Wilma was not thrilled either about paying an expensive repairman for something that didn't seem to be a problem in the first place, especially so close to Christmas. Still, she suspected it would be cheaper than the bill for Edgar's ambulance ride and the ensuing emergency room visit. But noticing how determined he seemed to be, she reluctantly backed off. "Well, dear, you be very careful on those stairs. And hold onto the handrail."

"Sure thing, hon."

§

While holding tightly onto the handrail, Edgar took one slow and cautious step down. He focused intently on his joints; the ones that could at any moment give out and send him tumbling the rest of the way. By the third step he was questioning his motive, and by the fourth he was wondering why Wilma had not been more resistant. Still, he kept going.

When he finally reached the bottom, he paused to catch his breath and relax his tense muscles. The basement was not warm, but cold and dark, with only a hint of daylight seeping in around the curtains of the two small windows along the left wall. Neither one showed any movement due to air coming in. The warm breeze was gone also, replaced by an unpleasant combination of smells: old cardboard, dust and a hint of mold.

Since they had bought the house from his parents in the 1960s, the basement had not been used much at all. Most of his parents' belongings stayed behind when they moved out, and most of Wilma's parents' things had been stored down here as well. Wilma had used the basement for laundry up until the time he retired, at which point they had the washer and dryer moved upstairs and into the converted back bedroom. After that, the basement had become nothing more than a dumping ground for empty boxes and things that no longer worked. Instead of throwing old and unusable things away, Wilma would have him move them to the basement, for reasons he could never quite understand. He grumbled, of course, but did it anyway. And all the boxes, well, Wilma just insisted on keeping them in case she needed to pack or mail something. Edgar, to the best of his recollection, could not remember using even one of the boxes from the basement for anything. In fact, he couldn't remember the last time they actually shipped a package.

With his hand still aching from the descent, Edgar felt along the wall until he found the light switch. With a flip, it illuminated a single bulb in the middle of the room. There were other light fixtures hanging from the ceiling, but the bulbs had burned out unknown years before and were never replaced. Why spend good money on light bulbs that were never going to be used anyway? With only that dim light to see by, Edgar surveyed the site. Laid out before him were dozens of boxes, some stacked neatly in various spots around the room, while others were strewn about. Scattered throughout were packaging materials, wrapping papers and decades worth of old and no longer used household items. Metal shelves lined the center wall. Edgar had installed those himself right after they moved in, and that was where they kept their extra dishes, games, puzzles and collectibles—all now covered in years of dust.

Edgar glanced to his right, toward the doorway leading into what used to be the laundry room, and his father's old workshop in the back, which was nothing more than an oversized closet with a workbench. He hadn't been back there more than once or twice since he was a kid. With the door to the laundry room closed, he assumed that the breeze was not coming from that direction. But since he was downstairs anyway, he might as well check. He opened the door and felt around for the light switch, hoping nothing would crawl on his hand. Without incident, he found what he was looking for and switched on another single bulb, this one hanging above the spot where the washing machine once sat. Two more windows with matching curtains were high on the wall on either side. He scanned the room, hoping to find the source of the leak. The furnace sat silently to the left like a soldier waiting for its next command, and the door to the workshop in the back was closed up tight. As far as he could tell, everything looked normal.

With no clear problem to fix, Edgar flipped off the light, closed the door and headed back toward the stairs. As he did, the furnace behind him clicked and rumbled to life. *Maybe that's all it was; just the furnace.* He paused at the base of the stairs to think. *But the door was shut and the vents out here are closed; I sealed them up ages ago.*

No sense in wasting good money on heating a basement we don't use.
He looked around again, but nothing out of the ordinary caught his
attention. Yet there was a distinct feeling in the air—a sense that he
was not alone—and of being watched. Scanning the mess in front
of him, he wondered what might be living in there. Certain that his
imagination was just getting the better of him, he shut off the light
and began his slow ascent, glad to be leaving the messy old basement
behind. At the top of the stairs, he paused and glanced back down
into the darkness. Relieved to see no-*thing* there, he pulled the light
chain and closed the door good and firm. This time it stayed shut.

§

Edgar tried to go about his morning routine. His attempt at reading
the paper was futile though; his mind refusing to stay focused on
the words, preferring instead to dwell on what might be below the
floorboards. *Was there really something watching me, or was that just
my imagination?* He got up and went to his room, passing Wilma
along the way. Sitting on the edge of the bed, he put his hands over
his face and took a few slow, deep breaths.

"Edgar, dear, are you all right?"

Startled, Edgar looked up to see Wilma standing in the doorway.
"Yeah, hon, I'm fine. I was just relaxing here for a few minutes."

"Edgar, you don't look well," Wilma said. "Are you sure you're
okay?"

"Maybe a little tired. I think I'll just lie down for a while."

"What did you find in the basement?" she asked. "Did you find
the leak?"

"Oh, nothing that I could see," Edgar replied as he kicked his
shoes off and lay back on the bed.

Wilma helped him under the covers and then placed her hand
on his forehead. Satisfied that he didn't have a fever, she kissed him
on the cheek and pulled the curtains closed. "Edgar, you just call me
if you need anything, okay?"

"Thanks, hon."

Edgar lay motionless as his eyelids became heavy and his mind began to slow down. A rustling sound came from down beneath the floor, and the buzzing in his ears surged briefly. He imagined mice running around in the heat ducts. *They must have gotten in through a crack somewhere.* He cursed himself for not looking more closely. *I may need to go down there again, with a flashlight this time.* That was the last thought he had before drifting off.

§

Edgar woke up just after noon, feeling refreshed and hungry. He made his way to the kitchen, where the smell of something grilling reminded him of how well Wilma took care of him. She was pouring iced tea into a glass when she paused to glance his way; her eyes scanning him like an X-ray.

"Edgar, how do you feel?" She put the pitcher down and walked up to him, and for the second time that day put her hand on his forehead.

"I feel great, hon. That nap sure did the trick."

Seemingly content with his response, Wilma went back to the stove, flipped two grilled cheese sandwiches and stirred a pot of soup. They ate lunch together and talked about the upcoming holidays. Wilma filled out her grocery list with the same holiday ingredients they had been having for the past fifty years. After cleaning up and putting the leftovers away, she headed off to fold the laundry while Edgar scoured the sports section one last time. With nothing left to read, he tossed the paper into the recycling bin and put his glass in the sink. Outside the window, the sky was a cold blue and the ground a dirty gray under patches of melting snow. He longed for spring, and did his best to imagine lush greenery, blossoming flowers and the sounds of baseball coming from his radio. Even though time seemed to be moving so fast now, at his age, the wait for spring training was still painfully long.

Edgar's longing was interrupted by a creaking sound coming from behind him. "Hon?" There was no reply. He turned around, but nobody was there. His already somber mood sunk even lower when he noticed the basement door standing open, again. Without moving, he spoke softly toward the dark opening, "Wilma? Hon, you down there?" Even though there was no verbal reply, he felt that something was there. He stepped cautiously toward the opening and, almost without conscious thought, inhaled deeply through his nose. What he smelled seemed illogical, so he sniffed again. Yes, it was the unmistakable scent of grass.

Edgar pushed the door closed and grabbed for the knob, as if trying to hold off an intruder. It was warm like before, but there was something more. *Was that there before?* Very faintly, he could feel a tingling sensation in his hand—a vibration—like the doorknob was attached to a very fast running electrical motor. Squeezing tighter, the sensation moved up his arm to his shoulder. Before allowing it to go any further, Edgar let go of the doorknob and wiped his hand on his pants—to liberate whatever contaminant might have been present.

"Edgar?"

Startled, Edgar jumped and turned quickly; a sharp pain shot through his side. He noticed Wilma standing in the doorway to the living room with a concerned look on her face. She seemed somehow distant, like they were both there together, but in a dream instead of reality.

"Edgar, can you hear me?" Wilma moved forward and put her hands on his shoulders, and then shook him gently. As she did, the distance began to evaporate.

"Hey, hon."

"Edgar," she said, "are you okay?"

This time he thought for a moment before replying, mostly because he was unsure himself of the answer. Maybe it was all just his imagination. He looked from Wilma to the basement door, considered his options and then replied, "Yeah, I'm fine. I must have just drifted off there for a moment. Daydreaming I guess."

"Edgar, you don't look right. I think you should go sit down while I call Dr. Slawoski."

"No, I'm fine, hon." He wasn't completely sure, but he definitely didn't want another visit to the doctor; once in a month was more than enough, thank you very much.

"Edgar, I'm a bit worried about you," Wilma said, backing up to get an overall view of him. "You're acting strange."

As she spoke, Edgar thought of something. Yes, of course, he just needed confirmation from another source. He took her hand and pulled her toward the basement door. "Wilma, put your hand here," he said, placing her hand on the doorknob. "Okay, now tell me what you feel."

"Feel? Edgar, what are you talking about?"

"Tell me what you feel. How does the doorknob feel?"

"It feels like a doorknob, Edgar. Like a doorknob."

"Just hold it there." Edgar put his hand over hers, so she couldn't move it, and then squeezed. "Do you feel the vibration? Do you feel how warm the knob is? Do you feel it?"

"No, I don't feel anything, Edgar. Now you're scaring me." Wilma pulled her hand away and looked at Edgar with frightened concern.

Oblivious to her worry, he put his own hand back on the doorknob and closed his eyes. But there was nothing; it was gone. "I felt it," he mumbled. "It was warm just a minute ago...and vibrating."

"Edgar, the doorknob was warm because you've been holding onto it, that's all. Please come and sit down; I'm going to call the doctor." Wilma grabbed his arm and led him to the living room.

"I'm fine, hon," he pleaded weakly, without conviction.

After Wilma had Edgar settled on the couch, she hurried back to the kitchen, where the doctor's phone number was on one of the refrigerator magnets. She picked up the phone and dialed.

Edgar stared at the television, but his mind was still on the basement door and what might be happening down below, as well as in his own head. He thought about the sensations—the heat coming from the vibrating doorknob, the warm air that now smelled like grass. *Good thing I didn't mention that to Wilma; I would be in an ambulance right now for sure.* He then tried to rationalize each part, starting with the warm air. *That was just the furnace. The vibration was coming from there, too, just the old blower motor vibrating. Yes, that's all it was; the furnace vibrating up through the floor. And I could feel it in the doorknob.*

Wilma returned with a glass of water and two pills. "The doctor said to take two of these and keep an eye on you. He said if you're not feeling better in the morning, to bring you in."

"Sure, hon," Edgar replied.

Wilma looked into his eyes as he took the pills. He could sense that she was assessing his condition, most likely guided by the doctor over the phone. After a moment, she seemed satisfied and returned to the kitchen.

§

Over dinner that evening, Edgar decided to tell Wilma everything. He was not looking for a return trip to the doctor, or to a mental institution for that matter, but he needed to share what he was going through, and hoped that she could make more sense of it than he had. She already knew about the creaking door that wouldn't stay closed, the warm doorknob and the vibrations. He added the ringing in his ears, the smell of grass and finished with the strange feeling from the basement—of being watched.

Wilma took a slow sip of tea as she considered what he had told her. He was worried that in her silence she was searching for a kind way of telling him that it might be in everyone's best interest that he be moved to a place where he could be properly cared for. His mind drifted to the old Eloise Mental Hospital, and he imagined being chased by mad doctors wanting to do unthinkable experiments on him.

"Edgar," Wilma said, "do you know what I think? I think you're right. There is a leak down there somewhere and it keeps blowing that door open. The smell of grass, well dear, I think you probably imagined that—just wishing for baseball to start again. You know how you are with that. The doorknob was warm because the sun was coming through the window over there. And what you felt when you were down in the basement was just a mouse or something that probably came in through a crack. I hate to say it, but maybe even a squirrel or a raccoon. It was probably looking right at you, and that's what you felt. And you even said yourself that you heard some scratching. Well, that just confirms it; something got into the basement."

Feeling like the tie-down straps had been loosened and the drug needles and electrical shock wires removed, Edgar breathed an enormous sigh of relief. Leave it to Wilma to find the answer. Yes, she was right; he was certain of it. So filled with relief that he almost cried, Edgar reached out and took both of her hands in his and kissed them. "That's good news, hon. I feel so much better now." He thought for a moment, then added, "What do we do now?"

"Edgar, I'm going to find someone to come out and look at the basement. We need to find the leak and have it repaired, and we might need an exterminator to clear out what's living down there."

"Oh, hon, that sounds expensive."

"Edgar, I don't care," Wilma said. "We need to find out what's down there and get it out."

The discussion was over.

8
THE DRIVE

The shiny blue Plymouth had been backed down the driveway and was sitting quietly when Edgar appeared on the front porch, right at noon. The ladies were sitting on the bench, but stood up and began *oohing* and *aahing* as soon as they saw him. He was dressed in his nicest summer clothes: navy colored shorts and a clean white shirt that his mother had ironed. In his hand was his new glove.

Edgar's grandfather appeared from the side of the house; a faint cloud of smoke lingered around his face. He tried unsuccessfully to hold back a burst of coughing. He had changed his clothes as well, and was wearing light gray slacks, a white shirt and thin dark tie hanging between black suspenders. On his head was a gray wool hat.

"Aw, look how handsome you both look," his grandmother said, looking from one to the other.

Edgar looked at his grandfather, who winked back at him and smiled.

"You boys have fun at the game," his mother said as she brushed something off of Edgar's shirt.

"Give your old grandmother a hug, too."

"Sure, Grandma." As Edgar moved in, she wrapped her hearty arms around him and squeezed tightly.

"Come on, pal, let's hit the road," his grandfather said, trying to save Edgar from the attack. He opened the driver's door and slid behind the wheel. Edgar hopped down the steps and raced toward the car. As he grabbed for the handle of the rear door, his grandfather said, "No, pal, you're riding up front—with me."

"Oh, okay." Edgar looked back toward his mother, to make sure it was all right. She smiled and nodded her approval.

The inside of the Plymouth was much nicer than his father's car. There were no holes in the seats and it smelled good, clean, but with a hint of tobacco and his grandmother's perfume. Edgar settled into the wide bench seat and looked around. The dashboard was filled with an assortment of knobs and dials; there were chrome grilles and polished details everywhere. It was like being in Flash Gordon's rocket cockpit. In the center of the dash was a small radio dial. He had heard about radios in cars, but had never seen one himself.

"What do you think?" his grandfather asked. "Nice car, huh?"

"It's the nicest car I've ever seen, Grandpa."

With a quick turn of the key, the car rumbled to life. The men rolled down their windows and pushed open the air vents. The ladies stood on the porch and waved. Edgar did the same as the car backed down the driveway, the wheels crackling over the gravel before finding smoother ground in the street. After the gentle meshing of gears, the car changed direction and accelerated down Hawthorne Street with a soft *put, put, put.* The temperature was making its way toward 80 degrees as the two best friends headed toward the big city and a day at the ballpark.

§

The city of Detroit grew prominently around them; the buildings becoming larger and more condensed. To the south, gray smoke from unseen factories rose high into the air.

"It sure is nice here," Edgar said as he watched the happenings all around him. "I wish we could live here."

"Yes, Detroit sure is beautiful; it's one of the finest cities in this great country of ours. Lots of people here working to make all sorts of things. All this smoke," he said, waving his hand, "is from all the factories making parts and building new cars; that's what your father does. They call Detroit the Automotive Capital of the World."

As they drove under a tangled maze of overhead freeways, the small clock on the dashboard ticked past the 12:40 mark.

"About a mile to go," his grandfather said.

§

"There she is!"

"Where?" Edgar replied.

"Up there, about five or six blocks," his grandfather said. "See the white building rising above that row of stores?"

They were still a ways off, but Edgar could already sense the scale of it. It dwarfed the smaller brick buildings around it like a mountain hovering over smaller hills.

"That's Briggs Stadium," his grandfather said with a hint of hometown pride, "one of the nicest ballparks in the whole country."

"Really? Wow!" Edgar thought about the baseball players who got to play there, and wondered how that must feel. Important, he imagined. He had never really felt that way, or thought of himself as special in any way. Those things were for other people, from special places. But the thought of it made him think of something he had never even considered before. Did you have to *be* special first, before you could feel that way, or did you have to *feel* it first before becoming it?

"Yup, she holds over 50,000 fans," his grandfather added.

Edgar's mind shifted to that. He couldn't imagine what so many people would look like all in one place. And then, as if his grandfather had read his mind, he said, "That's like a whole city's worth of people. Not a big city like Detroit, but maybe a good size city, like Dearborn."

"Wow," Edgar said without taking his eyes off the stadium, getting closer and closer.

On their right was a large parking lot. Standing in the street, waving an orange flag, was a man wearing greasy work overalls; a rag dangled from his back pocket. He was shouting, "Cheap parking! Easy out! Come on, folks, the best parking is right here!"

As they slowed to a stop beside him, the dirty man said, "Hey bub, that'll be fifty cents." His head disappeared outside the car as he pleaded for more customers. "Only a few spaces left! Come on in, folks, best parking in town! Easy in and out!" The man's head reappeared and his grandfather flipped him two quarters. "Enjoy the game, fellas," he said enthusiastically before turning to address the people walking along the sidewalk. "Make way, folks! Let the car through! Make way, please!"

They rolled slowly through the opening in the fence and into a large lot that took up half the city block. They passed several open spaces without stopping. Edgar observed quietly, knowing that his grandfather had a good plan; he always did. They pulled up to the fence in the very back and stopped. His grandfather maneuvered the large lever on the steering column upward and turned off the ignition.

"It should be safe to park here," his grandfather said. "And we won't have to worry as much about careless people walking by and scratching the paint. And a few extra steps never hurt anyone."

They grabbed their gloves and got out. A leaf was stuck to the side of the car. Edgar watched as his grandfather pulled it off and released it to the wind. He pulled out a handkerchief from his pocket and wiped the spot clean.

"Take good care of your things," Edgar said. They both chuckled, and then headed across the lot, out the gate and merged into the street traffic along Michigan Avenue.

"Stay close, pal; lot's of activity here."

"Yeah," Edgar replied, looking around and taking it all in. People were everywhere, smiling and laughing. It was like going to the world's largest movie theater for a really good movie.

"I haven't been to a *Tigers* game in years," his grandfather said. "I just love it here."

Scattered along the sidewalk were street vendors selling their wares. A boy about Edgar's age had his bike leaning up against a light pole. A large canvas saddlebag was draped over the seat and on the side was printed: *The Detroit Free Press.* The boy was waving a paper in the air and shouting, "Get your paper here!" He paused for a moment and then blurted out again at the top of his lungs, "Get the latest on the communists in Eastern Europe!" Just a few steps down from the paperboy, an old man was sitting on a wooden stool behind a rickety, folding metal table. On top of the table was a large cardboard box filled with small brown paper bags. On the front of the box was written: *PEENUTS.* Edgar saw the writing and chuckled to himself.

"Pee-nuts, only fifteen cents for pee-nuts!" The man shouted, as if he were competing with the paperboy for air space. Edgar noticed that most of his front teeth were missing. "Get your pee-nuts, folks! Don't pay a quarter inside; only fifteen cents right here!"

"Hey, pal, should we get some pee-nuts?"

"Yeah, let's get some pee-nuts," Edgar replied. They both giggled as the old man watched them curiously.

"We'll take two bags, please," his grandfather said politely, handing the man some coins. "And keep the change."

"Thank you, sir!" the toothless man replied. "Enjoy your pee-nuts!"

§

"Tickets please," said the man standing at the turnstile. He was wearing a dark blue uniform with a *Tigers* patch on the front. Stitched on his jacket was the name: *Floyd.*

Edgar handed him the tickets.

"Thank you. Come on through and enjoy the game," Floyd said as he returned the stubs to Edgar.

Inside the stadium, the incoming crowd dispersed down long corridors running off in both directions. Every fifty feet or so there were openings leading into the grandstands, with bright summer daylight shining in through each one. Scattered along the hallways in both directions were counters where vendors were selling food and souvenirs. People dashed around in every direction, stopping for a beer, a hot dog or one of the many other treats. A subtle pattering sound came from nearby, and the smell of buttered popcorn caused Edgar's mouth to water. But that time his grandfather didn't seem to pick up on his thought.

"Come on, pal, I want to show you something."

Edgar was led through the growing crowd, weaving left and right to avoid oncoming fans. Above each opening into the stadium were section numbers printed in white letters over dark green walls. Edgar tried to see out to the field, but there were too many people moving and standing around, blocking his way. He watched as the section numbers changed from the 140's down to the 130's. When they reached the marker that said section 122-123, his grandfather turned and led them up the ramp. They stopped behind a small group of people who were waiting in front of them. Edgar could just see the blue sky above their heads, and waited patiently as they inched slowly forward. Someone up ahead was calling out directions, "Section 123, row 16, right this way, folks." When the group in front of them turned and disappeared toward their seats, the space in front of Edgar opened outward in a great rush of expansion. The image before his eyes was beyond anything he had ever imagined. "Whoa!" he blurted out. He was standing in the lower level grandstands directly behind home plate, looking out over the largest baseball field he had ever seen. "It's huge!" He gazed out past the pitcher's mound, beyond the infield and toward the empty flagpole standing erect in center field; it looked like it was a mile away. He thought of their small baseball field at the local park and concluded that this place was probably bigger than the whole block.

"Quite a place, huh?" his grandfather said.

"Yeah!" Edgar replied, trying to take it all in.

Around the perimeter of the field, the grandstands were built on two separate levels, each filled with endless rows of dark green seats and a scattering of excited fans. There were several *Indians* players out on the field practicing, and some other men were raking the dirt around the infield.

"Let's move aside, pal. There's a whole line of people behind us."

"Uh, okay," Edgar replied as he was gently guided to the walkway on the left. They continued along the third base side of the stadium until they arrived at their seats, located near the foul pole down the left field line. They settled into their seats and watched as a continuous stream of people appeared from the entrances all around the ballpark and dispersed into the grandstands. When Edgar's attention returned to the playing field, he noticed that it was empty. The players and the grounds crew were gone and the field looked spectacular. The grass was a bright green, glimmering in the afternoon sun and perfectly cut. The dirt around the infield was a deep reddish brown, and without a single rock as far as Edgar could tell. The only thing missing were the players and the game itself. As that very thought went through his mind, a crackling sound came from the speakers hidden within the overhang above. "Ladies and gentlemen, please welcome your Detroit Tigers." As the announcer spoke his lines, the *Tigers* players appeared from the dugout along the third base line and jogged out to their positions on the field; the growing crowd cheered wildly. Edgar leaned forward in his seat and looked across the vast field toward the pitcher's mound, where the *Tigers* pitcher began warming up. "Is that Hal Newhouser?" he asked, turning toward his grandfather, whose expression told him he wasn't going to like the answer.

"Sorry, pal. That's Fred Hutchinson."

"Isn't Hal Newhouser going to pitch today?"

"I guess not."

"Why not?"

"Well, he's a starting pitcher and only one starting pitcher plays per game. I guess today is Fred Hutchinson's day to pitch."

Edgar was disappointed, but he didn't really know the players all that well anyway. Hal Newhouser was just his favorite because he had his baseball card and his grandpa talked about him all the time and because he was a lefty and an MVP. Regardless of who was pitching though, it was still great to be at Briggs Stadium for a real live *Detroit Tigers* baseball game. And with his grandfather now in his life, there would be plenty of opportunities in the future to come back and see Hal Newhouser pitch.

The crowd went suddenly quiet, and Edgar looked around to find the cause. Appearing from the gate behind home plate was a small group of soldiers with flags, marching in perfect formation toward the outfield. When they reached the flagpole, they stopped. The men in the crowd began removing their hats. Edgar looked over at his grandfather, who had removed his as well.

"Grandpa, what's going on?"

"They're going to sing the national anthem," his grandfather said softly.

Suddenly, a large American flag unfurled and began its rise up the pole. Once it reached its highest point, the soldiers took several steps back and saluted. The soldier in the center of the group stepped forward, raised a trumpet to his lips and began playing.

"Put your hand here," his grandfather said, "like this—over your heart."

9
A HELPING HAND

It was an early Sunday afternoon, two weeks before Christmas, when Wilma returned home with a smile on her face. It was the kind of look that came with finding something she really wanted at a great discount. While Edgar decided to sleep in, she had gone to church alone and then stayed for the potluck—not just for the food—but also to ask around for someone who might be able to help them with the basement. She was eager to resolve that little problem before it became a big one. Closing the front door, she noticed Edgar curled up in a comforter on the corner of the couch, staring at the television.

"Hi, hon. How was church?" he asked.

She put her purse down and sat next to him. "Edgar, I talked to the pastor after church today, and he told me that Mr. Johnson's son—you know Mr. Johnson—the short, heavy set man that sits up front during the service. Well, the pastor told me that Mr. Johnson's son works for one of those pest companies. So I asked Mr. Johnson about him, just casually, to see what he would say. Well, Mr. Johnson was so happy to talk to me, and he did confirm that his son, Tom Junior, works for *PEST-B-GONE*, and that he could help us with the basement. He gave me Tom Junior's number and said to go right ahead and give him a call."

"Sure, hon, but that sounds expensive," Edgar said. "You know how those places are. Maybe I can just put some traps down there myself."

"No, Edgar," Wilma replied. "I don't want you going up and down those stairs. It's too dangerous, and we already agreed to call someone for help. I'm going to call him now." Without waiting for further debate, Wilma went into the kitchen and dialed the number.

Edgar stared blankly at the television, but turned the volume down, hoping to hear the conversation, especially the part about how much it was going to cost. Unfortunately, the buzzing in his ears made that impossible. A few minutes later, Wilma returned.

"Good news," Wilma said. "Tom Junior said that he would come over after work on Wednesday and look at the basement for us—for free. He said that he would only charge us for any traps or chemicals he might need to buy."

"I suppose that's all right," Edgar replied. "I would hate to spend a lot of money on that basement,"

"Edgar, dear, that's enough. If something is down there, we need to get it out."

"Okay. Sorry, hon."

Although Wilma seemed satisfied, Edgar remained unsure, not about Tom Junior coming over and putting out traps, but what was really down there. Even though it made sense logically, it didn't *feel* like a mouse or a squirrel to him. But for Wilma's sake, he kept that to himself.

§

On the Wednesday evening that Tom Junior arrived, the temperature outside was in the low twenties and snow flurries were blowing hard. The knock on the front door startled Edgar, as he'd completely forgotten about the appointment. Wilma remembered though, and had the porch light turned on ahead of time. She scurried across the living room and opened the front door. Tom Junior was a short, heavy-set man about the size of his father, and in Wilma's estimation, about thirty years old. He had wavy brown hair flowing out from under an old baseball cap. On the front was a graphic image of a mouse running away from a giant lightning bolt. Below that was printed: *PEST-B-GONE*. In his hand was a long black flashlight. He offered a warm, genuine smile that stretched across his entire face.

"Good evening, Mrs. Howard," he said.

"Good evening, Thomas," Wilma replied.

"Please, ma'am, you can just call me Tommy. Everyone calls me Tommy, except my dad. He calls me Junior, but I prefer Tommy."

"Oh, okay," Wilma replied. "My goodness, it's cold out there. Come on in Tommy before you freeze to death."

"Thank you, ma'am." Brushing the snowflakes off his jacket, Tommy stepped into the house and Wilma quickly closed the door behind him.

"Let me show you to the basement," she said.

"Yes, ma'am," Tommy replied. "Just let me put these on first. I don't want to get your nice carpets dirty."

Tommy leaned up against the door and slid blue plastic slippers over his work boots. Wilma then led him through the living room and into the kitchen, where Edgar was sitting at the table eating his dinner. When he saw Wilma and Tommy appear, he started to get up.

"Oh please, Mr. Howard, there's no need to get up for me." Tommy reached out and offered his hand as Edgar fell softly back into his chair. "I'm Tommy Johnson, sir. If you recall, we met once in church about a year or so ago. I usually attend the later service, but I know you folks go earlier, like my dad."

"It's nice to meet you, Tommy," Edgar said. "We're glad you could come by and look at our…little problem."

"It's my pleasure, folks. I'm glad to be of service. It sounds like you might have an unwanted intruder. I'll take a look and see what I can do to take care of that for you."

"Mrs. Howard thinks there might be something living down there," Edgar said. "And that door there has been blowing open. So we think that whatever it is, it probably came in through a crack somewhere." Edgar thought of being watched as well, but decided not to share that. "I was down there recently," he continued, "but didn't notice any serious damage or openings. Also, that basement hasn't been properly cleaned out in oh, let me think now, close to fifty years I'd say. I think we straightened it up a bit when we bought the place from my folks. Did we ever clean it out after that, hon?"

"It doesn't really matter, dear," Wilma replied. "I'm sure Tommy doesn't need to know that."

"Sure, hon. I was just getting at, well, that it's a bit of a mess down there. It may be hard to find whatever *it* is."

"Well, folks," Tommy said, "if there's anything living down there, I'll find it; that's what I do. You would be surprised at what I've found over the years. He caught himself before elaborating further—nearly forgetting how those gory details might sound to these nice folks. "When it's cold outside," he continued, "like it is now, all the critters want to be in where it's warm, just like us humans do."

"That's wonderful, son," Edgar said. "What do we need to do?" Edgar pushed his chair back and began to get up.

"Oh, nothing at all," Tommy said. "You folks just relax and finish your dinner; this is my department."

"Edgar," Wilma scolded, "you stay put."

"Oh, okay, hon." Edgar slumped back into his chair.

Wilma opened the door to the basement. Some cold air drifted out, but not enough for it to be consider it a breeze. Under the circumstances though, it was all she had to work with. "There's that breeze Mr. Howard mentioned."

Edgar was not close enough to feel it for himself, but he did wonder if it was warm and smelled like grass.

"Well, the source of the breeze is probably where they're coming in," Tommy said. "I'll take a look and see." With that he moved past Wilma and into the basement doorway. He noticed the light string and pulled it until it clicked. He switched on his flashlight and surveyed the wooden stairs, and then took a cautious step down, feeling for the strength of the old wood. Confident that the steps were strong enough to hold his weight, Tommy pulled the door closed behind him and continued down.

Wilma sat down to finish her dinner.

"I sure hope he can get rid of whatever is down there," Edgar said.

"Oh, I'm sure he can," Wilma replied. "Like he said, that's what he does for a living."

§

Each step creaked in response to Tommy's guarded but heavy descent. Once at the bottom, he waved his flashlight slowly from left to right and gasped, "Whoa, what a mess!" He raised his open hand to his mouth, hoping that his voice had not traveled upstairs. He found the lower light switch and flipped it. A single, low-watt bulb came to life in the center of the open room to his left. *What are they doing with all of these boxes and junk?* Along the right side were metal shelves filled with smaller boxes, trinkets and other junk. There was an old toaster, some china and glasses, games, puzzles and model ships. Out toward the center of the room, mixed throughout more boxes, were suitcases, an old brass floor lamp and stacks of clothes. Leaning against the back wall was a small mattress. Next to that, a vintage looking baby crib and high chair sat in dusty silence. Wrapped around the backrest of the high chair was a faded pink bow. Closer to the stairs, the junk and boxes were more randomly tossed and scattered, as if there were a point in time in which the Howards had given up on any sense of organization and just began dumping.

Tommy moved along the wall to his left, where there was a door to the closed in area under the stairs. After undoing the latch, he pulled it open. Inside were rows of plywood shelves; it looked like the small space was used as a pantry at one time. It was mostly empty, except for some old canned vegetables and a few items scattered here and there. Along the bottom of the wall, dead insects and mouse droppings were everywhere. An old rusty metal toolbox was pushed back under the stairs. Tommy checked the wall for cracks and openings, but there was nothing big enough for a rodent to get through. He left the pantry and re-latched the door.

Continuing along the outer wall, Tommy pushed aside several empty boxes. As he approached the first of two windows, another pile of boxes blocked his way. He put his hand on top and pushed lightly; they were full of something heavy and did not move. He shined the flashlight down the narrow gap between the boxes and the wall, where something caught his attention. Getting down on his knees, he reached his hand as far back as it would go. He felt the object with the tips of his fingers and managed to grab it. He stood up and laid it on the top box. Staring at it curiously, he then turned it over to examine the other side. After observing both sides closely, he picked up the dusty twenty-dollar bill, folded it in half and slid it into his jacket pocket.

At the first window, drab green curtains with an outdated gold floral pattern hung from a corroded brass curtain rod. Tommy pulled aside the fabric, revealing a window coated with a film of dirt and age. In his mind, he imagined the ammonia-filled scent of window cleaner. He examined the area closely, running his hand around the edge of the frame, feeling for cold air. There were no cracks in the glass or gaps around the edges. It was sealed well enough to keep out anything with four legs. Satisfied with the condition of that window, he worked his way toward the next one, maneuvering around and over more debris. He came across another pile of stacked boxes, and resisted the urge to open one and see what was inside. *A good Christian would not do that.*

At the next window he found what he was looking for—a breeze. He didn't even need to feel around to find it. The large crack in the concrete near the bottom of the frame made it clear where the air was coming from. He pushed gently on the glass and the whole window and frame creaked and moved. He presumed the crack to be at least partially responsible for the door opening upstairs; an imbalance in air pressure from the cold basement. *A good caulking all around with some spray foam should seal this up nicely. That will take care of anything trying to get in, and then some traps along the walls should take care of what's already inside.*

Tommy headed back toward the stairs. Along the way he began to feel a sense of unease settling over him. He had been in hundreds of basements and cellars and attics far worse than this one—but had never felt anything quite like it. It felt unnatural—a presence he could not define. He approached the closed doorway that led to the other side of the basement. Reaching for the doorknob, a part of him hoped that it was locked, that there was no key to be found and he could just get out of here. Unfortunately, the knob turned with ease and the door opened with a creaking moan. He shined his light around and located the light switch. A room full of bright light was exactly what he needed, but a flip of the switch caused a disappointing pop from the nearby bulb. "Crap."

The old laundry and furnace room was filled with more discarded memories of the Howard's' past. Two old suitcases sat just to the right of the doorway. On the opposite side of the room was a laundry tub next to a bare spot on the floor, where a washer and dryer had obviously once stood. Dust, pieces of lint and an old sock outlined the area. Near the top of the wall was another window with the same green and gold curtains, and further down a second one was partially blocked by a rolling garment cart; two white dress shirts dangled from the top bar. Opposite that, on the left side of the narrow room, was the furnace sitting next to an outdated water heater. At the far end was another closed door, and from what Tommy could discern, the room on the other side was quite small, probably a closet or a storage room. He chuckled at the thought. *This whole basement is a storage room.*

At the first window, a slow sweep of his hand under the curtain indicated more cold air. Tommy flipped the curtain up and shined his flashlight. The glass was still intact, but like the previous one, the seals around the frame were badly deteriorated. He moved to the final window and, just as he was about to grab the curtain, a creaking sound came from just behind him. Startled, he dropped the flashlight. As it hit the concrete, the room went pitch black. His heart raced as he turned and pressed his back against the wall, and then lowered himself to the floor. He felt some invisible force closing in around him, and had to resist the urge to scream out for help. Sweeping his hand frantically across the floor, he found what he was looking for. Just as he clicked the flashlight back to life, the furnace, just a few feet in front of him, did as well. The sensors and solenoid crackled and the glow plug ignited the chambers. *What's wrong with me?* After composing himself, Tommy stood up and turned back to the window, where cold air was seeping in through the seals.

The room at the end was the last place that needed to be checked. Although Tommy wanted desperately to get out of the basement, and away from whatever this strange feeling was coming from, a promise was a promise. He walked up to the door, whispered a prayer and grabbed the doorknob. As if God had granted his wish for being a good Christian, the door was locked. Out of habit more than desire, he tried turning it again. *What are you doing? Just get out of here.* He did a quick check for leaks, then turned and hurried back toward the stairs. As he grabbed for the handrail, a new feeling came over him, causing him to stop in his tracks. He glanced at the stairs in front of him and then slowly around the room. The beam of the flashlight revealed nothing to confirm his suspicion, yet as he turned off the dim overhead light and started up, he was certain that something down there was watching him.

10
AN IDOL IN THE MAKING

People were still searching for their seats when Fred Hutchinson wound up and delivered the first pitch of the game. Edgar watched intently as the ball shot out of the pitcher's hand and on a line toward the batter. A popping sound followed, a brief silence, and then the umpire's arm rising for a strike. The call was met with an agreeable cheer from the crowd. At first, Edgar thought the crowd was cheering the umpire, but then realized his mistake. His grandfather put an arm around his shoulders and together they waited for the next pitch. After a single, double-play and a strikeout, the top of the first inning was over.

"Looks like this kid has good stuff today."

"Grandpa, why do you call him a kid?" Edgar asked. "He looks like a grown-up to me."

His grandfather replied with a chuckle, "When you're as old as I am, Edgar, everyone is a kid." That initiated another bout of coughing. "I need to get something for this cough." He waved down a vendor carrying a red metal tub with a white *Coca-Cola* logo on the side.

"Are you thirsty, pal, or hungry?"

"Yeah, both," replied Edgar, opening his bag of pee-nuts.

Large icy *Cokes* appeared, followed by hot dogs and *Cracker Jacks*. As Edgar chewed and watched the action, a bag of buttery popcorn made its way into his lap. He looked over toward his grandfather, who smiled and winked.

§

The fourth inning came to a close with the *Tigers* leading 1-0. A scattering of fans began making their way toward the aisles.

"I need to use the restroom," his grandfather said. "Gotta go?"

"Naw," Edgar replied as his hand dug deeper into the popcorn bag.

"You okay sitting here by yourself?"

"Yeah."

"Okay, pal. I'll be right back."

Edgar watched the activities as his stomach grumbled from the onslaught. Blurs of people came and went from every direction and vendors enthusiastically pushed their wares. The *Tigers* players moved out onto the field and baseballs started flying around, seeming to hover from player to player, as if gravity had no affect on them. Edgar turned his face upward and closed his eyes, to enjoy the warmth of the sun on his face, which caused the inside of his eyelids to glow a brilliant orange. Swirling movements and gradating textures made the color come alive—like viewing the surface of the sun. Then a strange sensation began to form—a tingling feeling that started over his skin before moving inward. Curious, he kept his eyes closed. As he focused in, a weightlessness began to permeate everything. The seat underneath him seemed no longer connected to the concrete, but rather floating above it. It felt good, in a curious sort of way, like the feeling he got on the roller coaster at the carnival, that sensation in his stomach and down below.

The intense glow on Edgar's inner eyelids began change. Starting at the perimeter of his vision, it faded from that fiery orange to gray and then to black. The heat of the sun on his face settled down to a gentle warmth—like a hot summer day evolving into a comfortable evening. Edgar suspected it was just the clouds moving past the sun, so he kept his eyes closed and let the experience continue. His attention shifted from the physical sensations to the sounds coming from all around, which were expanding and distorting. It felt like the fans watching the game with him and his grandfather were moving further away, while something unexplainable was moving in closer. Blurry and dreamlike, ghosted forms moved against his own shapelessness. In some form of non-physicality, he could feel hands touching him on his back and shoulders—powerful sensations of camaraderie and oneness filling his mysterious inner space.

A tiny dot of light appeared in the center of Edgar's vision, far in the distance. He sensed something peculiar about the space between himself and the light, like the distance could not be measured in feet, but rather in time. Then, as if it had noticed his awareness upon it, the light began to grow, taking the form of a vertically oriented rectangle. Rather than approaching, he realized it was actually he himself who was moving. His inner eyes looked down but he could see no legs or feet, or even feel them touching the ground. Still, he knew that he was walking down a long tunnel, and the light was not just an illumination, but rather a doorway—an exit from where he was into someplace else. The thought of that alone elicited a tinge of fear in Edgar, not of death per se, but of something unimaginable—grander.

The panel of light was now just a few steps away, hovering above where the ground should have been. Edgar could sense subtle colors and abstract movements deep within the depths of the light, even though it appeared as only a dimensionless film, like a sheet of vellum separating him from another world. He squinted, but there was no focusing through it. A deep rumble appeared and began to build, shaking everything. It came not from a singular source, but rather from thousands of scattered vibrations, all synchronized by some mysterious commonality. Goose bumps appeared on his formless body as the movements around him became more animated—the energy of the space intensifying. One by one the ghostly figures passed by, and as each one faded into the light, the vibration surged.

Desperate to see what lie beyond, Edgar stepped up to the edge of the light. As he did, the veil of haze dissolved. The colors, that before were muted and translucent, washed across his vision with a dream-like intensity that bordered on surreal. A carpet of the most vibrant green spread out endlessly. Set between the field of green and the dark sky above was what Edgar recognized instantly as the inside of Briggs Stadium. There was movement all around as thousands of tiny bodies filled every available space. Hanging everywhere were red, white and blue circular banners; the American flag blew proudly in the distance. Sensing that something was missing, he looked out over the field, where baseball players he didn't know, but somehow did, were warming up. His gaze crossed the infield and stopped at the pitcher's mound. It was empty, and that was the answer. The sky drew his attention back upward, and that's when he noticed them—the giant stars beaming down from all around the roof of the stadium; hundreds of individual lights formed into strange rectangular constellations—floating—transforming the night into day.

Edgar stood alone at the threshold and stared out into that strange and magical realm. The humming intensified, drawing him outward with an energy that was so utterly foreign, while also immensely powerful and intoxicating. He looked down and noticed that his feet had appeared. He was now standing at the edge of the grass, looking out toward the empty pitcher's mound. He raised his weightless foot, ready to take his first step—

§

"Edgar?"

Edgar jumped in his seat. He opened his eyes and squinted into the bright sun. A face hovered above, talking to him in a blurry distortion of words. As his outer world came back into focus, he recognized the smiling face.

"Edgar?"

"Huh?" he replied.

"Hey, pal, I didn't mean to startle you," his grandfather said as he settled himself into his seat. "Not sleeping on game day, are ya?"

"Uh, no," Edgar said, "just resting my eyes for a minute, that's all." Edgar felt a little foolish as the imagery of the dream began to dissolve. But the feeling of being *there* lingered—and it felt wonderful. He wondered what his grandfather would think about such a crazy dream, right in the middle of the day like that, and at the ballpark of all places. His grandfather already thought he was sleeping on their special day, so he decided to just keep the whole silly thing to himself.

"Are you okay, pal?" his grandfather asked. "You seem a little spooked."

"I'm okay, Grandpa."

After settling himself back into his body, Edgar asked, "Grandpa?"

"Yeah?"

"Do they play baseball games here at night?

"Sure. They have lights up there, see?" He pointed to the large metal towers sitting on top of the roof, spaced evenly around the stadium. "They just put them in earlier this year, I believe. Why do you ask?"

Edgar stared up toward the light towers, surprised that he had not noticed them before. Or maybe he had, and his dream had somehow brought them into his awareness. He then said, "Someday, I'd like to see a baseball game at night."

"I've never been to a game at night," his grandfather replied. "I guess an old fellah like me believes baseball was meant to be enjoyed during the day, beneath the sun and the blue skies, the way God intended."

As Edgar watched the next pitch, a new thought appeared in his head. "I think it would be fun to *play* baseball here at night," he said, "under the giant stars."

§

At the end of the 7th inning, with the *Tigers* leading 4-2, his grandfather leaned over and said, "Come on, pal, let's go." He patted Edgar's arm and raised himself from his seat.

"Are we leaving?" Edgar asked nervously, not wanting to miss a minute of the game.

"Nope. Just follow me; I've got an idea."

They walked the middle isle back toward the infield and continued around until they were behind home plate. Edgar waited as his grandfather talked to the usher guarding the top of the isle. With the noise of the crowd, he couldn't hear what they were saying. His grandfather pointed down toward the screen behind home plate, and the usher said something back while gently shaking his head from side to side. Then, the two men shook hands. Edgar noticed a folded up dollar bill of some denomination being passed from his grandfather to the usher, who looked down at it. His eyes grew wide and he smiled nervously, then nodded and started down the steps toward the field.

Still smiling, his grandfather said, "Come on, pal."

"Where are we going?"

"New seats!"

They made their way down the steps until they were just a half-dozen rows from the screen and the field. The usher wiped down two seats with a dirty rag, backed out, pointed to the two slightly less dirty seats and said, "Enjoy the rest of the game, fellas." He turned and disappeared back up the steps.

"New seats," his grandfather said again.

"Really?"

"You bet! Best seats in the house!"

Edgar moved in and sat down next to a nicely dressed older lady with gray hair who offered him a pleasant hello. He could smell her immediately, like she couldn't decide on which perfume to use, so she used them all, and lots of each. On her head was a bright green hat with an assortment of bows and ribbons. Her hands were decorated with large rings set with colorful stones. To her left sat an equally well-dressed man that Edgar assumed was her husband. He noticed that everyone in their new section was dressed up nice, like they had all come from church or a family wedding. Looking back out toward the field, he could not believe how close they were; he could almost talk to the players from where they now sat.

§

The joy of the moment was short-lived as the *Indians* began to rally. After two singles and a home run, they took the lead by the score of 5-4. Parts of the booing crowd began to move toward the exits. But Edgar kept his attention focused on the game, which had stopped between plays as an older *Tigers* player came out of the dugout and walked slowly toward the pitcher's mound.

"Who's that, Grandpa?" Edgar asked.

"That's the manager. He's either going to talk to him to calm him down, or he's going to take him out of the game."

"Can he do that?" Edgar asked. He thought of the boys at the park and wondered what would happen if someone tried to take one of those bullies out of the game. Turning back toward the field, he wondered if a fight might break out.

"Oh, sure," his grandfather said. "The manager can change pitchers if they are not playing well. Actually, he can take any player out of the game, if he wants to."

The manager took the ball from the pitcher, whose head dropped as he began to walk off the mound and back toward the dugout. An unenthusiastic mixture of boos and cheers came from the thinning crowd.

"Looks like he's coming out."

"Who's going to pitch now?" Edgar asked.

"One of the relief pitchers," his grandfather replied. "Their job is to come in when the starter is struggling, and try to pitch the rest of the game without giving up more runs."

As Edgar listened, a fresh murmur of excitement began to spread throughout the nearby crowd. Fans that were leaving paused and waited while others began to stand up and look over toward the *Tigers* dugout. A burst of applause came from that direction. As

Edgar stood to get a better look, the cheers from the crowd grew until most of the remaining fans were standing.

"What's happening, Grandpa?" Edgar asked.

"I'm not sure; I can't see what's going on down there."

With a little bit of maneuvering and leaning forward into the next row, Edgar caught a glimpse of a *Tigers* player standing near the team dugout, looking in. He then turned toward the field and took a few steps forward until he reached the edge between the dirt and the grass. He paused with his head down, as if he were looking at his shoes. The stadium vibrated as the crowd cheered even louder. Then the pitcher stepped onto the grass and continued toward the mound. Before he reached his position on the field, Edgar noticed the number on the back of his jersey; it was 16.

"Will you look at that?" his grandfather said.

Edgar looked toward him and asked, "What, Grandpa, what?"

"Do you know who that is out there? Number 16?"

"No," Edgar said as he looked back toward the infield.

"That's Hal Newhouser."

"Really?" Edgar replied, straining for a better look.

As the fans began to settle back into their seats, Edgar remained standing, and watched as the man on the mound began throwing warm-up pitches.

"That's very unusual," his grandfather said, "for a starting pitcher to come in as a reliever. The coach must think this game is pretty important to bring in Hal Newhouser to finish it out."

For Edgar, it was the most exciting moment of the whole day. He couldn't explain it, this mysterious connection to a player that he'd never seen before, and until just a couple of weeks ago, had never even heard of. He focused on Hal Newhouser as the next batter approached the plate. With the pitcher staring down the batter, Edgar sensed something else coming from out there on the mound. It was different, a feeling that he had never really experienced himself, yet he knew instinctively what it was—confidence.

With a long and graceful windup; his arms swinging forward and his right knee raising almost to his chin, Hal Newhouser delivered his first pitch. The ball shot out of his hand like a blur and hit the catcher's mitt with a resounding pop. The excitement of the game, that seemed lost just moments before, had returned. As Edgar looked on, absorbing every detail of the action, he wondered what it must have taken Hal Newhouser to reach the big leagues and become an MVP. Certainly it was more than just practicing a lot. He imagined Hal Newhouser as a kid, and was pretty sure that *he* was not afraid of any bullies.

§

Hal Newhouser closed out the 8th inning without giving up another run, leaving the *Tigers* in a 4-5 deficit. Fortunately for the remaining fans, the *Tigers* came back with a vengeance in the bottom of the inning. They tied the game with a single and a double, chasing the *Indians* pitcher from the mound. After two walks and a double, the *Tigers* took the lead 7-5, and the crowd was thundering with delight. For Edgar though, the real excitement came two batters later when number 16 approached the plate. He remembered what his grandfather had said about pitchers not being good hitters, but he didn't care. To see Hal Newhouser there, standing at the plate just steps from where he was sitting, was magical. With two outs on the board, someone nearby said, "At least we'll go into the 9th with a two run—" Before the man could finish, Hal Newhouser swung at a pitch that seemed too far outside to hit; his long arms stretching as the bat moved with grace and power. The crowd paused and held its collective breath as the bat made contact. The ball returned to the field as a line drive deep into left center. The two outfielders converged upon it, but it dropped between them and continued all the way to the wall. The crowd went wild as the other two base runners raced around and scored easily. Hal Newhouser slid safely into third base under a cloud of dust. Along with the remaining fans, Edgar jumped up and down with excitement. His grandfather stood as well, whistling so loud it nearly drowned out the cheers.

"He's really good, isn't he, Grandpa?" Edgar asked. "Is he the best player on the team?"

"Yeah, I think he is. That's what an MVP looks like, Edgar. Never forget that."

"Most valuable player," Edgar repeated. And no, he would never forget.

§

"Let's just sit here for a while," his grandfather said, "and let the crowd clear out a little."

"Okay," Edgar replied, happy to keep the day going.

"What do you think?" his grandfather asked. "Great game, huh? *Tigers* take it 9-to-5 and Hal Newhouser gets the win."

"Yeah," Edgar replied, "great game."

There was a short period of silence as they watched the few remaining fans trickle out the exits.

"Grandpa?"

"Yeah?"

"This was the best day ever."

"Come on, pal, it's not over yet. We have one more thing to do."

They made their way up the steps and down the long inner corridor, where workers had replaced fans and large garbage cans were being filled with waste. They exited the main gate to the street, where the sun had moved from its earlier peak in the sky and was now casting long shadows across Michigan Avenue. Edgar followed his grandfather's lunging strides, his eyes focused on the sidewalk in front of him. His mind still on the game, he replayed each pitch, and the way the ball traveled to the plate; some were fast and straight and others with big curves. There was the movement of Hal New-houser's body as he wound up and pitched. Edgar filed everything into his memory. When they finally stopped, he noticed that they were standing within a crowd along the outside of the stadium. There was a commotion somewhere off to the left. He drifted back to the game as his grandfather talked to some people nearby.

"Edgar? Edgar, you there, pal?"

"Uh, yeah," Edgar mumbled, looking around. His grandfather had somehow gotten behind him and his hands were resting on his shoulders. They were standing up near the front of the crowd, close to the side of the stadium. To Edgar's left was a large doorway, with a police officer standing guard on each side. There was a tall man standing directly in front of him, so he had to lean to his left to get a better view. He also noticed that people were turning and forming a circle around him. From behind, his grandfather chuckled, followed by laughter from the nearby crowd. Edgar couldn't see what was funny, with the tall man blocking his view.

His grandfather leaned down and said into his ear, "Edgar, I would like you to meet someone."

"Huh?" Edgar looked back up over his shoulder at his grandfather's smiling face. "Who?"

"Well, this man standing right there in front of you."

Edgar turned back toward the man who was blocking his view. He was very tall, and nicely dressed in a light gray pinstripe suit and a matching hat that he held in his hand. His hair was short and golden blonde, with a large sweeping curl on top. Under his right eye was a large scar. He was looking down at Edgar with a friendly smile, but said nothing.

His grandfather rubbed his shoulders and asked, "Edgar, do you know who this is?'

Edgar felt his heart beginning to race as the people all around seemed to be staring at him. The man did look familiar, but he didn't want to guess and say the wrong thing.

His grandfather seemed to sense his discomfort and said, "Edgar, this is Hal Newhouser."

Edgar's body tensed, and his now racing heart seemed determined to break through his chest. "Huh? Really?"

The tall, well-dressed man reached out his hand and said, "Pleased to meet you, Edgar."

Edgar froze, not sure what to say or do. He couldn't believe that Hal Newhouser, a real *Detroit Tiger*, was standing right there in front of him. He felt like he should say something, but his lips refused to move. His lungs moved short, rapid bursts of air.

"It's okay, pal, you can talk to him," his grandfather said.

Edgar reached out a shaking hand and Hal Newhouser grasped it firmly in his.

"Did you enjoy the game, Edgar?" Hal Newhouser asked.

As nervous as he was, Edgar knew that this was a once-in-a-lifetime opportunity, and if he didn't say something he would feel like an idiot for the rest of his life. So he let it all out, "Yeah, it was the greatest game ever! It was my first real baseball game and it's very nice to meet you, sir!" There were more chuckles from the crowd, but Edgar didn't notice.

Hal Newhouser placed his hat on his head and reached inside his coat pocket. He felt around and pulled out a short stack of baseball cards. From another pocket he withdrew a stubby yellow pencil and scribbled something on the top card. "These are my first baseball cards, Edgar," Hal Newhouser said with a chuckle, "and I want you to have one." He handed Edgar the signed card.

Edgar took the card. "Wow, thank you, sir!" He remembered that he already had a Hal Newhouser card, but decided right there that if he had to keep only one of them, it would be this one.

"It's a pleasure to meet such a great fan, Edgar. It's really swell that you were able to come to the game today, and I hope you and your grandfather will come again real soon."

"Thank you, Mr. Newhouser!" Edgar said, beaming.

"Edgar, you can just call me Hal."

Edgar smiled as Hal Newhouser looked up at his grandfather. The two of them reached out and shook hands. "Sir," Hal said, then turned toward another fan.

§

On the drive home, Edgar could not stop talking. He recounted, over and over, every detail of the day, from how big the stadium was and how perfect the grass looked (no rocks or weeds at all) to all the happy rich people who filled the seats. There were the players throwing balls that just floated across the air and the pop of the ball in the catcher's glove. The hot dogs were the best he'd ever had and he just loved *Cracker Jacks* but his mother hardly ever bought them. The game was amazing, too. He loved watching the pitchers working to keep the batters off balance with different types of pitches—fast ones, curves and breaking balls. And, of course, meeting Hal Newhouser in person and getting his very own autographed baseball card was his favorite part of all. *You can just call me Hal.* Edgar could hardly believe he was on a first name basis with the great Hal Newhouser.

As Edgar bounced excitedly in his seat and chatted on, his grandfather sat behind the wheel, smiling and listening to every word with the joy of a grandparent who got exactly what he wanted, an unforgettable day at the ballpark with his favorite grandson.

§

Later that night, Edgar settled himself under the covers and looked across his bedroom. Sitting on top of his dresser, leaning against his new baseball glove, and seeming to glow in the dim moonlight, was his signed Hal Newhouser baseball card. He couldn't stop thinking about the best day he'd ever had. As soon as they got home, he replayed every detail with his mother and grandmother, and even shared the day's events with his father over dinner; he couldn't help himself. Afterwards, he raced over to Jimmy's with his card and spent the evening sitting on the porch, reliving the day yet again. By the time he had left Jimmy's house, he and Hal Newhouser were the best of friends and would probably be spending more time together whenever Hal didn't have a game. But now, unable to keep his eyes open any longer, Edgar let them close. As they did, his mind drifted back to Briggs Stadium, now his favorite place in the whole world. His imagination ascended until he was the one standing on the mound, the crowd cheering his every pitch. Above him, hundreds of giant stars glowed beneath a deep indigo sky.

11
DOWN BELOW

Thundering footsteps echoed up the stairwell, causing Wilma's prized Norman Rockwell prints to rattle on the wall above the kitchen table. Tommy appeared, pulling cobwebs off his hat and brushing at his shoulders. The expression on his face was not the same jovial Tommy that had gone down twenty minutes earlier. He moved across the kitchen, put his flashlight on the counter next to the sink, turned on the faucet and proceeded to splash cold water on his face.

As the creepiness faded in the light of the kitchen, Tommy wondered what he was going to tell the Howards, and what he wasn't. He turned around to see them sitting at the table, staring at him with looks of concern. He quickly shifted to his *it's not as bad as it seems* face and took a deep breath. "Well, folks, I did some looking around down there. I found cold air leaking in through some of the window seals. One has a nice gap where the caulking has fallen out and a bit of the concrete around the frame has broken loose. I don't think it's big enough for a raccoon, but mice could get through there, and possibly a chipmunk or a—" He caught himself before saying *rat*. It was a word that the warehouse and factory owners could handle, but for homeowners it was a different story. He once told a couple that they *may* have rats in their basement and a for-sale sign was in the front yard by the time he returned for a follow up visit. It was *PEST-B-GONE* policy to present the customer with the truth, or in his critical opinion, the worst-case scenario version of the truth, as that tended to improve sales. It was not how he would prefer to do things, but he did follow the rules. Since this was a pro-bono job though, he didn't feel obligated to share the doom and gloom sales pitch. "Those cracks are probably the cause of your draft," he said. "The cold air is coming in and forcing the warmer air up the stairs and pushing on that door. I can fix the cracks and gaps pretty easy with a little bit of spray foam."

"Did you find anything *living?*" Edgar asked, his eyes shifting from Tommy to Wilma.

"Well, Mr. Howard, I didn't see anything moving, but there are some mouse droppings. But that's normal. Mice can get in through the smallest of openings, so it's hard to keep them out completely. I can put some traps down there and seal everything up good and tight. That should do the trick."

"That's so kind of you, Tommy," Wilma said.

Tommy was surprised at how much he didn't want to return to this particular basement, but he had no intention of breaking his promise to help. "I'm going over to the *Home Depot* now and get some traps and sealant," he said. "I can't use what's in the truck; the company keeps track of that stuff. I should be back in about an hour, if that's okay with you folks."

"Oh, sure, we're not going anywhere," Wilma replied as she moved toward the living room. "Let me get my purse. How much do you think all those things will cost, Tommy?"

Edgar cringed in anticipation.

Tommy thought for a moment. "No more than twenty dollars, maybe less."

Wilma returned with her wallet and opened it up on the kitchen counter. She pulled out several small bills and laid them out in front of her. She counted out a total of seventeen dollars in fives and singles as Tommy watched on.

"It's okay, Mrs. Howard, that should be enough."

"No, no," Wilma replied. She opened a drawer and retrieved a small glass jelly jar filled with coins. She poured out a pile of change and separated the quarters until she had 12, scooped them up and poured them into Tommy's open hands. "You let me know if it cost a penny more, Tommy."

"Yes, ma'am."

Wilma waited for Tommy to put the money in his pocket and followed him to the front door. She thanked him again for his help, then let him out into the cold December night, quickly closing the door behind him. She headed back toward the kitchen as Edgar made his way down the hallway toward his bedroom.

"Hon, I'm going to go and rest my eyes for a few minutes."

"Okay, dear."

§

A little more than an hour from the time he left, Tommy returned. This time he was carrying his flashlight in one hand, and in the other was a brown plastic bag with *Home Depot* printed in dull orange. "Sure is cold out there," Tommy said as he stepped inside.

"Well," Wilma said, "I have something that will warm you up nicely." She paused as he covered his boots, then led him back to the kitchen. On the table were two grilled cheese sandwiches cut into triangles and a large mug of steaming tomato soup. Iced tea in a commemorative *Detroit Tigers* glass sat next to it.

"I've made you some dinner," Wilma said.

"Oh, Mrs. Howard, you didn't have to do that."

"Well, I already did. So you just sit yourself down and eat young man."

"Yes, ma'am. This is very kind of you." After sitting down, Tommy laced his hands together and did a quiet prayer while Wilma waited respectfully.

Tommy ate while Wilma put the dishes away and wiped down the sink and counter top. After his last bite, he asked, "Mrs. Howard, do you have some more cheese, or maybe some peanut butter?"

"Are you still hungry?" Wilma replied. "I can make you another sandwich." She grabbed the bag of bread off the counter and started untwisting the tie.

"No, ma'am," Tommy said, "I could just use it for the traps. Mice like cheese, as everyone knows, but I find that peanut butter works better. They have to work a little harder for it." He was about to share how it kills them quicker—when their heads are further in the opening trying to get at the peanut butter, but thought twice about it. He decided that was a trade secret better kept to himself.

"Yes, Tommy," Wilma replied, "I have some peanut butter. Mr. Howard loves peanut butter sandwiches, too. Not as much as grilled cheese, but I like to mix things up for him. But he only likes the creamy peanut butter, not the chunky kind. I think the chunky gets stuck in his dentures. Will the creamy peanut butter work?"

"Yes, ma'am. The creamy kind will work just fine."

"Oh, good." Wilma pulled a jar of *Skippy* out of the pantry cabinet and set it on the counter. From the silverware drawer she pulled out a butter knife and started opening the bread again. She was about to pull out two slices when she realized what she was doing. "Oh, silly me. You don't want a sandwich, do you? You just want the peanut butter. Sometimes I don't know where my head is at."

Tommy smiled without saying a word as Wilma put the bread away, and then invited him to do what he needed to do. He washed and dried his hands before opening the jar. With the knife he scooped out a large portion, then closed the jar and put it aside. One by one he proceeded to take each mousetrap and spread a small amount of peanut butter along the back of the tongue, and then placed the unset traps into the *Home Depot* bag. Discretely, he wiped the remaining peanut butter on the inside of the bag, and finished up by running the knife under the faucet.

"Oh, Tommy, you don't have to do that," Wilma said as she hurried back toward the sink. "I'll clean up."

"Oh, thank you, Mrs. Howard." With that, Tommy grabbed his flashlight and the bag, and then opened the basement door. "This shouldn't take more than half an hour or so."

"Okay, Tommy, you take all the time you need," Wilma replied.

§

After switching on his flashlight, Tommy pulled the light string and proceeded down the steps. The feelings from earlier were gone, at least for the moment, washed away by the trip to *Home Depot*. He had turned the heat off in the truck and put the windows down, just enough to feel the frigid air blow across his face. That helped to clear his mind, and a trip to *Home Depot* always made him feel better. He loved walking up and down the aisles, looking at tools and parts and imagining having a place of his very own, where he could fix things up and make it just the way he wanted it. A real fixer-upper, that's what he dreamed of. Just thinking about his own place improved his mood dramatically, and by the time he had left the store with the traps and spray foam, he was whistling Christmas tunes.

Tommy moved quickly to the farthest window in the basement. He always worked his way back toward the exit, so he wouldn't accidentally step on a trap. Sitting the bag down on a box, he pulled out the can of spray foam. A thin clear hose was taped to the side, which he removed and inserted into the opening. After placing the open end of the hose into the large crack in the concrete, he gently pressed down on the nozzle, causing a hissing sound as air escaped from the end, blowing small bits of dust and debris all about. After a few seconds, a yellowish colored foam appeared from the hose, flowing into the crack. He continued around the perimeter of the window until all the gaps were filled and overflowing.

After the window was sealed, Tommy removed and set a mouse-trap, then placed it on the floor along the wall. He made quick work of sealing the other frames and setting traps along the walls, near doorways and in the corners he had identified earlier. Once he had all the traps set, he proceeded to the furnace. He knelt down on the floor and placed the *Home Depot* bag beside him, then reached in and pulled out a much larger trap. This one was nearly seven inches long and had four metal spikes protruding from the hammer bar. He had kept it hidden in the bag, as he didn't want Mr. or Mrs. Howard to see it. He thought they were unusually upset with just the possibility of mice in the house, and didn't want to worry them about a rat, or something else.

With his finger, Tommy scooped the peanut butter from the inside of the bag and spread it firmly along the catch part of the trap. He wanted to make sure the unwanted visitor did not eat the bait before getting what it had coming to it. He set the hold-down bar and carefully slid it up against the wall behind the furnace.

His work complete, Tommy moved back toward the stairs. He turned off the lone light in the main room and was about to start up when the strange feeling returned. It was the same sensation of being watched, but there was even more to it than that. It was like being felt, in some non-physical way, all the way through his skin. Agitated by the thought of some hidden rodent scaring him, and causing him to think such ridiculous thoughts, Tommy swept the light beam slowly across the room, looking closely into the spaces between boxes, across each shelf along the wall and up into the ceiling beams. "Just wait," Tommy said. "I'll get you; that's what I do." With that, he turned and headed back up the stairs.

§

Wilma was putting the dishes away when Tommy re-appeared. She looked over and noticed that he seemed a bit frazzled again. "Is everything all right, Tommy?"

Not realizing that his expression was so obvious, Tommy forced out a smile. "Oh, yes, Mrs. Howard. Everything is just perfect. I sealed up those windows and put out the traps. If you don't mind, I'd like to come back next Wednesday after work and clean them out for you. No charge, of course."

"That is so kind of you, Tommy," Wilma said. "You are such a blessing."

"It's my pleasure, ma'am."

As Tommy headed toward his truck, he tried to imagine what exactly might be lurking in the Howard's basement. He hoped that on Wednesday he would find it—in one of the traps.

§

Throughout the following week, Wilma scurried about the house—baking, cleaning and decorating. She went out almost daily, shopping for gifts on sale or to the grocery store for baking supplies or to the Post Office to mail cards. She frequented the church to help out in any way she could and dropped off food for the homeless. She kept a close eye on Edgar's behavior and, like a pre-holiday prayer answered, everything appeared to be back to normal. Whatever Tommy had done in the basement, it was working. With *Home Depot's* gross sales for the month of December increased by $19.64, courtesy of Edgar's Social Security check, and the basement scattered with *You Can Do It* products, the problem seemed to have been solved. Unless Edgar had been hiding something, the basement door had remained closed and there were no more scratching noises. All was good.

§

While Wilma went about her holiday preparations, Edgar spent his time under the guise of being his old self—but it wasn't easy. His curiosity about the basement door had turned into a borderline obsession. Whenever Wilma wasn't around, he was there checking it. But he wouldn't have had to do that if the gosh darn thing didn't keep opening. At one point the doorknob was so hot it left a red mark on his hand. That one almost forced him to bring Wilma back into the game. But she seemed so happy with her holiday planning and decorating that he didn't have the heart to upset her. On top of everything else was the buzzing in his ears, which seemed to have migrated right into the middle of his brain. He stared for hours at the television, much to Wilma's delight, yet he didn't hear a word of it. He spent the time focusing inward, and the more he did, the clearer it became that the noises in his head were anything but a normal part of aging.

12
THE LAST DAY

G randpa has to get back home," Edgar's mother said. "He has…
he has some appointments this week, and he cannot miss
them. He will try to come back soon, I promise. Maybe at the
end of the summer. Or, if not then, maybe for Christmas."

Edgar sensed no certainty in his mother's voice as she sat on the
edge of his bed, her fingers fiddling with her apron, the way they
did when she was nervous. She was keeping something from him;
he was certain of that. Her words seemed like lies; not the mean
kind, but the kind that were told when the food was really bad or
the gift was not what you had hoped for. He decided not to push
it; there was no sense in making her mad at him. Instead, he shifted
the subject just a bit. "Why can't they just move here," he said, "and
live with us?"

A more genuine smile appeared on his mother's face, as if she
liked the idea as much as he did.

"We'll see."

§

Their final walk to the park that morning was decidedly more somber than the first one several weeks before, when Edgar was appre-
hensive about the arrival of his grandparents, and wondered how
much they were going to disrupt his life. On this day, few words

were spoken until they reached their familiar spot. They sat at their table, the one they had visited every day, where they laughed and talked about baseball, life and the things that best friends share. For Edgar, it was an escape from his otherwise un-special life. It had become his safe place, where he could talk and be heard like a real person, not as a dumb kid saying stupid things to adults— who were too busy or impatient to listen. There at the picnic table his thoughts and ideas were taken seriously; responses were never harsh, but thoughtful and considerate.

His grandfather stared off toward the empty baseball field and said, "If all goes well…and the weather is good, maybe we can get back for a quick visit by the end of the season; maybe go to another game."

Edgar observed the sadness in his grandfather's eyes as he spoke, and something disturbing in his voice. His mother must have sensed it as well. "Yeah, Grandpa, that would be really swell."

Edgar had been spending more time than usual lately inside his own head, mostly at night in bed as the final minutes of the day burned away, before his ordinary old dreams got going. He would think of his father, sweating his days away in gloomy factories, year after year, and wondered what *he* dreamed of when he was twelve. Did he get the life he wanted, or was it just given to him? What about Hal Newhouser? And who decided such things? Was it God? Or did someone just pick lives from a hat and you got what you got? Edgar had no idea how it all worked, but since his grandfather had arrived he had begun to believe that maybe he wouldn't end up at the back of the line, only to find out that no good dreams were left. And he knew exactly which one he wanted when his number was called. He looked across the picnic table at his grandfather and said, "Grandpa, when I grow up, I want to be a baseball player—a great pitcher—just like Hal Newhouser."

Out of instinct, Edgar still half-expected his idea to be shot down, and to be told not to waste his time with such foolish thoughts. *Work hard and one day you might get to be the foreman of the factory*, his father once said. But this time there was no incredulous scowl waiting. The expression on his grandfather's face was completely void of judgment or disappointment. His eyes brightened and his face warmed into an approving smile. He spoke as if acknowledging a truth so absolute it could never be questioned, "Of course you will, pal. And you know what, I'm going to be right there watching you—from the front row."

§

The late afternoon sun presented itself briefly through an opening in the gloomy gray clouds, sparkling over the shinny blue Plymouth as it idled quietly in the driveway. The picnic lunch held earlier in the back yard was a happy, yet somber event. Even Edgar's father was relaxed and pleasant as he cooked hot dogs and hamburgers on the grill. Everyone talked and shared memories of the visit, with anticipation of more to come. After desert was served, cheesecake with an assortment of fresh fruits and a large watermelon, the mood turned as the inevitable end was in sight. Edgar did his best to keep the conversations going, and the car parked in the driveway, but finally it was time to go.

The trunk was loaded and both grandparents sat in the front seat, talking quietly to each other and fiddling with the maps. Hugs and good-byes had already been shared. Edgar's mother stood in nearly the same spot as when her parents had arrived and wiped tears from her eyes. So did Edgar; he couldn't help it. As he wiped his face, the driver's side window rolled down and his grandfather called out, "Hey, pal, come here a minute."

When Edgar appeared at the side of the car, his grandfather opened his wallet, pulled out a clean new five-dollar bill and handed it to him. "Buy yourself something really nice with this," he said. From behind, his mother lightly protested but, luckily for Edgar, she lost.

"Thanks, Grandpa!" Edgar said as he leaned in and hugged his grandfather again. Fresh tears rolled down his cheeks. When they finally pulled apart, his grandfather's eyes were red and watering as well, and this time it wasn't from coughing.

"Remember, Edgar, never give up on your dreams, and they will never give up on you. Can you make me that promise—to never give up?"

With a broken voice, Edgar replied, "Yeah, Grandpa, I promise."

As the rain began to fall, the car backed out of the driveway, changed direction and rolled slowly down Hawthorne Street. Edgar waved one last time to the grandfather he would never see again.

13
TRY AGAIN

Tommy arrived right on schedule. He was wearing a white uniform with a matching jacket; his name was scripted in red on the left pocket. In one hand was his flashlight and in the other a crumbled up plastic grocery bag. A small white pickup with a matching cap on the back, and the *PEST-B-GONE* logo printed along the side, sat in the driveway.

Wilma opened the door and looked past Tommy, out to the truck.

"Yeah, I was working late today," Tommy said as he looked down at his uniform. "I'm trying to make a few extra bucks—with the holidays and all. I want to buy one of those nice charm bracelets for my girlfriend. You know, where you put a little charm on it for each special occasion. We're also hoping to get married in the spring, and we need to save up some money for that; it costs a lot to get married these days. And I'd like to take her somewhere extra nice and romantic for our honeymoon, maybe to Niagara Falls."

"That sounds lovely, Tommy," Wilma said. "Won't you come in out of the cold?"

"Sure. I shouldn't be more than five or ten minutes, Mrs. Howard." With that, Tommy covered his boots and moved quickly to the basement door and disappeared down the stairs. His first scheduled stop was the laundry room and the trap behind the furnace. But even before reaching the bottom, he could feel the familiar dread coming on. It was as if he were the unwanted guest of an unwanted guest, an intruder into some mysterious family matter that did not concern him. Determined not to be bullied by some rodent he couldn't even see, Tommy forced the feeling aside and moved into the laundry area, shining his light into the eerie darkness. As he approached the furnace, he paused in anticipation. He took a deep breath and aimed the light back into the corner, hoping for something no worse than a rat. He was both disappointed and relieved to see the trap empty, and the peanut butter still there. Moving up for a closer look, he noticed that the peanut butter was not only still there, it had not been touched at all.

Despite the unexpected situation with the rattrap, and the disturbing sensation of being watched again, Tommy continued on, hurrying from trap to trap. Along the way he shined the flashlight into every corner, between boxes, up in the ceiling, wherever he sensed something could be hiding—and watching. Nothing jumped out at him and, to his surprise, all the other traps were empty as well, and the bait untouched. It occurred to him that perhaps the basement's smaller intruders might have something more concerning to deal with than basic sustenance. With nothing to show for his efforts, and concerned homeowners upstairs depending on him to solve their infestation problem, Tommy picked up some crumbled up pieces of paper and other small items from the floor and tossed it all into the *Home Depot* bag.

§

Reappearing from the basement, flashlight in one hand and the *Home Depot* bag in the other, Tommy closed the door firmly behind him. "Well, we got a couple," he said, shaking the bag.

"Oh, that is good news," Wilma said.

"I thought there would be more," Tommy added, "but it's a start. I left the traps down there, to hopefully catch some more. Sometimes these things take a bit of time."

§

Wilma closed the front door behind Tommy and went to check on Edgar. Halfway down the hall, the doorbell rang. "Oh my," she said, "he must have forgotten something."

"Mrs. Howard?" Tommy said, shivering on the porch.

"Yes?" Wilma replied as she welcomed Tommy for the second time that day.

"Well, I wanted to tell you something I nearly forgot about. Would it be all right for me to come in for just a minute?"

"Sure, Tommy, come on in."

"I feel really bad about this, Mrs. Howard. But I asked the pastor at church and he said I did the right thing."

"What is it, Tommy?"

"Well, ma'am, when I was here that first day—well, I did find something in your basement."

"Oh?"

"No, ma'am, not something *living*." Tommy reached into his coat pocket and pulled out a plain white envelope and handed it to Wilma.

"What is this, Tommy?" She opened the envelope and pulled out a strange looking twenty-dollar bill.

"I found that in your basement," Tommy said. "It was down between some boxes and the wall. I wasn't looking through anything, just looking for, you know, pests. It was all dirty, you see; it must have been down there for a long time. I thought nothing of it at first; just a twenty you know, and I figured I'd give it to you or Mr. Howard right away; it's yours of course. Then I took a closer look at it and—well—I don't know much about money, other than how to spend it, but it looked different somehow. At first I wasn't even sure it was real money."

"In what way, Tommy?"

"Well," Tommy said, "I noticed that the design was different, and saw that it was old—from 1922. Then I turned it over, and as you can see, the back is all printed in orange. That got me to thinking that maybe it might be worth a little something extra. I thought of my buddy, Mark. He owns a little collectibles shop over by the mall and knows a lot about coins and cards and such. I thought I'd have him take a look at it. I've known him since I was a kid, and he's a real honest, straight up guy. I know I should have talked to you about it right away, but I got busy downstairs and by the time I came back up, I completely forgot." Tommy considered mentioning being distracted by unseen eyes watching him, but decided against it. "When I got home later, I found it in my pocket as I was doing my laundry. That's when I got to thinking that it would be a real nice surprise for you and Mr. Howard, especially if it was worth something, you know—more. So I showed it to Mark, and he looked it up. He called it a gold certificate, and it turns out I was right. He said it's a bit rare, and worth about two hundred dollars. That's what he said he'd pay for it; then he would sell it and make a few bucks more for himself. He also told me I should get a finder's fee; that's a small percentage for bringing a seller and buyer together. But I told him that's not necessary."

"Oh my, Tommy, that sure is a lot of money."

"So I hope you will forgive me for taking something that wasn't rightfully mine. I never meant to keep it, but I'm also really glad it's worth more than the twenty dollars. I'm sure you folks could do something real nice for the holidays with an extra two hundred dollars; I know I could. That is unless you just decide to keep it; that would be nice, too."

"Thank you, Tommy," Wilma said. "That was very noble of you. I'll show this to Mr. Howard when he wakes up; maybe he'll remember where it came from."

"Yes, ma'am. And if you do decide to sell it, and need some help with that, I would be glad to help you out there. No finder's fee; it would be my pleasure."

"That's very kind of you, Tommy,"

Tommy opened the door and stepped out. "Stay warm, and please give my regards to Mr. Howard."

Wilma closed the door behind him and looked again at the bill.

§

Tommy was pleased with himself for returning the bill; it had been weighing on his conscience ever since he found it. As he drove home, his mind shifted to his concerns about the Howard's house. But even as the eerie feelings dissolved the further away he got, he couldn't help but wonder if *Home Depot* or *PEST-B-GONE* had the kind of traps or chemicals needed to exterminate that basement, and rid those kind folks of whatever was down there. He then wondered again if they had felt anything unusual, like being watched. Wisely, he decided to keep that to himself—and not scare them with his own paranoid nonsense.

§

Edgar woke from his nap, eased his feet into his slippers and headed toward the living room. He was already thinking of the door and the strange feeling from the basement. It occurred to him that Tommy was supposed to come back and check the traps. If he was still at the house, Edgar wanted to pull him aside and ask if he had smelled anything unusual down there, or if he felt like he was being watched. He would have to handle it carefully; the last thing he needed was for someone else to question his sanity. His hope dissolved though when Wilma informed him that Tommy had just left. He had caught some mice and, according to Wilma, everything was going as planned. As pleased as he was for Wilma, Edgar was not convinced. He was certain that something, in addition to small rodents, was scurrying about down there. And in his closely held opinion, it was unlikely that *PEST-B-GONE* or *Home Depot* had the kind of chemicals or supplies needed to exterminate it.

14
ALONE AGAIN

Standing at the back door, Edgar looked down at the old baseball resting in his glove. It was not his nice new one, but the one his grandfather had found in the garage when he was working on the Plymouth. Edgar wanted to keep the new one for special occasions—like for when his grandfather returned. But right now he wanted to have a catch, hoping it would relieve the empty feeling he felt inside. There was nobody to play with though. Being seen at the park alone was out of the question, and so was playing catch with Jimmy. Jimmy hated sports of any kind and would just complain the whole time. Edgar looked out the window and around the back yard. There was no room to throw there, for fear of damaging his mother's gardens. He glanced toward the alley out back and an idea came to him.

The side door to the garage creaked as Edgar opened it. He looked around cautiously, then slipped into the darkness. There was a small window on the left wall facing out into the yard, but it was covered with years of dust and blocked by stacks of paint cans piled on top of his father's old workbench. Except for a small open space in the middle, too small for a car, the rest of the garage was filled with junk. It smelled dirty and old, and he tried not to imagine what kind of bugs and other crawly things were living in here. His eyes scanned the space, but he didn't know exactly what he was looking for. On the other side was an old wooden crate on top of a pile of old boxes. "That might work," he said, maneuvering toward it. Reaching up, he grabbed the crate and pulled. Something fell from it onto to the ground behind the boxes and shattered like glass. He stood silent for a moment, hoping nobody had heard, then hurried out. Once outside, he checked the crate for bugs, then grabbed it and headed across the back yard, through the gate and out into the alley.

Edgar liked the alley. It was mostly used for garbage pickups, but it was quiet and the bigger kids in the neighborhood rarely used it, except to smoke and drink beer, but that was usually at night. Just outside the gate was an old stump from a tree that had been cut down years before. It was roughly two feet high and a foot wide. He put the crate on top of the stump and positioned it so that it was sitting vertically, with the opening facing diagonally out into the alley. Standing next to it, he noticed that his shoulders aligned near the top edge of the crate, while the bottom edge was just below his waist. "Good enough," he said, and then began backing out into the alley. Once satisfied with the distance, he took the front edge of his *Keds* and scratched a line in the dirt. With his pitching location set, he began gathering gravel, kicking it toward his line, building a crude mound. Getting down on his hands and knees, he spread the smaller piles into one larger one, and then stomped the whole thing down until it was packed good and tight. Once it looked reasonably usable, he stood back and observed his work. It was not the pitcher's mound at Briggs Stadium, but it was still pretty good.

Looking up and down the alley, to make sure nobody was watching him, Edgar turned back toward the crate. He brushed the dirt off of his hands and slid his glove on. On his makeshift pitcher's mound, standing tall and facing the crate, he closed his eyes and thought back to how Hal Newhouser stood that day. He tried to remember everything his grandfather had taught him; how a pitcher holds a baseball and where to put his fingers for each pitch. Opening his eyes, Edgar stared at the crate for the longest time. Both excited and nervous, he looked around again, just to make sure the coast was clear. Taking a short, clumsy wind-up, he threw the ball tentatively toward his target. It arched softly through the air and hit the front of the tree stump, fell to ground and rolled back out into the alley. "Crud." He retrieved the ball and returned to the mound. His second pitch missed as well, hitting the chain link fence behind the crate. "Ball two," he mumbled in disappointment.

All that afternoon, Edgar threw balls at the milk crate. After each pitch, he picked up the ball and returned to his mound. He thought about his previous throw and how to correct what he had done wrong. He made adjustments and threw again. Every day that week, and throughout the rest of July, Edgar threw balls into the wooden crate sitting on top of the old tree stump in the alley. As his strength increased, each pitch became harder and harder, and he was hitting the crate more than the fence behind it. When his shoulder was sore from too much throwing, he rested it and played war or read comics with Jimmy, or listened to the *Tigers* games on the radio. When his shoulder felt better, he went back to throwing balls in the alley.

§

It was an unusually cool and quiet August morning as Edgar walked to the park with his glove and new baseball. He had been practicing in the alley for weeks with the old one, but his confidence was still a delicate thing. His arm was rarely sore anymore though, and all of his pitches were hitting inside the crate. He was getting pretty good at placing the ball where he wanted it, too. He even had to move everything up against the fence, to keep the crate from being knocked off the stump.

The park was deserted, except for a few robins wandering the grass for food. Edgar thumped across the piece of wood that was home plate and stopped at the pile of dirt and rocks in the center of the infield. He stood on the mound, wondering what the park version of baseball would be like, pitching to a real batter instead of a wooden crate. Would any of the boys be able to hit his pitches? Could he strike out nearly every batter, just as he did daily in the alley? In the quiet of the morning, his mind drifted inward to his latest fantasy. He was Hal Newhouser on the mound at Briggs Stadium. It was the biggest game of his career and he was pitching to the great Ted Williams. With eyes half closed, he took a slow wind-up and follow through, only pretending to throw the ball. In his head, the crowd cheered wildly as Williams swung at a sinking curveball that seemed to defy the laws of physics—coming in right at the letters and then, at the last second, pausing in mid air before falling down to his imaginary ankles. *Strike three! Take that Williams!*

The sound of laughter in the distance jolted Edgar out of his daydream. He turned to see some older kids carrying bats and crossing the street the next block over, moving toward the field and where he was standing. He hurried off the mound and toward the back of the park, where he sat down in the grass and leaned back against a towering oak. It was the first time he had been to the park since that last day with his grandfather, and he missed that sense of protection, among other things. He watched the baseball activities unfold, certain that he could get away safely if anyone saw him and wanted to start trouble. He wondered again what Hal Newhouser must have been like as a kid. Probably the toughest kid on the block and not afraid of anyone, but too nice to be a bully himself.

Several innings into the game, something happened on the field that caused play to stop. A few of the boys huddled together and were looking at the ball. It appeared to Edgar that the ball's covering had torn off. Confirmation came when one of the boys ripped it off the rest of the way and threw it to the ground. While the boys in the distance stood around staring at each other, Edgar looked down at his glove and clean white baseball lying in the grass. The ball was still perfect; no scuff marks or anything. Having a catch with his grandfather, it landed in the grass many times, but that was all. And he always wiped it down afterwards. *Take good care of your things, and they will take good care of you.* He picked up the ball and ran his thumb over the smooth leather and across the red stitches, noticing how perfectly even they were. He then looked back toward the field.

Opposing forces of apprehension and desire swirled through Edgar's mind. He knew what was being presented to him. In his short life, he had been afraid of a lot of things, but in that moment he was terrified. His father's voice scolded him for being clumsy and uncoordinated, and told him that he needed to stop daydreaming. *Real men get jobs and work for a living.* He closed his eyes tightly, while rocking forward and back with his arms wrapped around his knees, the ball tight in his grasp. He sensed a movement to his right and looked over, almost expecting to see his grandfather. But there was nobody there. Instead of his grandfather, a voice without sound spoke inside his head: *Edgar, there will always be things in life that scare us. What's important is what we do in those moments.* Then it was gone.

Edgar stood up and brushed bits of grass and dirt from his pants. He looked across the way, knowing what he had to do. Picking up his glove, and with all the courage he could muster, he started walking. His eyes stayed low to the ground, and his strength came from imagining his grandfather walking by his side. Questions loomed with each step. What was he going to do once he got there? What would he say? Who would be the first one to beat him up or steal the gifts his grandfather had given him? He thought back to that first day, when they walked to the park together, sat at the picnic table and watched these same boys play ball. His grandfather seemed so certain that he could just join in the game and be one of the fellas. The idea was still terrifying, but what if that could actually work? What if his grandfather was right? What if it really was that easy— to just walk up to them and ask to play, and be accepted with open arms?

The boys paid little attention to Edgar as he approached. Some were discussing the game situation while others were talking about girls—a subject Edgar felt even less comfortable with. There was the new girl that had just moved in down the street, but he had yet to get close enough to see what she looked like. She did have that curly blonde hair though, and if she wasn't always walking around with

Stupid Sally Morgan, he might actually try talking to her. His heart was beating frantically as he neared the crowd—his mind scrambled with thoughts of curly blonde hair, a perfect white baseball and a sickening fear for his life. Sam Broadman, one of the few kids he knew by name, was the first to engage him. "Hey, stilts, can we help you with something?"

Some of the other boys turned around and conversations stopped. To Edgar, it felt like even the birds stopped chirping, happy to be watching from the safety of their branches. Cold sweat ran down his back and caused his body to quiver. With his head hanging low, he glanced up with his eyes and looked around, but avoiding direct eye contact. He stopped several feet from the edge of the group, definitely too close now to outrun them if it came to that. Standing there, he was all in, as his father's drunken chums sometimes said while playing poker. All eyes were on him, and it felt like the beginning of his worst nightmare coming true. Whispers and chuckles moved through the crowd.

Edgar was too nervous to wait a second longer. He had to get it over with, one way or another, so he asked, "Can I play?" It was barely a whisper, but all that he could manage to get out.

"Huh? Couldn't really hear ya there, bub," came from somewhere in the crowd.

I can do this. I can do this. Unable to control his vocal chords, Edgar shouted, "Can I play!"

"Hey, take it easy, partner," some overweight kid said. "No need to get excited. Thanks for the offer, but we're done for the day. Our last ball just bit the dust."

Lying in the nearby grass was the leather covering. Some other kid was holding the inside part of the ball, unraveling the string. There was a moment of uncomfortable silence, and then most of the boys seemed to lose interest and returned to their own conversations.

Some unknown kid moved closer to Edgar and said, "Hey, do you even know how to play baseball? That glove of yours looks awfully clean." A snickering of laughter rose from those who were close enough to hear.

"Well, I never played in a real game before," admitted Edgar, "but I can throw real good. And I listen to the *Tigers* games on the radio and I've even been to Briggs Stadium once." Edgar felt stupid for babbling, knowing good and well that listening to games on the radio did not mean he could throw a ball or pick up a bat.

"Well, slugger," the boy said, "maybe next time. Come back tomorrow, and if we can find a ball, we'll think about it."

Did he really say that? Did he actually imply that they might let him play? This was far better than what Edgar could have imagined. He was proud of himself; he had actually worked up the nerve to talk to them and nobody had punched him or took his things. He breathed a sigh of relief as the other boys began gathering their equipment. He then looked down at his glove, which he had been holding tight to his chest—just in case someone tried to steal it. He pulled it away a little bit, just enough so that only he could see the bright white baseball hidden inside. It was so clean and new, and he had dreamed of keeping it that way forever. His grandfather taught him to take good care of his things, and that had become very important to him as well. But there was that other promise, too, the one about dreams, and never giving up. That one didn't make much sense to him before, because he never had a real dream to hold on to. But in that moment, standing there at the edge of the field, he did. He realized that those two things together might have something to do with choices, and he knew that one promise would always be more important than the other. He took a deep breath, looked up and spoke firmly, "I've got a ball we can use!" He pulled the ball from his glove and held it up high for everyone to see. The boys that were walking away stopped and turned back; the ones nearby looked up. Although the baseball was a basic necessity for the game, it rarely got special attention. That was unless they didn't have one and wanted to play, or it was a new ball. In Edgar's case, it was both.

Some tough looking kid named Charlie Moore, who Edgar later learned was the leader of the group, moved in and grabbed the ball from his hand.

"Hey, that's mine!" Edgar shouted. He then took a precaution-ary step back.

"Don't worry, bub, I ain't gonna take it'" Charlie said. "I just wanna see it." Charlie turned the ball in his hands and nodded in admiration before tossing it over to Sam, who did the same.

"Hey, this is a nice ball," Sam said. "Not one of those cheap ones; a real official baseball. Where'd ya get it?"

"My grandfather bought it for me; please give it back," Edgar pleaded.

"Take it easy, take it easy," Sam replied.

Edgar watched as his ball was tossed around the group, certain that someone was going to steal it. But after visiting nearly every pair of hands, the ball made its way safely back.

"Okay, you can play," Charlie said. "But you have to be the catcher."

"But I want to pitch!" Edgar said. He had naively assumed that his role would be pitcher; it never occurred to him that he would be forced into another position.

"Hey, calm down there, sport!" Charlie shot back. "We already have teams here, and an important game on the line." He paused, and then added with a sly look on his face, "And you don't become part of a team until you fulfill your duties. If you want to play, you need to catch. Everyone catches when they first start out; it's called being an apprentice. You don't get to bat either; only catch. If you do a good job with that, then maybe you'll get a shot at playing another position. That's called being promoted."

Edgar remembered that word, but it sounded better before, like a possibility. This sounded like they might be taking advantage of him. Some kids were chuckling softly, which only made him more uncomfortable. But he didn't want to instigate any trouble. He was still standing, yet to have been beaten up, and he didn't really know the rules of the field. The most worrisome thing though was what might happen if he actually tried to take his ball and leave.

"Okay, fine," Edgar said. "I'll play catcher."

"Good choice," said Charlie. "Come on fellas, let's finish this game!"

Edgar made his way back behind the splintered piece of plywood, and actually felt somewhat relieved. As much as he had dreamed of standing out there on the mound and staring down a batter, being an apprentice would give him a chance to see how things worked up close, before having to participate.

As the game continued, some of the boys introduced themselves and seemed friendly, while others paid him little attention. As the final innings passed, Edgar spent most of his time behind home plate, far behind it in fact, chasing wild pitches and foul balls. At one point near the end of the game, without realizing what he was doing, he returned the ball to the field with a long wind-up and a pitch. Ernie, the actual pitcher on the mound, yelled back at him, "Hey, just throw the damn ball, will ya! Who ya pitchin to anyway?"

"Fine," Edgar mumbled in embarrassment. It didn't take him long to realize that the apprentice part of baseball was no fun.

15
THE VOICE

Mother Nature had thrown a fresh blanket of cold, powdery snow over the entire region. The storm was not as bad as the Channel 4 weatherman had predicted, but with only a week to go, it was now certain to be a white Christmas. From his place at the kitchen table, Edgar glanced out the back window and saw the late morning sun reflecting off the snow-covered branches. The frozen flakes twinkled like millions of diamonds scattered beneath the dense blue sky. Feeling a chill, he pulled his sweater up tight and rubbed his hands together. The heat was set at his daytime limit of 67 degrees, but his body felt colder. Turning the heat up was simply out of the question; who had the money to run the furnace all day?

As much as Edgar disliked winter, he loved Christmastime. Wilma always did such a wonderful job of decorating the house. She baked lots of cookies and treats—even though the doctor warned them both about diabetes. The sweets were mostly for holiday bake sales and other church events, but Edgar still managed to grab more than his share. Well into his seventies, with a body that creaked and moaned and cursed him with every movement, strange vibrations running through his head and a basement cursed with something still unknown—and apparently unwilling to go away, Edgar felt like sugar was the least of his concerns. He dipped a colorful Christmas tree shaped sugar cookie into his warm coffee, crammed the top half into his mouth and stared at his newspaper.

After reading a few insignificant baseball blurbs, Edgar folded the paper up neatly, dropped it into the recycling bin at the end of the counter and glanced back out the window. As he watched the winter wind move the dusty snow back and forth across the yard, a familiar breeze, this time strong enough to rustle the curtains above the sink, blew across his back. In its warmth came that distinct and pleasant scent of freshly cut summer grass. With both curiosity and reservation, Edgar turned to face the (as expected) wide-open doorway leading to the basement. He stared blankly until the aroma rising out of the darkness became too intoxicating to resist. His body moved autonomically forward as his mind sunk deeper into the sensations emanating from within the breeze—beyond the heat energy and scent molecules. The ringing in his ears intensified, as if alerted to his awareness. His rational mind felt a sense of fear, but not in a physical way, and no slimy, fluid-dripping creature from some Stephen King novel was poised to lunge out and pull him mercilessly into the basement, and then further down into some deep underground catacomb, where his body and mind would be harvested for food and things unimaginable.

Edgar moved his hand to the door surface and then down to the doorknob. Both were warm to the touch, and the tingling vibration was clearly there as well. Resting his head up against the doorjamb, he realized that the vibration there matched perfectly with the buzzing in his ears, like they were connected together, or emanating from the same unknown source. The sensation began to lull Edgar in deeper. He felt the presence of another world—perhaps another existence of himself—and with that came an entirely new realization. The humming in his ears and the sensations running through the doorknob were not from a small electrical motor running erratically, or even Tinnitus as the result of *just getting older*. It was a voice. Yes, a voice—calling out to him in a language that seemed to have no words. With his eyes closed, and teetering dangerously at the edge of the open staircase, speaking in barely a whisper, he said, "I'm listening."

§

Wilma was in her bedroom, finishing up the laundry and listening to the Christmas music coming from the CD player on her nightstand. She folded the last towel and placed it neatly on top of the others, then gathered the pile and turned to put them away. When she saw Edgar standing in the doorway, leaning his head against the doorjamb, his eyes glassy and distant, she dropped the towels and gasped, "Edgar!" His arms were hanging limp at his sides and he was mumbling incoherently. She moved quickly and put her hands up on his shoulders, fearful that he was having a stroke. "Edgar, can you hear me? What's wrong, dear?"

§

Wilma faded into view before him; her arms were on his shoulders and a frightened look on her face. She was speaking to him, but her words were distorted, as if she were talking under water. When she started shaking him, he felt himself returning—the sensations fading. "Hi, hon," was all he could think to say. He looked around and noticed that he was standing in the hallway, but had no idea how he got there.

"Edgar, what's wrong?" Wilma repeated.

Still disoriented, Edgar struggled to form a more respectable response. There seemed to be so much to tell her, but he didn't know where to start. She was obviously upset, but that was probably because he startled her and made her drop the laundry. That was not important though. What was important was back in the kitchen. Trying to convince her with words was useless; he needed to show her—right away—before it faded again. He took her hand and without another word led her across the house toward the kitchen and to the basement door. He placed her hand onto the doorknob and said, "Okay, hon, tell me what you feel." He stepped back to observe her reaction.

"Not again, Edgar," Wilma said. "You're really scaring me now."

"Just hold your hand there and close your eyes," he said, "then tell me what you feel."

With a deep sigh, Wilma closed her eyes. "Edgar, I don't *feel* anything; we went through this already."

Edgar pulled her away from the door, grabbed the doorknob himself and felt for the vibration—the voice— whatever the hell it was. But it was gone. His shoulders slouched in exasperation. *It felt so real; the vibrations inside and outside of my head, the smell, the warmth—all of it. It couldn't have been just my imagination.* For the second time he had dragged Wilma to the basement door, and for the second time he was left feeling like a fool. All he wanted was for her to feel it as he had, and then he could tell her about the voice. Or maybe, God willing, she could hear that for herself. But right now she didn't believe any of it, and with the look on her face, he began to regret pulling her back in. He decided that for the time being, at least, he needed to keep the latest development to himself, and pray that the whole thing would not continue to escalate.

"Edgar, I want you to come and lie down while I call the doctor." Wilma closed the door, took his hand, led him to his bedroom and helped him into bed. His symptoms did not indicate a stroke or heart attack, but something was seriously wrong; that much she was certain of. While getting Edgar settled and relaxed, Wilma formulated her plan—take his temperature, check his pulse and blood pressure with their home monitor, then call the doctor. After that, she had something else to take care of. There was a lot to do; it was going to be a busy day.

§

After returning the phone to the hook, Wilma breathed a sigh of relief. Even after going through her full list of Edgar problems, the doctor assured her that he had most likely not suffered a stroke. Nonetheless, he did want Edgar to come in the following day for a checkup, and to discuss some additional tests. She noted the appointment time on the calendar and moved toward the bathroom. In the vanity she found the pill bottle she was looking for. There was only one left, but it would do until tomorrow, when Edgar would most certainly be getting a fresh prescription. She took the pill and a cup of water to Edgar, watched him take it, insisted that he not leave the bed, kissed him on the cheek and left.

Back in the kitchen, she ran her hand over the surface of the basement door, and down to the doorknob. Both felt cool to the touch, and there were no vibrations or anything else out of the ordinary, as far as she could tell. Regardless, she had a plan and would not be deterred. One option required her to go outside and into the garage. The second involved going down into that dreadful basement. She could slip outside or she could fall down the basement stairs. Either way, something could get broken. With Edgar in his current condition, she didn't want to leave the house, so she chose the basement; at least there was a handrail to hold onto. She looked over at the phone on the wall, and the cord hanging down, and wondered how far it would reach. She thought about those little portable phones that everyone else in the world had, and for the first time wished she had one. After retrieving her safest outdoor shoes, the small flashlight she kept in her nightstand and a warm sweater, she was ready.

With all of Edgar's erratic behavior lately, imaginary or not, Wilma was a bit nervous about opening the basement door. But not one to linger once a decision was made, she turned the knob and pulled it open. There was no rush of warm air that smelled like grass, just the cool darkness of their musty old basement. There was no shrieking, rabies infested rodent lashing out, just an empty staircase. She pulled the light string and peered down, then flipped on the flashlight for a better look. The only thing leering up at her was a tired old slab of concrete. With the flashlight in one hand, she grabbed firmly onto the handrail and took her first cautious step down.

Safely at the bottom of the stairs, Wilma flipped the light switch and looked around. It had been at least a few years since she had been down here, and while she knew it was a mess, it was much worse than she remembered. For the first time, she felt bad about holding onto all these worthless things—and having poor Edgar run up and down the stairs all those times. But in her mind, she had always been certain that they would need every bit of it—someday. Her parents had struggled through the Great Depression, and kept everything; nothing went to waste. Standing there in a moment of self-realization, she supposed that in some way that same obsession had been genetically passed onto her. Moving carefully along the wall to her left, she came to the door to the small space under the stairs, which was used as a pantry back when Edgar's parents owned the house. She grasped the hook and wriggled it back and forth until it unlatched, and then pulled the door open. She shined the flashlight beam around. When it reached the bottom, back under the stairs, she paused. The light illuminated what looked like a small metal toolbox. *I thought I remembered that being there.* Pleased with her memory, she carefully made her way toward it. Being careful not to hit her head on the underside of the stairs, she reached down (her back reminding her of her age) and grabbed the handle. It was heavier than she expected, but she was able to slide it out.

The toolbox landed on the stair with a metallic thump, and the rusty latch gave way with an annoying squeal. Under the light of the flashlight, Wilma was pleased to see tools inside, especially the small, wood-handled hammer sitting on top. Underneath were more dusty relics; their intended purposes a mystery to her. There were fuses, pieces of wire and various nuts, bolts and screws lining the bottom. Satisfied that she had found at least something to help her implement her plan, she left the toolbox where it was and headed through the doorway and into the old laundry room. After a quick glance around, and not seeing what she needed—it was more likely in the garage—she closed the door and headed back toward the stairs.

Before heading back up, Wilma paused at the base of the stairs. A feeling of warmth began to envelope her—like a comfortable blanket next to a warm fire. There was no accompanying anxiety or fear of any kind, rather quite the opposite. Scattered memories of her life floated in and out unexpectedly—feelings of love and nurturing, hope—and something else. But just as quickly as they had appeared, they dissolved back into the coldness of the basement. *That was only my imagination. Edgar's behavior is just getting the better of me.* Wilma thought of how ridiculous it seemed anyway. What would Edgar think if she told him about seeing flashes of their life together? And what would he say if she mentioned smelling something in the basement as well—not grass—but saltwater?

§

Wilma kept her own arthritis medicine in the top drawer next to the silverware. She put two pills into her mouth and swallowed with a sip of cold tea. She turned back to the filthy toolbox sitting on her clean counter and opened the lid. She removed the dirty hammer and washed it in the sink. Still short two of the three items she needed, she continued looking through the toolbox. Hoping not to do anything that would require a Tetanus shot, she reached down into the bottom. After some digging around, she came across a long rusty nail. *That should work. But I need another.* She dug around and found a matching nail, then put it next to the other one on the counter. There was one more item to go, but she knew that it would not be found in the toolbox, or anywhere upstairs for that matter. She needed a board, long enough to secure that door closed. But she dreaded the thought of a trip out to the garage. Without a plan, she grabbed a nail and the hammer and walked over to the basement door. Looking it up and down, she was rewarded with an idea. Positioning the nail up against the crack between the door and the frame, she turned it at an angle, so that the nail protruded out and in front of the closed door. With the hammer, she tapped at the end of the nail. After a few solid strikes, the nail began to penetrate the wood of the doorframe. She continued tapping and, when the nail was halfway embedded into the wood, she stopped and pulled at it—testing her work. It didn't budge. But the important thing was not the nail, but rather the door itself. She grabbed the doorknob, turned and pulled. To her delight, the door was locked firmly in place, by that one rusty nail.

Pleased with her handy work, Wilma returned the hammer and the other nail to the toolbox and closed it up. With the basement now secured, she placed the toolbox on the floor and moved it with her foot up against the door. *There, now that door will not only have to open past the nail, but it will have to push the toolbox aside as well.* Smiling, Wilma washed her hands and the counter thoroughly, then proceeded to stir the pre-dumpling chicken stew that was simmering on the stove.

§

Edgar awoke; startled out of his sleep by the sound of pounding coming from somewhere in the house. "Wilma?" Pushing the covers off, he swung his legs over the side of the bed and listened. When the pounding failed to return, he got up. *Just my imagination.* He was hungry, enhanced by the smell of dinner drifting pleasantly through the house. In the kitchen, Wilma was standing at the stove stirring the contents of a large pot. By the smell alone he knew that it was his favorite, chicken and dumplings. His shuffling across the Linoleum caught Wilma's attention, and she turned to face him.

"Dear, how are you feeling?" she asked. "Are you okay?"

"Yeah, I'm fine, hon," Edgar replied. He wasn't completely sure, but now wise enough to know how to respond properly.

Without thinking, he turned toward the basement door. To his relief, it was closed up tight. But it was the nail sticking out of the doorjamb and the toolbox on the floor that caught his attention.

Noticing his gaze, Wilma acted quickly to avert the subject. "Edgar, dear, why don't you come into the living room and watch some television. Your supper will be ready shortly. I set out the TV trays and I'll bring it out to you when it's ready." She took him by the arm, gently led him out of the kitchen and settled him into his recliner. After handing him the remote, she kissed him on the forehead and returned to the kitchen.

For the rest of the evening, Wilma refused to let Edgar anywhere near the kitchen. She encouraged him to sit and watch television, and gladly brought him whatever he needed, even more Christmas cookies. At 9:00 she gave him his nighttime pills, including a sleeping pill—doctor approved—and soon Edgar's head was drooping. After helping him to bed, she returned to the kitchen to put the last of the dishes away. Once her chores were finished, she turned on the small nightlight over the sink and then wandered over to the basement door. As expected, it was closed up tight. For now, the basement seemed fine—but she was still worried about Edgar, and prayed that the doctor would have some answers tomorrow.

16
THE LAST PITCH

The summer of 1948, that started out so wonderfully for Edgar, with an unforgettable visit from his grandparents, fell apart less than a week after becoming a baseball apprentice. He was finally getting into the routine of showing up at the park around 10:30 am and taking his place behind home plate. The other kids were not mean to him, but he did get scolded a few times for missing tags and letting balls get by him. He was expected to catch anything thrown his way and tag out the runner at the plate if necessary, even the big ones coming at him full speed. He got knocked down a few times, and on those nights he would lay wounded in bed, wondering if baseball was the right game for him. But the only way to know for sure would be to get a chance at the only thing he really wanted—to pitch.

It came on a muggy Friday afternoon while they were playing an important 6th game of the World Series. With the score tied in the bottom of the ninth, Timmy Wilcox was on the mound pitching, determined to strike out Charlie, who had been taunting him all game. In Edgar's short time with the group, he knew that Timmy was the best pitcher out there and Charlie by far the best hitter—so it was a great match-up. With two strikes on Charlie, Timmy's mother pulled up along the curb in a tattered old Studebaker roadster. She blasted the horn and waved insistently.

"Aw, Ma, not now!" Timmy cried out. "I can't leave yet; it's the bottom of the ninth!"

The figure in the car sat silently and glared while everyone waited in silence. After a brief stare-down, Timmy ran over to the car and stuck his head in the open window. Unintelligible words and dramatic hand gestures were shared back and forth. Finally, Timmy turned toward his teammates and said, "I've gotta go." Without another word, he tossed the ball toward Edgar, got into the car and was gone, leaving behind a plume of blue smoke and an unfinished game.

The boys on each team looked at one another. Edgar watched as he tossed the ball to himself. While the others mumbled and conversed, he realized that his moment had come. He had done his apprentice duties, hardly ever complained, and now it was time for a self-promotion. He gathered his courage and said casually, "I can pitch."

"Huh?" Charlie asked as he watched Edgar step over the plate and walk past him.

"I'll pitch," he repeated without breaking stride.

The other boys began to debate the subject at hand. Most of the discussion had to do with whose fault it would be if either team lost such an important game. The overall consensus was that it would be the skinny new kid who spent his time daydreaming behind home plate. But as Edgar waited on the mound, it was finally agreed upon as the least undesirable option. He would become the full-time pitcher, as long as he could get the ball over the plate, which many considered highly doubtful.

As the new pitcher, Edgar stood nervously on the pile of dirt and rocks and looked down. He tried to get his feet planted firmly, but the rocks felt awkward. He laid his glove and ball in the nearby grass and got down on his hands and knees. Working the dirt in front of the mound, trying to get his landing spot just right, he removed some smaller rocks and tossed them aside. He picked at a larger, protruding one, but couldn't get it out.

The other boys watched and chuckled. Charlie made a swirling, crazy gesture and shook his head.

"Come on," someone said, "let's get going here! Plant the damn flowers later, will ya!"

"Okay, okay," Edgar replied. He stood up, brushed the dirt off his knees and put his glove back on. Looking around, he noticed that some of the boys were laughing at him, while others were visibly agitated. He tried his best to shake it off and focus on what he was there to do. He was as prepared as he could be. He knew that he could hit the old milk crate easily, and get the ball from behind the plate back out to the mound. But this was real pitching, and the plate was not an old crate, and there was a batter standing beside it, and that batter was Charlie Moore, the toughest kid on the field. Even though Edgar had gotten somewhat comfortable playing ball with them, and for the most part they had accepted his presence, this was different. By opening his mouth, he had thrown himself in. Not just a toe in the water, as his grandfather once said, he had jumped right into the deep end—and it was now sink or swim.

Charlie stood impatiently, swinging his bat. Edgar sensed the tension and wondered if this was what pitching in the big leagues was like. Even though he was scared to death, a small part of him liked being there in the center of everything. He wiped his hands on his pants as Charlie positioned himself at the plate, his bat now back up over his shoulder, his eyes glaring out at Edgar. It was a critical at-bat, and everyone knew that Charlie had no intention of being the last out. With everyone watching and waiting, Edgar rolled the ball over in his hands and looked in. Someone from behind him shouted, "Come on, we're getting old out here! Pitch the ball, will ya!"

Edgar took his setup position, just like he had seen Hal Newhouser do for almost two innings. Winding up slowly, his mind spinning wildly and his eyes trying to see a wooden crate instead of a batter much bigger than he was, he threw his very first pitch. The ball landed a good two feet in front of the plate, hit a rock and bounded into foul territory. Both teams burst into laughter. Edgar was horrified. He wanted to run, but held back the urge with all his might. Charlie kicked the ball back out toward him and said,

"Come on, stilts, just pitch the ball." As Edgar retrieved it, the laughter turned back into baseball chatter. He composed himself with a deep breath, just as he had noticed Hal Newhouser doing when the pitch count was not in his favor. He stared at Charlie, who slowly swung the bat a few times before holding it in position right over the middle of the plate. "Just throw it right here," Charlie coaxed. "I'll do the rest."

Edgar wrapped his fingers around the ball and re-focused on his batter. A sense of something he had never experienced before welled up inside of him—a feeling of competition. He was now pitching to the best hitter in baseball—Hal Newhouser pitching to some bully named Charlie who was looking an awful lot like Ted Williams. The hushed crowd waited with bated breath.

The sounds from all around faded. It was Edgar's moment and he knew it. This was the big game. Radios throughout the country were tuned in. All businesses were on-hold as the world anxiously awaited the outcome. The great Hal Newhouser was staring down Ted Williams; the World Series on the line. Edgar took a deep breath and held it as his upper body began to twist and turn. He pulled his glove in tight toward his body. His windup was steady and controlled as his arms and legs moved in a fluid, graceful motion. When he reached his fullest contraction, the point where his body could turn no more, and without ever taking his eyes off the plate—which was no longer a piece of plywood, but an official white home plate mounted securely in the ground at Briggs Stadium, Edgar released the ball with everything he had. As it shot forward toward the batter, his right foot landed on the edge of that large rock, causing his ankle to twist. He lost his balance and fell forward—never seeing the pitched ball after it left his hand. Charlie did though; he saw it perfectly, and with the game on the line he swung the bat with everything he had.

17
WHAT IS WRONG WITH ME?

They kept the remote opener in the small plastic bracket on the wall, just to the right of the back door. That's where the nice man who installed the garage door some twenty years earlier had mounted it. Push once to open and push again to close, he told them. Next to the remote was the calendar, which showed the date as December 21st. To the right of that was the same telephone that had been on the wall since the seventies; it worked just fine. Without removing the remote from the bracket, Wilma pushed the big brown button in the middle until it clicked, which caused the garage door to rumble in the distance. Pulling her scarf tightly around her neck, she opened the back door and stepped out into the arctic December air. The men who shovel their snow, but only when it is more than four inches deep, had been there a few days before. Per her request, they had put down extra salt. According to the nicely designed pamphlet on aging, the one the doctor had given them years before, after strokes and heart attacks, the greatest concern for the elderly was falling down. Wilma watched her steps closely as she made her way toward the garage, her shoes crunching over the salty pavement.

Standing next to the driver's door, Wilma retrieved a small bundle of keys from deep within her purse. She pressed the correct one into the lock and turned. She slid in behind the wheel and placed her purse on the cracked and cold vinyl seat. Although

Edgar had been forced to stop driving a few years earlier, she still enjoyed it. Like a teenager, she loved the freedom of going wherever she wanted. Her closest friend, Estelle Lacey, was still driving, even though she did have those two small accidents in the past year. Her family was to the point of insisting that she not drive anymore, and with three kids and five grandchildren all on the road, there was always someone to take her to the store or the doctor's office. Not Wilma though, she was on her own in that regard. She pushed the key into the ignition and turned. After a few slow cranks the car fired to life. A sputtering of gray smoke blew out the exhaust pipe and hovered briefly before being carried away by the winter air.

Wilma backed the car slowly through the gate and came to a stop in the front driveway. She maneuvered the gearshift lever up and into the park position, then sat motionless in the cold; the steam of her breath lingering after each exhale. As the car struggled to warm, she wondered how long it would take for Edgar to come out on his own. Knowing that he was anxious about the doctor, she suspected that he might need some more nudging—in addition to her earlier reminders, including the *I'll be in the car so please don't make me wait* she had given him just before heading out the door. With Edgar's delay harder to bear than the cold car, she let out a deep sigh, opened the door and pulled herself out. Anxious or not, Edgar was going to hear about it—making her come after him in this frightful weather.

She walked up the two front steps and opened the outer screen door. The enclosed porch was empty, except for the lawn chair and wooden crate set back in the corner. She unlocked the front door and went inside. Edgar was nowhere to be seen; his coat still draped over the couch where she had left it. "Edgar, where are you? We need to get going, dear, or we're going to be late." She found him in his bedroom, slowly buttoning his shirt.

"Almost ready," he said.

Wilma stood as patiently as she could, not knowing if she should be irritated with Edgar for not being ready or grateful for the warm car that would be waiting for them. With his shirt buttoned, Edgar glanced around. From the look on his face, she could tell that he was searching for another delay. "We've got to go, Edgar; the doctor will be waiting." She took him by the hand and urged him toward the door.

§

Their destination was exactly 4.3 miles from the house; Edgar had measured it several times. The clock on the dashboard said it was 9:35, and Edgar's appointment was at ten. Wilma had planned for 30 minutes of driving time, which now put them five minutes behind schedule. With Edgar settled into the passenger side seat, she backed out of the driveway, shifted the red Caprice Classic into drive, gently depressed the accelerator and proceeded forward at a steady 20 mph.

As she drove along in silence, Wilma wondered what the doctor might find. Senility and dementia seemed like the most likely places to start. She worried also about strokes and Alzheimer's, but Edgar wasn't forgetting anything, and least no more than usual. But if his behavior continued to get worse, she wondered how much longer she would be able to take care of him. It made her sad to think that her dear Edgar might be fading away, and that he might have to spend his final days in a nursing home, or someplace worse.

§

Edgar was also wondering what was wrong with him, but he didn't think this particular doctor was going to find it. He could feel poor Wilma's worry radiating across the seat like the heat blasting from the old Chevy. He had told her most everything, except about the voice, of course, but even without that little tidbit, he wouldn't be surprised if she were sitting there trying to decide what home to have him committed to. They had never really discussed such possibilities; what they would do with the other should something unfortunate or inevitable happen. As Wilma put on the turn signal, Edgar thought that perhaps they should have one of those talks, and probably sooner rather than later. Maybe right after the holidays, over a glass of brandy and a nice fire. No sense ruining Christmas over talk like that. It could wait. He hoped.

§

The doctor's office was located in a complex of scattered, single story brick buildings that were built in the 1960's. Edgar and Wilma had been going there since it was new; their dentist's office was in one of the buildings around back. The parking lot was nearly full, but they were lucky enough to find a spot up close, in the first row near the doorway.

Wilma turned wide and pulled cautiously into the narrow spot. After checking both mirrors, she backed out, adjusted the steering wheel and pulled back in. Once satisfied with the car's position, she turned off the engine. Looking over at Edgar, she watched as he tried to unlatch his seat belt. She wanted to tell him that everything would be okay; the doctor would take care of him, but that seemed like too much to say at the moment. She just smiled and put her hand gently on his knee. He turned toward her and smiled back. Without saying a word, they both got out of the car.

Edgar stepped forward, as he always did, and opened the door to the building, allowing Wilma to walk through. Inside the main entrance was a wide hallway with doors on either side, each with gold printing that identified the business within. At the end was a glass doorway with *Eugene Slawoski, MD, Family Practice* printed in bold type.

The heat inside the waiting room was a shocking departure from the cold outdoors. As Edgar took Wilma's coat, he wondered how much they were paying for heat. He suspected that with how much doctors charged those days, they could certainly afford it. Or maybe that was why they charged so much. Overhead, the acoustical ceiling was scattered with dozens of bright fluorescent lights. Edgar wondered what those were costing him, too.

While Edgar hung up their coats, Wilma stood at the counter

and watched as the young receptionist stared into a computer monitor. After a few seconds, the receptionist said, "I'll be right with you." Wilma waited patiently. She had planned on two hours and, since traffic was light, they were back on schedule. Everything was fine, except for Edgar, she feared.

Edgar hung their coats on the rack by the door and settled into one of several open seats by the window. Watching Wilma across the waiting room, he did his best to relax. Looking around, he noticed the other patients, all of them old. It was a sea of white hair, except for one woman sitting off in the corner by herself. Her hair was dyed a bright orange with white roots glowing from beneath. He thought she looked like the top of an orange sherbet sundae. A wooden rack, carelessly stuffed with magazines, hung on the far wall while more reading materials were scattered around the room. For Edgar, it was impossible to concentrate on reading while waiting for the doctor to tell you the bad news. With nothing to interest him anyway, he just sat and thought about being old, and now possibly crazy. Wilma appeared and sat down next to him, grabbed a magazine with a huge holiday meal on the cover and began to browse through it.

§

"Mr. Howard?"

Edgar waved at the nurse standing in the open doorway that led into the depths of the office. Both he and Wilma rose from their seats and made their way past her.

"Room six, please," she said. "That's the second room on the right."

The walls in the windowless room were painted a bland shade of light gray, as if the decorators could not decide on the best hue to improve the health and mood of the patients, so they decided to forego color altogether. Adding to the affect were several dull pastel prints of flowers stuck to the back wall. A variety of charts and warning posters covered the others: don't smoke, eye chart, the signs of stroke and heart attack. On the desk was a life-sized model of a hip joint—another reminder of being old. Edgar took his place on the end of the exam table while Wilma lowered herself into the chair by the wall. She pulled out the waiting room magazine from her bag and continued reading. The nurse settled into the chair at the computer desk and began clicking.

"How are you folks today?" she asked in a cheerfully young voice.

"We're fine, thank you," Wilma replied politely, without looking up.

Edgar said nothing.

"Excellent. My name is Rita and I'll need to take your blood pressure, Mr. Howard, and ask you some questions before the doctor gets here."

Edgar grumbled to himself while sitting up straight and doing his best to appear in good health. The nurse pulled the sphygmomanometer from the mount on the wall and wrapped the cuff around his thin bicep. Once it was settled, she pumped and listened with her stethoscope. Edgar sat motionless and stared forward; he had been through the routine a hundred times and knew the drill. After getting the reading, Rita unwrapped the cuff and put it back into its mount. Without sharing the details, she returned to the desk and clicked some more. After a few general health questions, she swiveled around, got up and headed for the door.

"The doctor will be with you shortly," she said and, without waiting for a reply, left the exam room.

The term *shortly* combined with *doctor* had no measurable meaning to Edgar. The words were like repelling magnets unable to touch—two words never meant to come together within a single sentence. He wondered what *shortly* actually meant in official medical terminology. Was it different than the *Webster* version that defined it as *in or within a short time*? As Edgar wondered how the medical establishment could create its own polar-opposite definition of a word, the door opened and the doctor appeared.

"Good morning, folks. How are you today?"

Edgar shifted his attention to a new thought. Did doctors really wonder if people were having a good time while sitting in an exam room, or having their bodies picked at, probed or scanned? He wisely resisted the urge to share that out loud.

Wilma put her magazine down and jumped right in. "Doctor, I'm very worried about Edgar. He's had this problem with the ringing in his ears, which seems to have gotten worse. And now he's obsessed with our basement door. He says it's hot and vibrating or some silliness, and that it smells like grass." She paused internally to consider the smell she herself had experienced. But surely that was just her imagination; it had nothing at all to do with Edgar's condition. "But I can't feel anything," she added. "What do you think it is, doctor? Do you think it could be dementia or senility? What about schizophrenia?"

Edgar's head fell forward into his chest.

Doctor Slawoski let Wilma talk. He astutely concluded that Mr. Howard was not the party responsible for the appointment. "Well, I doubt it's any of those things, Mrs. Howard," he said, "but let's take a look." The doctor examined Edgar; just the basics: eyes, ears, nose, throat, reflexes, pulse and heartbeat. "How do *you* feel today, Mr. Howard?" he asked.

"Well, doc, I feel okay for an old man. My knees have been bothering me a bit. The hip has been pretty good, but it's hurting a bit more today, probably from all the walking. And I did go down into the basement recently. It's also getting harder to get up and down anymore. My hands have been throbbing, too, with the arthritis. The aspirin helps, but—"

"Edgar!" Wilma said. She rested her hands in her lap and composed herself before continuing. "That's not what the doctor asked you, dear."

"Oh, sorry, hon."

"Mr. Howard," the doctor said, "tell me more about what you're hearing. We discussed the possibility of Tinnitus during your last visit. Are these symptoms the same, or are you experiencing something different altogether?"

Edgar had been dreading this conversation all morning. Every scenario he had played out in his mind had turned out badly—for him. He had intentionally *not* told Wilma about the voice, even though that's exactly what it felt like. But the more he thought about it, the less crazy it seemed. In fact, it felt perfectly natural to call the sound a voice, once that realization had come to him. It was like those *Stereogram* images, the ones that take forever to see the hidden image within, but once you do, you could then never *not* see it. In his case, it was a voice instead of a harmless picture. But sitting there with both Wilma and the doctor waiting, he realized that there were two options: ignore it altogether or just come right out and say it. And wasn't that what doctors were for anyway, to help? What if the doctor actually understood? Maybe he'd seen similar cases a thousand times before, and the solution was just a pill away. Hoping for that scenario, Edgar took a deep breath and decided on option two.

"Well, doc, it started out as those strange vibrations that I told you about when I was here back in, oh, I can't remember exactly. Just a few months ago, right? I think it was in late October. Hon, do you remember when I was here last? Wasn't it October?"

"It was October," Wilma replied, "and it doesn't matter, dear."

"Oh, okay, okay. Doc, these sounds, well, since then they've been changing. I mentioned before about the ringing, that it was coming from inside somewhere. But I don't think it's coming from in here," Edgar said, tapping his head. "I think it's coming from—" He paused to choose his words carefully. "I want to say that it might be coming from outside of me, but I feel it inside, too. Does that make sense? I think it's connected to me somehow, but originating from somewhere within our house. But Wilma can't hear it. Is that possible?"

"Do you hear it now?" the doctor asked.

"Well, not as much actually. It's there—but further away. I hear it stronger at the house, but it feels more urgent here." Edgar considered what he'd just said. It just flowed out of him that way, and even though he hadn't realized it consciously, it was true—that urgency.

Dr. Slawoski contemplated the situation before continuing. "Well, Mr. Howard, people can hear sounds and frequencies differently. Perhaps what you're hearing is the furnace, or the washing machine." "No, I don't think that's it, doc," Edgar pleaded. "I went down into the basement; the furnace was off and I could still hear the sound. But I couldn't tell where it was coming from. I'm also feeling these warm breezes near the basement door, and the smell of grass. Does that make sense, or am I just crazy?"

"Perhaps your skin is just sensitive," the doctor suggested. "Did you say that you also smelled grass?"

Wilma again ignored her own irrelevant experience and jumped back into the conversation, hoping to diffuse the situation. "Doctor, we had some leaky windows in the basement, and cold air was coming in. Our maintenance man (she liked the sound of that; having someone around to fix things whenever she needed; it sounded extravagant.), well, he fixed the leaks this past week, so we're hoping the *breezes* are a thing of the past."

"Well, there you go," Dr. Slawoski said with diluted optimism. "You were just feeling the air from the basement rushing up the stairs. And there are probably some bushes just outside those windows—and that's what you smelled."

"Sure, doc, but—" Edgar thought about it. Yeah, the broken seals might have explained that in the beginning, but it didn't explain how warm air could be coming up from a cold basement when the heat vents were closed and the furnace off. Wouldn't that air actually be colder? "That may explain the breeze, doc, but the *sound* has changed, too. How do you explain that? It feels like it has slowed down. And there is something else. Somewhere inside the sound is another noise." He paused again, tapping his fingers together. "Well, doc, I just have to tell you—" He looked at Wilma, fearful of how she was going to react to this. "Inside these noises, it's like something is— *talking* to me—and I can't understand what it's saying."

"Saying?" The doctor asked; his *don't worry* expression showing its first signs of fracture.

Edgar was relieved to have said it out loud, yet worried in a new and different way. With Wilma and the doctor observing him with identical looks, he wondered if he should try to rescind. But he was already in too deep, so he continued. "I've been asking it to speak slower, doc. I told it that I'm listening, but I can't understand what it's saying." He glanced toward Wilma, but averted her eyes; he could only imagine what she was thinking.

While Edgar talked, Dr. Slawoski considered how to proceed with a patient that appeared to be suffering a psychological problem more than a physiological one. Before a full analysis could be made, and next steps determined, he needed to get a better sense of his patient's perception. "Who do *you* think it is, Mr. Howard?"

Both the doctor and Wilma look at him—in anticipation of an answer that would likely determine his fate. Softly he replied, "I don't know; I just don't know."

The weight of concern hung heavy in the room, and the doctor was the first to lighten things up. "I'm sure there is nothing serious here to worry about, folks."

Wilma didn't think he sounded very convincing. "Doctor, are there tests you can do to rule out dementia or Alzheimer's or things like that?"

Edgar's head dropped again. He despised tests, and this was starting to feel like the beginning of the end for him. Wasn't that how it worked? You feel sick, go to the doctor, who prescribes a bunch of tests and drugs and then before you know it you end up plugged into a hospital bed, living out your final days on life support. Edgar wanted no part of that, and now he regretted opening his mouth in the first place.

"These are not symptoms of Alzheimer's or dementia, Mrs. Howard," the doctor said. "But we could consider other degenerative mental disorders and schedule some tests for those. I still suspect it's a case of Tinnitus, or nothing more than an inner ear canal issue. These sounds can be upsetting in the beginning, and I suspect that Mr. Howard's imagination is playing a role. I would like for him to first see an ear specialist and get a CAT scan. Until then, I suggest that you folks go home, enjoy the holidays and not worry about this. We'll schedule these tests for after the New Year. Also, we did some blood work back in October, and that showed nothing abnormal for a man of your age, Mr. Howard. But we'll take some blood again today and do some more extensive testing. I'm also going to give you a prescription for some Benzodiazepine. That will help relax you, which may be all you need. The doctor smiled, then looked to Wilma and said, "Please call me in a few days and let me know how he's doing."

"Yes, Doctor, I certainly will," Wilma replied. "Thank you."

Edgar couldn't tell which one of them the doctor was trying to appease. Either way, he was happy to be pushing out any tests until after the holidays. As far as he was concerned, they could move them out to June.

The doctor shook Edgar's hand and turned back to Wilma. "The medicine should help to relax him. I'm sure everything will be just fine. We'll have the results of the blood tests in a week or so, and that will show us if there is anything abnormal."

"Thank you so much, Doctor," Wilma said. "I'll feel so much better just knowing what's wrong with him."

With that, the doctor left the room.

Several minutes later the door opened again and a different nurse entered. She was older, wearing a modern nurse's uniform with a bright floral pattern on it. On the desk she placed a plastic basket with dividers that separated the needles, bandages and vials. "Hello, Mr. Howard. How are you today?" she asked in a pleasant yet rehearsed tone.

"Oh, fine I suppose," Edgar replied in his own *get me out of here* tone, the one that doctors and nurses who take care of the elderly must hear dozens of times a day. The nurse quickly took the blood sample, informed them that they were free to go, and left the exam room.

Edgar continued to the waiting room while Wilma stopped the doctor in the hall. He got their coats from the rack and waited by the front door, noticing a new crowd of tired old faces in search of relief. He wondered if any of them had a strange voice talking in their head. Wilma reappeared from the back, then stopped at the desk to sign papers and pay whatever was required after *Medicaid's* contribution. He then helped her with her coat and held the door open as she passed through to the outer hallway. While zipping up his own coat, Edgar looked back at one of the grim realities of being old. Letting the door close behind him, he followed Wilma out into the cold, leaving Dr. Slawoski's office for the last time.

18
THE BIG HIT

The bright white official baseball hit the sweet spot of Charlie Moore's bat with a force that would have sent it over the fence, had there been a fence, and had it been hit in that direction. Instead, the trajectories were such that the ball returned to the field as a line drive back up the middle. Stumbling forward, Edgar glanced up just in time to see it coming at him, and fast. The old crate in the alley never actually hit the ball, and when he played catch with his grandpa, it always arced gently toward him, landing softly in his glove. For this he was not prepared. Within that split second he struggled to recall the proper way to hold his glove. There was something about doing it the right way so you didn't get hit in the face. But the moment was happening so fast he couldn't remember. All he could think to do was try and protect himself. Unfortunately, he was not quick enough. The ball nicked the top edge of his glove and ricocheted up, hitting him squarely in the neck. He fell forward onto his knees and grabbed at his throat with his open hand. His eyes watered up instantly and he started choking and gasping for air. As his face flushed with fear and embarrassment, roaring sounds of laughter came from all around. *Why are they laughing at me?* It was too much to take, and the tears started to flow. He was certain that his throat was going to swell up and he would die of asphyxiation while they all stood around laughing.

There was movement everywhere, but Edgar couldn't make out

the details through his tear-filled eyes. *Are they coming to help me, or are they just getting in for a closer look?* He wanted so badly for his grandfather to be there, to make him feel better and tell him what a real athlete, or someone like Hal Newhouser would do in that situation. He thought of just shaking it off, taking it like a man and pretending it was nothing, but he couldn't. He was trembling and unable to get control of himself. There was no way to know if the play was still going, or where the ball was, but he didn't care; they could have it. He managed to get himself up; his foggy eyes fixated on the ground by his feet. He could sense them all around him as he stumbled slightly, then pushed himself through the crowd and started running toward the alley. The boys started yelling something, but he couldn't tell what they were saying; he didn't want to know and he didn't care.

Edgar's legs burned as he exited the alley and shot across Hawthorne Street. He wasn't going back to that stupid park—ever. And he never wanted to play baseball again. He just wanted to get home where it was safe. His mother could check his throat to make sure he wasn't going to die. She might have to take him to the hospital, but even that would be better than playing that dumb game. If he survived, he was going back to hanging out with Jimmy, reading comics and playing war with their airplanes. He should never have tried to play baseball in the first place; what was he thinking?

§

As Edgar burst through the front door, crying and holding his throat, his mother rushed from the kitchen. His neck was already swollen and he could feel a painful bruise forming. His mother had him lie down on the couch while she put an ice pack on it. She wrapped his head with a cool rag, trying to calm him down, asking over and over if he was breathing okay. He pleaded that he was fine, but the worried look on her face told him that her attention was not going to end soon. She went back into the kitchen, and he knew that she was calling the doctor's office. He heard the words *ambulance* and *hospital,* and he cried out for her to stop, "I'm fine, Ma, really."

She returned and the nurturing turned to scolding. "I told you, Edgar, those balls are too hard." Adjusting the ice pack on his neck, she continued, "That game is just too dangerous. How are you feeling? Open your mouth and breathe in and out for me."

As Edgar did as he was told, his mother observed him closely. She seemed at least momentarily content with his condition. "I talked to the doctor on the phone," she said, "and he said you should be fine. But I need to keep an eye on you for 24 hours. If the swelling gets any worse, we'll have to take you in."

As his mother returned to her household duties, Edgar was forced to stay on the couch. Except for his sore neck, he felt fine physically. Beyond that he wasn't sure. In his mind he ran through a summary of everything that had happened since his grandfather had left. He thought about that brief moment back there at the park, standing on the mound. He really did feel a spark of something special, like maybe he actually belonged there. What happened though? What did he do wrong? Or was baseball just never meant to be?

§

As the worst day of his life came to an end, Edgar crawled into bed. The swelling in his neck had gone down, but it still hurt to swallow. He pulled the covers up over his chest. Through the open curtains, moonlight crept in while abstract shadows moved throughout the room. He turned and caught the silhouette of his glove sitting on the dresser. In the fading seconds of that horrible day, he stared at his glove and noticed the subtle contrast of something else, a lighter object showing through the webbing. In that distorted space between awake and dreams, where logical minds begin to give way, Edgar wondered. Then he drifted off to sleep.

19
HOME AT LAST

After the ordeal at the doctor's office, and now feeling like a full-blown mental patient, Edgar wanted nothing more than to get home, make a cup of tea and take a long nap.

Wilma had other plans. She had Edgar's prescription in her purse and her next stop was the drug store; she had no intention of going home without his medication. After Edgar left the exam room, the doctor told her to make sure he was somewhere safe after taking it, and to not let him shower, drive or go up and down any stairs. The doctor also suggested that she keep a close eye on him for the next few days, and be aware of any side affects or more unusual behavior. Wilma promised to diligently follow the instructions, although she wasn't sure what unusual behavior was anymore; it all seemed unusual.

Since the pharmacy was on the way home, Wilma didn't have to change her route, leaving Edgar unaware of her plan until she put on the right turn signal. He began to grumble in disagreement, but she shot him one of her *don't start with me* looks. His head dipped and he wisely went silent. She pulled into the closest spot she could find, turned to Edgar and gently but firmly instructed him to stay in the car. Heading toward the door, she wondered if leaving him alone in his condition was a good idea. She thought about going back and grabbing the keys, but decided to leave the car running. She didn't want him to freeze to death, and she was pretty sure he wasn't going to try and drive away on his own. In less than 15 minutes she returned with a small white bag in her hand, and a prescription receipt stapled to it.

They were quiet for the rest of the drive home—each exhausted and lost in their own thoughts. Wilma pulled the car up the driveway and through the open gate, stopping in front of the garage to let Edgar out; there was not enough room for both of them to safely exit the car when it was in the garage. She pushed the button on the remote clipped to the visor and, before the door was all the way open, pulled into the garage and shut the car down.

Once inside the house, Edgar was the first to break the silence. "Everything is going to be fine, hon. I feel better already; just talking to the doctor sure helped a lot."

Wilma turned to him and smiled. "I hope so, dear. I still need you—and I'm not ready to let you go just yet." She put her hands gently on his chest and leaned up and kissed him on the mouth. "The *Tigers* need you, too. They still have a World Series to win, and they need their number one fan. And Edgar, it's the holidays; let's just do like the doctor said and relax and enjoy them."

Wilma put a pot of water on the stove for tea while Edgar hung up their coats. She opened the prescription bottle and removed a single pill. She filled a glass with water from the tap and called out, "Edgar, your pill is ready." There was no response. "Edgar, come on, dear. I have your pill ready." Again, there was only silence. She walked into the living room, but there was no sign of Edgar. She continued down the hallway toward the bedrooms and poked her head into his room. He was sitting on the bed, bending forward, working to untie his shoes.

"Edgar?" she called out softly.

He looked up. "Oh, hi, hon. I was just going to take a nap."

"No, Edgar. You need to take your medicine first."

"Couldn't I just—"

"No. You stay right there. I'll get it and bring it to you, then you can take a nap if you like. But don't even lie down until I get back." Wilma didn't wait for a response and hurried back to the kitchen.

Grabbing the pill and the glass of water off the counter, she returned to the bedroom where Edgar was still sitting—his head hung low.

"Edgar, dear, are you all right?"

He looked up. "I don't know, hon. I really don't know. Do you think this pill will help me?"

Wilma sat down next to him on the bed and handed him the glass. "Edgar, I'm sure whatever it is that's bothering you, the doctor will take care of it. If not this doctor, then another one." She handed him the pill. "I don't know about the pill, but the doctor said it will at least relax you and help to take your mind off these things. That's the best we can do for now. So why don't you take it and lie down. I'm sure you'll feel much better after your nap."

Edgar looked at the small pill and, without saying another word, put it in his mouth. He took a long drink of water, swallowed hard and put the glass on the nightstand. He put his hand over Wilma's and caressed it gently. His hand ached a bit from the arthritis; there would be another pill for that later. "Thanks, Hon. You sure take good care of me."

Wilma helped him with the covers and then kissed him on the cheek. He closed his eyes and was asleep almost immediately. She stood over him for a few minutes and then headed back to the kitchen to make herself some tea. Once the tea bag was done steeping to her satisfaction, she took the teacup and saucer into the living room and placed it on the small end table in the corner next to her knitting chair. She lit the special candle she had picked up recently—made especially for calming and relaxing, according to the label. After settling herself comfortably into her chair and taking a gentle sip of tea, her mind began to fill with more thoughts and worries. She closed her eyes and began to cry. Behind her tears was a prayer that Edgar would be all right.

§

When Edgar awoke, his stomach was growling so loud he could hear it. He rolled over and looked at the digital clock on the nightstand; the large red numbers showed the time as 7:07. Wilma had let him sleep right through dinner, but he knew that she would warm something up for him. Sitting next to the alarm clock was a glass of water and a small pink pill with the word *Xanax* embossed on the side—much too small for his old eyes to see. Edgar received the message loud and clear; don't do anything until you take your pill. He rolled onto his back and stared at the ceiling, allowing his awareness to focus in on any noticeable changes since taking the first one. He might have felt slightly more relaxed, but that could just be from the nap. Pushing the covers aside, he sat up. He scooped up the pill and popped it into his mouth.

Wilma was washing dishes in the kitchen sink when Edgar came up quietly beside her and put the glass on the counter. Lost in her own thoughts, and unaware of his presence, she jumped when the glass clanked on the hard surface. "Don't scare me like that, Edgar!"

"Sorry, hon."

She looked at the empty glass. "Did you take your pill?"

"Sure did."

Looking at him suspiciously, checking his eyes for anything unusual, Wilma asked, "How do you feel this morning? Can you feel the medicine working?"

"Yes, a little bit," he replied. "I think." When Wilma's last comment sunk in, he asked, "This morning?"

"Yes, dear, you've been sleeping for almost 15 hours."

"Oh, really?" Edgar looked out the window and noticed the angle of the morning sun.

"And you must be hungry," she said. "I've made you a nice big breakfast of bacon and eggs. Please sit down and I'll fix you a plate."

"Sure, hon, that sounds delicious. I'm starving."

After breakfast, Edgar moved into the living room and turned on the television. He lowered himself into his recliner and raised the footrest. Within a short time, the effects of his second *Xanax* appeared. He felt drowsy and light-headed, much like he did after taking his allergy medication in the spring, when the pollen was bad. The chemicals muffled the sound of the television, and whatever Wilma was doing in the kitchen. Instead of resisting though, Edgar closed his eyes and allowed himself to sink further into it. He had a distinct purpose in mind—to listen for the voice. With the outside world fading, Edgar searched within. After some measure of time he began to sense that the voice was still there, only different. It was still in the house, but the house itself had gotten much larger, and the room it was in was far on the other side. In his drug-induced journey, Edgar could hear it—only in a new and unique way. With his senses more highly tuned, without the chatter of the outer world, he was more acutely aware of the intonations of the still indecipherable voice. And his excitement began to grow as he realized something else—the voice was not merely speaking randomly—it was reaching out—It had something to tell him.

§

While Edgar napped restlessly, Wilma settled into her knitting chair for an afternoon break. While nibbling on a holiday cookie and rummaging through her knitting basket, she noticed the blank greeting cards tucked down in the side. She always kept a few extras, just in case she made a mistake or needed one unexpectedly. Flipping through the cards, she found one that suited her and placed in on top. She pulled a pen out of the basket and started writing. After scribbling a few words of gratitude and holiday cheer, she reached into her housecoat and pulled out the vintage twenty-dollar bill. She'd forgotten to mention it to Edgar, but with all that was going on with him, she decided he could do without the story. She unfolded it and placed it in the card, then slid both into a festive red envelope. She turned the envelope to the front and, in her best handwriting, wrote: *Tommy*.

20
THE AFTERMATH

The following morning, Edgar awoke late. He rolled out of bed and made his way to the bathroom. The reflection in the mirror was worse than he had expected. A giant purple bruise adorned his neck, and it hurt to even think about it. After enduring his mother's medical exam and a barrage of repetitive questions, he sat at the table and delicately ate the dry toast and extra juice she had prepared for him. When he was done, he wandered out the front door, turned right and headed across the lawns. Three houses down Jimmy was sitting alone on his porch, his head buried deep in a comic book. Edgar could see *Captain Marvel* on the cover with some helpless dame in a red dress, pleading to be saved.

"Hey, where were you yesterday?" Jimmy asked without looking up. "I thought you were coming over."

Edgar sensed Jimmy's annoyance right away. They had been best friends their whole lives and practically knew what the other was thinking.

"Playing ball with the *cool* cats?" Jimmy added.

Edgar replied in his best act of self-confidence, "Yeah, I was showing them how to play baseball."

Jimmy looked up, expecting to give Edgar a good eye-roll, and noticed the bruise. "Whoa, what happened to you? What's that purple bump on your neck?"

"A hickey," Edgar replied.

Jimmy giggled. "Which one of the fellas gave you that?"

"Funny," Edgar said, lowering himself to the porch.

There was simply no way Edgar was going to tell Jimmy about the events of the previous day. Jimmy was an accomplished liar, while Edgar preferred the truth, or at most a slightly enhanced version of it. Either way, he didn't feel like telling his best friend that he ran home crying from the baseball field while all the other boys laughed at him; he would never live that down. So his story included them practically begging him to pitch, because catching was not worthy of his obvious talent. He agreed, of course, and took the mound, proceeding to strike out batters left and right. They were all bigger kids, too, even some 15-year-olds. Admittedly, he was a little nervous at first, but once he started mowing them down he was fine. The one solid hit they got came right back up the middle. It hit a rock and the sun was in his eyes so he didn't see it. The ball bounced up and hit him clean in the throat, but he was still able to pick it up and get the runner out. "It didn't hurt at all," Edgar said. "I wanted to finish the game, but they told me I had to go get it checked out. They were afraid I might suffocate. As I walked off the field, they were practically cheering; you should have been there. My teammates said that they would win the game for me. When I got home, my mom made a big deal out of it, but I told her it was nothing."

"You going to play again today?" Jimmy asked, pretending to read his comic.

"Nah, I'm going to take a break. My arm's a little tight from pitching." Edgar rolled his left arm around in large sweeping circles. "Pitchers need a few days off between starts, you know. And the *Tigers* are playing this afternoon; I don't want to miss the game. You can come over and listen if you want."

"Nah," Jimmy whined, "I don't like baseball."

Edgar proposed a compromise. "We can just sit around or play a game, and I can listen."

"Maybe. What are you doing now?" Jimmy asked.

"I'm talking to you, dumb ass," Edgar said. "What do you think?"

Jimmy laughed, and then asked, "Wanna play war?"

"Yeah, sure," Edgar replied.

The boys headed into Jimmy's back yard to grab his airplanes, then through his back gate and out into the alley. All morning they ran around shooting each other and trading places on who got to be the allies and who were the Nazi pigs. When they got tired of air battles, they became bombers on search and destroy missions around the globe. At one point, Edgar's plane crashed into the mound of dirt and rocks off to the side of the alley behind his house. He stared at the pile while Jimmy was blasting his plastic toy soldiers with rocks further down. He turned toward the crate, still sitting on the tree stump where he had left it. Staring at it, he thought about his fastball hitting the back surface and the sound it made. He could feel the imaginary ball in his hand, turning it over with his fingers. In his mind he pictured his windup and pitch, and the ensuing strikeout.

"Come on you Nazi pig, stop daydreaming!" Jimmy screamed as he appeared in a full run, his airplane waving wildly above his head. "We've got a war to fight here!"

Before Edgar's attention shifted back to the battle, he looked again at the mound of dirt. With a sweeping motion of his foot he kicked the gravel back out into the alley—like a giant explosion—the result of a bomb hitting an enemy stronghold. He kicked a few more times for dramatic affect and, once the pile was gone, he turned back toward Jimmy. He raised his own airplane up and began waving it back and forth, then took off after his friend. "Whaaaaa, Pow-pow-pow!" Jimmy changed direction and Edgar's plane followed. "Captain Howard has the enemy in his sights. He is moving quickly into range. The enemy has no chance. Pow-pow-pow!" The bullets shot forward like flashes of light, meeting their intended target with deadly accuracy. "I got you!" Edgar shouted.

§

At the same time, the next block over, the boys were making their way to the field for their morning game. Two worn and tattered balls, one found in Stan Tully's basement and the other retrieved from a doghouse, were tossed around, as were the morning insults. Charlie brought a bottle of *Coke* and didn't share it with anyone. Stan chewed on a big wad of gum as some other boys made their way across the grass toward the infield. Billy Wilson was carrying two bats over his shoulder and tossed them carelessly toward the plate. Eventually, the regular teams had gathered, one out in the field and the other behind the plate. The first pitch of the final game of the World Series was about to be thrown. The practice balls were tossed in as each fielder settled into position. Charlie moved up to the plate. He stood there for a moment, confused and looking around. The boys in the field looked at each other, but not a word was said. Several others looked toward the alley across the street, and then back to the empty pitchers mound. Finally, Charlie shouted out, "Where's Edgar?"

21
TIME TO SAY GOODBYE

dgar awoke early on December 23rd—to the sound of Wilma moving around in the kitchen. The clock on his nightstand said 6:37, and the darkness of the room reminded him of the shorter days of winter. He turned onto his back and stared up at the dark ceiling. Taking slow, deep breaths, he concentrated his attention on each notable sensation in his body: the warmth of his toes, a dull ache pulsating softly in his knees, his right arm still tingling from sleeping on it too hard. None of those things really mattered though; they would dissolve with movement or a pill. The only thing that mattered was in his head, ears, or wherever *it* was. His attention settled there as he listened for it. However, for the first time since that rainy October evening on the porch, when that burst of "thunder" caused the ensuing ringing in his ears, which then started him down this most unpleasant path—the voice that nobody could hear but him—was gone. *Is this right? Is it really gone?*

A bit unsettled by the prospect of being normal again, Edgar decided to try and make the best of it. There would be no more crazy talk of voices, and whatever was in the basement was under lockdown, thanks to Wilma. With his head numbed, thanks to the fine folks at *Pfizer*, he pushed the covers aside and sat up. It was now only two days until Christmas, and he was going to enjoy this time with his wife.

§

Wilma went about her final holiday chores while refusing to let Edgar near the kitchen. His meals were served on the TV tray next to the couch. He took all of his pills right on schedule, even the magical pink ones, and relaxed the day away just as the doctor requested. She asked him several times how he was feeling, and each time he said better than ever.

For the most part, Edgar thought that was true. But even with the voice gone, there was still an unsettling feeling in his gut. In his mind was the image of a best friend from childhood moving away. As their family car heads off toward their new home, you can see him waving to you and his lips moving. And even after the car is gone from sight, you know he's still calling out to you.

After dinner, Wilma joined Edgar on the couch. They watched Christmas specials on television and even laughed a little, something that had been missing in the Howard household of late. As their last holiday special came to an end, with Rudolph taking his rightful place at the helm of Santa's sleigh, both were delighted at how the day had turned out. Wilma shut off the lights and lowered the thermostat before helping Edgar to bed. She watched him take his nighttime pills, pulled the covers up to his chin and kissed him on the cheek. "Goodnight, dear," she said sweetly. He wished her the same.

§

Somewhere in the earliest hours of the morning of December 24th, Edgar stirred from within a bubble of anxiety. He twisted and kicked under the covers before pushing them aside. A chill ran over his body, urging him out of his dream, if that's what it was. Half awake, he looked around, feeling for something solid to settle his mind on. He was certain that the lingering sensation had something to do with the expulsion of his strange inner companion, the one driven ruthlessly away by the exterminators from *Pfizer*. He searched deeper for what it meant, the cause behind the effect. Was the voice still out there, trying desperately to send him a message, but trapped in the chemical undercurrent? As his mind fixated on that, he felt a curious sense of loss—but more of a place and time than a thing.

Still unsure as to what any of it meant, Edgar became clear on one thing. It was something he must never share with anyone, not Wilma or Dr. Slawoski or the even the fine healthcare professionals he seemed destined to meet in the very near future at some facility for the elderly and mentally disabled. It was undeniable though—he didn't actually *want* the voice to go away after all. As crazy as it seemed, he wanted it back. He wanted to know it; a part of him needed to know it.

Getting up from his bed and stretching his creaking body, Edgar left the bedroom and turned into the hall bathroom. He quietly closed the door and pushed the lock button. The medicine cabinet behind the mirror was where Wilma kept some of their medications. He opened the door and stared at the rows of little plastic bottles lining the shelves. Wilma's were on the middle shelf; his were up top. The bottom held some over the counter drugs that either of them could take. One by one, Edgar removed a bottle from his collection, brought it up to his face and struggled to read the microscopic print. When he found the one he was looking for, he opened it. The container was filled a quarter of the way with tiny pink, oblong shaped pills, the ones that had separated him from—

As Edgar stared into the pill bottle, he imagined the scientists within the drug company creating microscopic warriors, programmed to relentlessly pursue the targeted enemy. When the carrier pod was swallowed, the soldiers broke free, sought out and formed a barrier around the problem area. They never questioned their role, whether it was right or wrong, they simply did as they were ordered. The validity of the enemy, whether it was really the actual enemy at all, never came into question. It was simply seek and destroy. Any collateral damage was just the cost of war, and for those who fought for and claimed their share of the billions of dollars in profits, that was good enough. All told, it was simply the business of destruction, rather than sitting down with the intruder and having a civilized conversation, getting to know it and understanding what it was doing there in the first place. Where did it come from, and why?

Edgar sat the open pill bottle on the sink and filled the plastic cup they kept on the vanity with cold water. He put that down and wondered if this was how God intended his journey to end. The voice was gone; the relentless soldiers seemed to have done their job, and now it was his time to finish the mission once and for all. He picked up the pill bottle and poured the entire contents into his open hand, careful not to spill a single one. He thought again of the tiny soulless drones, poised to do their work. He wondered if he was the only one who had considered the possibility that the voice was never the enemy to begin with, that somewhere behind that *effect*, the presence that had *caused* it was offering a gift—maybe something beyond human reason—yet infinitely worthy of the effort to discover it.

Or, am I just crazy?

Edgar closed his hand lightly around the pills and shook them gently. He stared at his reflection in the mirror and wondered how he had gotten so old, so fast. He raised his hand up to his face and opened it, taking a long look at the magical pink pills. *Is this enough?* There was no way to know for sure, but regardless, he had made his decision. He then squeezed the pills tightly in his hand, wished them well on their journey, and then reached over and released them into the open toilet. Watching as the tiny warriors floated helplessly, Edgar mercilessly flushed.

He removed his bottle of arthritis medicine from the medicine cabinet and opened it. He poured half of the pills into the empty *Xanax* bottle and then popped another one into his mouth, following it with a drink of water. After returning the arthritis pill bottle to the cabinet and closing it up, he looked again at his reflection in the mirror and smiled. Behind the tired old eyes and droopy skin and aching joints he caught a fleeting glimpse of something that he had lost a very long time ago—the child within.

Returning to his room, Edgar placed the pill bottle under his pillow. He thought about the voice and wondered how long it would take for it to return, but mostly what it had to say. As he calmed himself back down to a state where sleep was possible, he offered a request to whatever power was responsible for this recent madness in his life—that he and Wilma would have, if nothing else, a Christmas they would never forget.

22
A NEW FRIEND

A few mornings after that horrible day on the baseball field, the soft patter of Jimmy's bike could be heard faintly up and down Hawthorne Street. The wooden clothespin clamped to his bike frame held a baseball card that slapped against the rear wheel spokes as he rode. It wasn't exactly Mr. Johnson's Harley-Davidson Knucklehead, but Jimmy's imagination filled in the gaps. He liked the mornings; it was quiet and he could enjoy riding his bike before the other kids came out. Without warning, he slammed his foot down on the pedal of his 1930's era *Streamline Aerocycle*, the one his father had bought for himself right after the depression, and eventually gave to his son. He skidded to a screeching stop in front of Edgar's house. He turned and looked back at the thin black line that marked the pavement. "Bitchin." Several other streaks marked the street from previous competitions—to see who could make the longest skid mark. Their parents had yelled at them for wearing out their tires, and warned them that there was still a rubber shortage. Jimmy didn't know if that was true, or just a *we're not going to buy you new tires* said in a more convincing way.

Jimmy let his bike fall onto Edgar's lawn. He reached down and squeezed the clothespin, then removed the card. The edges were well frayed from the beating it had taken against the wheel spokes. He checked the player on the front, then flipped it to the ground. If it were a *Tigers* player, he may have put it aside for Edgar, who had been talking nonstop about that dumb game and the baseball cards his grandfather had bought him. It was annoying, but Edgar was his best friend, and his mother told him that's what good friends do sometimes; they just listen. From his back pocket, Jimmy removed one of the few remaining cards he had found while exploring his basement and attached it to the clothespin.

They had planned on riding their bikes to the store to get pops and *Hershey's* bars. Edgar got money from his grandfather and couldn't stop talking about that either. He wanted to buy some more baseball cards with it, too. A waste of good money in Jimmy's opinion. With no Edgar in sight, he laid back on the lawn and stared up at the sky. Soon he was daydreaming about his hero, *Captain America*, fighting bad guys around the world. Once small and weak, Steve Rogers was a disgrace to the service. All it took was the special serum, developed in the depths of some secret military facility, to turn the frail soldier into an invincible warrior. *Captain America* inspired Jimmy to have his own dream, to join the Air Force and become a great fighter pilot and an American hero. His mother told him, to *her* great relief, that they would never accept him because of his asthma. Secretly, he planned to lie his way around that. How would they know?

"Come on Edgar, shake a leg," Jimmy pleaded into the air. His outdoor time was limited, as he never knew when he might get an allergy or asthma attack. His medicine usually started wearing off around noon, and it was already after ten.

Edgar stumbled out the front door and down the steps, trying to button his shirt along the way. Squinting in the bright morning sun, he noticed Jimmy and his bike, but not his own. His mother nagged him constantly about putting it in the back yard so nobody would steal it, but he usually forgot and just left it at the bottom of the porch steps.

"Hey, fathead," Jimmy blurted, "what took ya so long?"

"I was taking a dump," Edgar replied, "and thinking of you."

"Well, are we still going for a ride or what?" Jimmy asked. "I've been waiting here all morning."

"Yeah, yeah, don't blow a fuse. Just let me find my bike; I thought I left it out here." Edgar looked around nervously. "I'll be right back." He didn't wait for Jimmy's approval as he ran toward the side of the house, through the gate and into the back yard. He yelled out toward the house, "Ma, where's my bike?" There was no answer. "Ma, have you seen my bike?"

His mother's head appeared through the kitchen window. "Edgar, how many times have I told you not to yell?"

"Sorry, Ma. I can't find my bike."

"Your bike is by the side of the garage. Your father put it there this morning after he tripped over it in the dark. Did you leave it by the front steps again?"

Edgar looked away. "I don't know."

"Well, your father does, and he wasn't happy."

Edgar's stomach tensed up. The line *not happy* meant trouble ahead, especially if his father had a bad day. His plans would have to be adjusted; the bike would have to be out of sight and he would have to do something extra around the house before his father got home. But even with the fear of his father's wrath, Edgar couldn't resist chuckling at the image of him stumbling over the bike in the dark.

The bike was right where his mother said, leaning up against the side door of the garage. It was at least as old as Jimmy's, but now in much better shape—after his grandfather had showed him how to put air in the tires, polish the chrome and oil the chain. Edgar hopped on, peddled through the gate and down the driveway. He came to a stop next to Jimmy, who was now sitting on his own bike near the curb. They sat together, side-by-side, facing in opposite directions.

Jimmy looked over Edgar's bike. "What's different about your bike? Did your grandpa buy you a new one?"

"No, I just cleaned it," Edgar replied while observing Jimmy's bike, which may have never been cleaned. "You should try it sometime."

"You're a real wise guy, aren't you?" Jimmy shot back, noticing that there was a clothespin stuck to Edgar's bike frame, but no card attached to it. "Where's your card?"

"Ah, I don't have any more cards," Edgar said. "I used all the old ones you gave me."

"Are you kidding?" Jimmy asked. "All those cards your grandpa bought you; what about those?"

"I can't use those."

"Why not?"

"I don't know," Edgar replied, not wanting to get into another baseball card debate with Jimmy." I just want to take care of them."

"Why? What else do you do with them?" Jimmy asked, thinking how strange Edgar had become since his grandparents' visit. Shaking his head, he reached into his back pocket and pulled out one of his own. "Here, I've only got a few left, but you can have one."

Edgar took the creased and tattered card, reached back and slid it into the clothespin. He rolled forward while observing the card, making sure it was positioned properly and in good contact with the spokes.

"Happy now?" Edgar asked as he started rolling forward.

"Yeah, but where ya going?" Jimmy asked, still facing the other way. "*Jake's* is this way."

"Heck, I don't want to go to *Jake's*," Edgar said. "Let's go to *Smitty's*."

"But that's twice as far, Edgar!"

Edgar looked back toward the alley and imagined the boys over there playing baseball. He knew that some of them stopped by *Jake's* for a pop and some gum before and after the game. Also, there was no easy way to get to *Jake's* without going past the park, and he had no intention of going anywhere near that baseball field, or seeing any of those boys. His secret had to be kept intact, as he could only imagine what might happen if they saw him. At the very least, they would laugh at him and Jimmy would find out that he had lied, and he would never hear the end of it. Yes, *Smitty's* was in the opposite direction and twice as far, but as far as Edgar knew, none of the boys from the park lived that way.

Sensing a debate over which store to go to, Jimmy knew he needed something more to support his argument. "Edgar, I don't want to ride all the way to *Smitty's*. What if I need my asthma medicine?"

"Come on, stop being a baby. Give it a shot," Edgar pleaded.

"But my mom will kill me if she finds out I'm all the way to *Smitty's* without my medicine."

Edgar couldn't give in; a ride by the park and the ensuing humiliation was simply out of the question. He felt the battle slipping from his grasp and needed more ammunition himself, something that was better than having asthma and needing to take medicine. He thought of becoming suddenly ill, and wondered if he could force himself to throw up. Probably not. Feeling his fragile world of deception collapsing before his very eyes, an idea came to him—and it was a good one. He looked over at Jimmy and smiled.

"What?" Jimmy asked, obviously annoyed.

"You know, Jimbo," Edgar said. "If we go to *Jake's*, we're going to have to go by the park."

"So."

"Well, the guys are going to want me to play baseball again; I already missed the last few days, you know. They are going to beg me to play, and actually they'll probably want *both* of us to play; they're always looking for more guys. Now I thought we would ride our bikes today, get a pop and hang out together. You know, just you and me. But we could play some ball instead. Yeah, that's a great idea. You wanna go play some ball, Jimbo?"

Edgar relaxed on his seat and struggled to keep a straight face. Jimmy stared off toward the alley; there was no smile on his face. It was cruel, but Edgar knew that he had won. He felt bad for attacking his friend that way, but he had his own problems to deal with. And as scared as he was about going anywhere near the park, he knew that Jimmy was sitting there, terrified. Aside from his lack of athletic skills, he was also a popular target with the bullies in the neighborhood, and Edgar knew that nothing would scare him more than facing that bunch at the park. Behind his fearful eyes, Edgar expected his friend's brain to be working on a way out. So he sat and waited.

"Okay, fine!" Jimmy screamed. "If you want to go to *Smitty's*, that's fine with me! I don't want to hear you bitching about it all day! Heck, let's go! If I die over there, just tell my mom it was your idea!"

"Okay," Edgar said.

Jimmy turned his bike around and, without another word, headed off down the street. Edgar followed. Their baseball cards pattered in their wheel spokes as their tires hummed and bumped along the rough pavement. Without saying anything out loud, both boys were relieved that they didn't have to go anywhere near the park.

§

Smitty's was a small brick building that sat at a residential intersection almost two miles from where Jimmy and Edgar lived. A wide concrete sidewalk separated the market from the street. Along the front was a row of windows sitting on top of a short brick wall, each plastered with signs that gave the prices of their most popular items: bread was 14 cents a loaf, milk was 86 cents a gallon and eggs were 79 cents for a dozen. Just above the door, which was cut into the front corner of the building at a 45-degree angle, was a hand-painted sign in sun-faded letters spelling out the name: *Smitty's*.

As the boys approached the intersection, Edgar took the lead while Jimmy fell a few lengths back. Their eyes darted back and forth as they checked for cars. With no traffic in sight, Edgar crossed the street as fast as he could, angling his bike toward the curb near the corner. An instant before impact, he pulled up on the handlebars and stood up on his pedals. The front tire leaped over the curb and landed smoothly on the sidewalk. With a bump the back tire followed. As soon as both tires were on the ground, Edgar slammed his foot backward on the right pedal and turned the handlebars hard to the left. The tires squealed on the pavement as the bike slid in a violent counter clockwise motion, screeching to a halt after spinning a full 180 degrees. Edgar watched as his friend did the same thing. Sitting side by side, they both looked down to admire their work. "Bitchin," they said together, laughing. Jimmy let his bike fall to the ground while Edgar lowered his onto the kickstand. They headed toward the door, unaware of the other boy sitting alone at the opposite corner.

Inside *Smitty's* was a counter on the left side that ran most of the length of the store. Behind it were layers of shelves that held boxes of cigarettes, bottles of liquor and other more expensive items. Along the front of the counter were boxes of cards, candy and other smaller items. Short rows of shelves ran perpendicular to the counter and divided the rest of the store into four equal aisles. Along the back wall were coolers that held pop, beer, milk, eggs and other perishables. Standing behind a giant antique cash register near the door was Mr. Smith, also known as Smitty. To Edgar, he looked to be about a hundred years old. He said nothing as his wrinkled eyes glanced emotionlessly in their direction.

They walked past the register and to the cooler at the end of the first isle. Edgar opened the door and grabbed two greenish colored bottles, passing one to his friend while the door closed with a solid thump. They returned to the checkout and slid their bottles onto the counter. Jimmy grabbed two *Hershey's* bars, dropped some coins next to the bottles and said, "My treat." Mr. Smith scooped them up, hit a couple of buttons on the large register and said nothing. The boys opened their bottles with the opener mounted below the register, left their caps on the counter and turned toward the door.

As Jimmy headed out, Edgar paused to notice the boxes of baseball cards sitting by the register. He thought about that horrible game at the park and about baseball in general. Playing was not in the cards for him, so to speak; that much was certain. But he sure liked listening to his grandpa tell stories about his baseball cards and the old days, and learning about the players and their statistics. He thought about adding more cards to his own collection, something to talk about when his grandparents came back to visit. He dug a dime out of his pocket, flipped it onto the counter and said, "Some baseball cards, please."

Jimmy was sitting against the wall outside, taking a long gulp of pop when Edgar appeared. "What took you?" he asked as Edgar sat down next to him.

"I was getting some cards," Edgar replied.

"Why?" Jimmy asked. "You can have another one of mine if you want."

Edgar knew the condition of Jimmy's cards, and in his head he heard his grandfather's voice. "No thanks," he said. "These are not for my bike. I just wanted to buy some."

"Yeah, yeah," Jimmy scoffed. "I just don't get it."

"My grandpa bought me some cards when he was here," Edgar said, wondering why he was defending himself. "I told you that, remember? He has lots of cards and baseball stuff and we had fun talking about it. I just wanted to get some more, just for fun. I was thinking about trying to get all of the *Tigers* players."

"Your money," Jimmy said.

"He's coming back to visit soon. Did I tell you that?" Edgar said. "Later this summer. If not then, at Christmastime for sure."

"Yeah, you said that," Jimmy replied.

The boys sat against the front wall of the store under a sliver of shade while cold pops were guzzled and fingers were stained with chocolate. Edgar was the first to notice the other boy, who looked to be about their age—stocky with a head of curly red hair. His clothes were old and worn, and he didn't look like the kind of kid you would want to mess with. The sole of one shoe was loose and a bare toe poked through the opening. Edgar tried to observe inconspicuously as the boy reached between his legs and pulled out his own pack of baseball cards. He opened it recklessly and shoved the stick of gum into his already full mouth, then crumbled the wrapper and let it fall to the ground, where many others littered the pavement. Next to the boy was a pile of cards. Edgar guessed that there were at least 50, maybe more.

Edgar turned his attention toward his own cards. Looking at the five packs in his hand, he sat four down and began to open the first one, carefully peeling the wrapper aside and setting it out on the ground next to his bottle. After sliding the stick of gum into his shirt pocket, he continued opening the other packs. Once all the cards were opened and piled neatly together, he gathered them gently and began going through them. One card at a time, he looked at the colorful picture of the player on the front, and then turned it over to study the statistical information on the back.

"Any good ones?" Jimmy asked.

"What's a good one?" Edgar replied.

"I don't know; they're your cards," Jimmy snapped.

"Don't know; haven't looked at 'em all yet."

Edgar continued examining his cards as Jimmy leaned back against the brick wall and closed his eyes. A moving shadow caught Edgar's attention. He looked up to see the boy from the other corner of the store approaching. He had his own baseball cards in one hand and a stick of pink bubble gum in the other.

The boy stopped directly in front of Edgar and said, "Wanna trade?"

"Huh?" Edgar mumbled.

"Wanna trade?" The stranger repeated, forcing more gum into his already crowded mouth.

Edgar didn't know how to respond. The question seemed honest enough, but it caught him off-guard. Jimmy perked up and slid further down the wall. Edgar half expected his friend to take off, leaving him to fend for himself.

"Huh?" Edgar replied again.

"Are you a dunce?" the boy asked. "I'm talking about a trade, partner. You know, I give you one of my cards that you need and you give me one of your cards that I need. A trade. Have you never heard of trading before?"

"I don't really know what to trade," Edgar said as he sorted quickly through his cards. He had not even looked at all of them and now some strange kid wanted to trade. He had often traded comic books with Jimmy, figuring they could read twice as many if they each bought different ones, and then shared back and forth. But this was different.

"Tell you what I'm gonna do, slim," the boy said. "I'll take a look through your cards and see if you have anything I need."

Edgar pulled his cards in closer to his chest.

The boy shook his head as if he were witnessing a poorly scripted comedy act. "Come on, what do you say? I ain't gonna steal 'em, if that's what you're thinking."

That's exactly what Edgar was thinking. Jimmy, too.

The strange redheaded boy held out his much larger stack. "Heck, you can look through my cards while I look at yours."

Edgar looked over at Jimmy, who was now several feet away. Together they both shrugged their shoulders as if to say, why not?

"Wow, that sure is a lot of cards you got there," Jimmy said as he moved slightly closer.

Edgar reluctantly accepted the offer and handed over his cards.

"Hey, what's your name anyway?" Jimmy asked.

"The name's Russell. Carl Russell."

"I'm Jimmy and this is Edgar Howard. Pleased to meet you."

"Same goes, fellas," Carl replied.

With the introductions complete, Carl started flipping through Edgar's cards. He paused for a moment to examine a card in the middle of the deck. He slipped it to the top of the pile like a professional card dealer, then tapped on it with his finger, wondering if it was one he needed.

"Hey, be careful with the card!" Edgar shot out. "You're going to damage it doing that."

Carl took a step back. "Egads! Ease up, partner! It's just a baseball card."

"But those are my cards," Edgar said, backing down a bit, but still determined to keep his cards from getting spoiled. "I just like to take care of my stuff; that's all. I don't want my cards bent or damaged."

"Well, I need this card for my collection," Carl said. "So if it's all the same to you, I'll give you any card in my pile for it. Then you won't have to worry about whether it's bent or not. What do you say?"

Edgar looked at the card in Carl's hand. It was not a *Detroit Tiger*, and he had never heard of the player before. He sorted carefully through Carl's cards, aware of the eyes on him. About halfway through the pile he found one he liked. It was Frank Overmire, a *Detroit Tiger*. He was about to agree to the trade when Jimmy interrupted, "Edgar, you should ask for two cards; he wants that one real bad."

Carl looked down at Jimmy. He didn't say anything, but the look on his face caused Jimmy to quickly glance away. "Only one-to-one trades today, fellas," Carl said with a forced smile, looking directly at Jimmy and challenging him to say something else. Jimmy grabbed his empty bottle and took a drink.

"Sure," Edgar said after giving it some thought, and deciding there was no downside to the trade.

"Good trade," Carl said. "Your guy is better than mine, but I've needed this one for a while." Edgar stood up, followed by Jimmy. They shook hands to complete the deal.

"How many cards do you have?" Jimmy asked Carl, hoping to get back into the conversation.

"Don't know; never counted 'em," Carl said. "Probably a few hundred; maybe more. I just finished collecting all of the football and boxing cards; now I'm collecting baseball cards."

"Gadzooks!" Jimmy said. "How'd you get that many cards?"

"I just buy them. I come here all the time and get cards."

"Where do you get the money for that?" Jimmy asked. "You must be rich."

Edgar looked away as his friend assaulted Carl with embarrassing questions.

Carl smiled but didn't answer. Noticing the empty bottles down near the end of the store where he was sitting, and the two others near Edgar and Jimmy's feet, he said, "Come on fellas, let's celebrate our deal with a *Coke*."

"I ain't got no more money," Jimmy said, patting hopelessly at his pockets. Edgar didn't bother to check; he already spent the money he had brought.

"They're on me," Carl said over his shoulder as he headed for the door.

Edgar and Jimmy looked at each other and smiled, then hurried to catch up. The three boys each grabbed a *Coke* from the cooler in the back and returned to the counter, where Smitty was standing with a clipboard, pretending to be doing important store business— not watching.

"Three *Cokes*," Carl said robustly, and then grabbed three *Hershey's* bars from the box on the counter. "We'll take these, too." He dug deep into his pocket and pulled out several coins, then flipped a few onto the counter. Smitty slid his hand across and grabbed them. The boys opened their bottles, again leaving the caps on the counter. Smitty said nothing as they left the store.

"Gee, thanks! You're aces!" Jimmy said as the three boys settled themselves against the wall of the store.

"Yeah, thanks Carl," added Edgar.

Raising his bottle, Carl said, "Glad to do it. Here's to new friends."

The three boys clanked their bottles together to seal the friendship. They sat for a while, the hot sun adding to their summer tans. Each boy took a turn gulping his pop and belching. They laughed and drank and ate melted chocolate until it was all gone.

"Catch you boys around," Carl said as he got up unexpectedly. "It's time to be on my way."

Before parting, Edgar and Carl agreed to meet the next day, same time, and trade more cards. Carl claimed to have some extra *Tigers* cards and promised to bring them. He assured Edgar that he would not bend them or damage them in any way.

Jimmy and Edgar mounted their bikes as Carl departed on foot in the opposite direction. He turned between two houses halfway down the block and was gone.

§

When Jimmy and Edgar arrived at the market, Carl was already there, sitting in the same spot the three of them had occupied the previous day. He waved as their bikes screeched to a halt near his feet, where more wrappers were scattered. A fresh pile of cards sat at his side.

"Hey, fellas, glad you could make it," Carl said.

"How long have you been here?" Jimmy asked.

"A while I guess. Long enough to open a few packs and finish off a *Coke*." With exaggerated care, Carl removed a few cards from the top of his pile, held them carefully by the edges and showed them to Edgar. "I brought the *Tigers* cards I promised."

"Where do you get the money for all these cards?" Jimmy asked again. "My mom only gives me a quarter for allowance, if I do my chores. You must be rich, because you're not old enough to work, are you?"

Edgar shot an annoyed *shut up* glance at his old friend.

Carl looked at him and smiled. "Naw, I don't work. My mom gives me all the money I want; she doesn't care."

"Gadzooks!" Jimmy shrieked, unable to imagine such a thing.

"Did you bring your cards?" Carl asked, looking first at Edgar, and then glancing sternly at Jimmy.

"Yeah," Edgar replied.

"My hard-earned American dollar is spent on comics," Jimmy added. "They're much more fun than baseball cards. What do you do with cards anyway?" He looked at the one stuck to the clothespin on his bike. "Except for that."

"I just like to have stuff," Carl replied.

While the boys casually compared and contrasted the merits of baseball cards and comics, Edgar pulled out a small package from his shirt pocket. It was wrapped in a piece of the morning newspaper, the edges neatly folded. He sat it on his lap and carefully peeled the paper open, revealing a short stack of about 20 cards. Carl and Jimmy watched, and then glanced at each other with puzzled looks.

Jimmy shook his head.

"What the heck ya doin with them?" Carl asked, chuckling.

"Just taking care of my stuff, that's all," Edgar replied without looking up, annoyed that he had to defend taking good care of his things. He folded up the piece of newspaper and put it back into his pocket, and then held out the extracted cards for Carl to see. "I'll trade any of these cards."

Carl raised his hands abruptly and shouted, "Hey, be careful with those! Don't touch the top of the cards or you'll ruin them! I'm not trading for damaged cards!"

Jimmy laughed hysterically while Edgar felt momentarily wounded, then he started laughing as well. They continued their back and forth jabs as Carl looked through Edgar's cards.

"Well, there aren't enough good ones here to trade properly. I have all of these, which means we're going to need more cards." Carl paused for a moment, then shouted, "Come on boys, let's get some more stuff!" Rushing toward the door, he added, "My treat!"

Jimmy and Edgar looked at each other and smiled. As they had done the day before, the three friends headed right past Smitty. Carl and Jimmy grabbed *Cokes* while Edgar found an *Orange Crush* in a different cooler. Three chocolate bars were grabbed from the same box on the counter and tossed near the register. Smitty was standing in his same position and wearing the same clothes as the day before; his lifeless eyes watched the boys as if expecting, or maybe hoping for, a great robbery—or anything to make his life more interesting. Before Smitty could ring up the items on the counter, Carl said, "Twenty packs of baseball cards, too. Ten for me and ten for my one friend here," nudging at Edgar.

Carl tossed more coins onto the counter, flipped the cap off his pop, scooped up his purchase and left the store without a word. Jimmy and Edgar followed.

"That's real swell of you, Carl," Edgar said as they regrouped on the sidewalk.

"Glad I could do it," Carl replied.

"Yeah, thanks, Carl," Jimmy added as he crammed half a chocolate bar into his mouth.

As the clouds began to darken overhead, the boys drank their pops and opened their cards. Edgar took a small bite of chocolate, folded the wrapper neatly, then slid the rest into his shirt pocket. He wiped his hands thoroughly on his pants and then carefully began to open his cards. For a while, the three of them traded cards and talked about baseball and comics and the silly things boys talk about. They laughed and joked and by the time their chocolate and pops were gone and their trades completed, a fine drizzle had begun to fall.

"Looks like it's time to go," Carl said.

Edgar scrambled to wrap up his cards before they got wet. He placed his new cards on the piece of newspaper, folded it up and carefully slid it back into his pocket. Jimmy took one of the extra cards Carl had given him, checked with Edgar to make sure it was not one he needed, and then stuffed it into the clothespin on his bike. The new cards really did sound the best—crisp, not muffled.

"How about we do this again tomorrow, boys?" Carl asked. "That is if the weather's right."

"Sure," Edgar and Jimmy said at the same time.

"We'll be here," Jimmy added.

§

Over the next two weeks the boys met almost every day. Carl continued to be more generous than Edgar and Jimmy could have imagined. He seemed to have an endless supply of money, more than a kid his age should have, but they were all enjoying themselves so much that even blabbermouth Jimmy had stopped questioning it. "Your money is no good here," Carl would say whenever they offered to pay for anything. Eventually, Carl started buying Jimmy comic books while he and Edgar continued collecting and trading baseball cards. The pop and candy and cards then expanded into other purchases: pocketknives, playing cards, anything that looked good on Smitty's shelves. It seemed harmless enough, so Edgar and

Jimmy just enjoyed it without question. The topic of Carl's unexplained wealth was frequently discussed on their rides home, and though they had formulated numerous theories, those were kept to themselves; there was no sense in killing the goose that was laying the golden eggs.

On their final day together, Carl was grabbing for change in his pocket when Edgar caught a glimpse of a large wad of folded up dollar bills, at least twenty of them. He pretended not to notice as Carl shoved the money back down. When it appeared that he didn't have enough change for the day's purchase, he carefully pulled out a single dollar bill and slid it across the counter, while looking around nervously—as if someone might be watching. Edgar said nothing.

23
CHRISTMAS EVE

Edgar, I'm making some eggnog. And I'm going to put a little rum in it, too."

"That sounds wonderful, hon," Edgar replied from down the hallway. "I'm dressing now; I'll be there in a few minutes."

"Good," she replied. "Now let's just enjoy the holiday, okay?"

"You bet."

With all the medication that Edgar was on, or no longer on, the doctor said no stimulation and no alcohol. But it was Christmas Eve, and they both enjoyed a little bit of rum in their holiday eggnog, just a few drops for flavor. What harm could it do? And besides, Edgar was doing so well. For the second day in a row there were no erratic episodes, no talk of voices and no obsessing over the basement. Since Wilma had driven the nail into the doorframe, that pesky door had not opened once, and she had not seen Edgar so content and relaxed in weeks. He watched television and read quietly most of the day, and even kept his new pills with him in the pocket of his sweater. He took them as soon as she reminded him it was time.

As Wilma was preparing the eggnog, a somber thought drifted into her mind. She tried to push it away, but it held on, as if needing a moment of her attention. It was a feeling, a wonder of just how many more holidays she and Edgar would have together. She knew thoughts like that were just part of getting older, but it also reminded her to make the most of each moment. A change was coming; she could feel it. Things were going to be very different soon, and even though Edgar seemed to be doing fine, that knowing still hung heavy in the air. Strangely though, she couldn't ascertain whether the change was good or bad. In a way it seemed like both potentials lingering together at the same time, and the answer was only a matter of perspective.

§

Edgar appeared from the hallway dressed in his favorite Christmas sweater and green corduroys. His hair was combed and he was freshly shaven. His shoes were even polished for the occasion. He loved their annual Christmas Eve celebration, and wanted to make this one especially perfect and uneventful—for Wilma. She had kept him out of the kitchen all day, and encouraged him to relax, which he happily obliged. Even after his toilet ceremony earlier that morning, he was still surprisingly calm; there was something about the process of total surrender. He had been monitoring his thoughts and feelings as well—wondering how long it would take for the effects of the medicine to wear off.

When Wilma saw Edgar all dressed up, a big smile came over her face. "Merry Christmas, dear," she said. She put her arms around his neck and kissed him gently on the mouth. "Aren't you handsome?"

Edgar smiled. "Merry Christmas, Wilma."

"Dinner is almost ready," she said.

The kitchen table was made up nicely, with their traditional holiday tablecloth and Wilma's favorite place settings. In the center of the table were two gold colored candles and nearby, two crystal wine glasses filled with just slightly alcoholic eggnog. Several pots simmered on the stove top while the scent of roasted turkey radiated out from the oven.

"It smells great, hon."

Wilma moved back to the stove to stir the gravy while Edgar looked around the living room. The Christmas tree was lit up and twinkling. Matching lights were draped within garland across the fireplace mantle. Wilma's holiday collectibles were placed lovingly around the room. Several *Precious Moments* figurines topped the small curio cabinet while a crystal snowman with a holiday scene within adorned the end table. A realistic looking baby doll in a shimmering holiday dress was sleeping peacefully in Wilma's knitting basket.

Wilma poked her head into the doorway. "Dear, why don't you light the fire and put some Christmas music on the phonograph?"

"Sure thing, hon," Edgar replied. "That sounds like a great idea."

The fire log was already in the fireplace, surrounded by their last few pieces of hardwood. Taking a long wooden match, Edgar lit the edge of the paper wrapper and within minutes the fireplace was glowing with a crackling fire.

Below the front window sat the stereo console, which had been in that location forever. Prior to the current one, which they purchased back in the 1970s, his parent's old radio had sat in the same spot. Edgar opened the cover, flipped the switch from radio to phonograph, and then slid the power lever to on. Below the turntable, between two speakers and hidden behind a heavy fabric mesh door, was the Howard's record collection. Edgar slid it open to reveal dozens of tightly packed LPs. He pulled out several albums before finding the one he was looking for—*Bing Crosby's White Christmas*. He slid the record out of the inner sleeve and placed it with care on the open turntable. After checking to make sure the speed setting was at 33-1/3 rpm's, he pulled the start lever. A motor hummed from within and the arm lifted, rotated and lowered itself onto the edge of the shiny black disc, causing a pleasantly soft scratching sound to radiate from the speakers below. As the music started, and Bing began to sing *Silent Night*, Edgar adjusted the volume and stepped back to admire his work.

"Oh, that's nice," Wilma said as she reappeared in the doorway. In each hand she held a glass of eggnog. She handed one to Edgar and said, "Merry Christmas, dear."

"You too, hon."

Their glasses clinked over the beautiful voice of Bing Crosby. Through the open front curtains, soft flakes of white drifted down from the night sky, and for the first time in months, everything was just perfect on Hawthorne Street.

§

After a fabulous dinner with all their favorites: roasted turkey with mashed potatoes and gravy, green bean casserole, cornbread stuffing and cranberry sauce from the can, Wilma and Edgar helped themselves to a second glass of eggnog and retreated to the living room. Edgar flipped the record over and Bing began his second concert of the evening. Wilma retrieved one of the presents from under the tree and handed it to Edgar, and he directed her toward a present for her. Without children, they never had the opportunity to play the Santa Claus game, to put out reindeer food and cookies and milk that would vanish by morning. Instead, they enjoyed dinner, music, sometimes a movie, and always the sharing of one present on Christmas Eve. On Christmas they opened the rest of their gifts throughout the day, enjoyed each other's company, ate leftovers and watched more holiday specials on television.

Wilma's gift to Edgar was the latest illustrated baseball encyclopedia. After unwrapping it, he momentarily wondered if the library might be getting a copy, and then decided for once in his life that he liked having his very own. It was thick and filled with glossy photos of players, historic games and artifacts. The front section featured, in alphabetical order, all of the great players from the history of the sport. "Thanks, hon," Edgar said. "This really is a beautiful book. I've never seen this one before."

"I'm glad you like it, dear," Wilma said, and then added with a chuckle, "And no returning it either."

"No, not this one. This is beautiful. Thank you."

Edgar's gift to Wilma was a picture book on the world's most exotic cruises, filled with high-quality photos and features on the most luxurious ships and destinations. From old-fashioned sailing vessels to private yachts for charter to the largest and most luxurious of ocean liners, the book was a tempting view into a world where wealth and extravagance came together. Edgar closed his book and watched as Wilma paged through hers. "I saw that magazine you had once," he said, "about those fancy ships. When I saw that book there, I remembered, and thought you might like it."

"It's a beautiful gift, Edgar. I love it."

Edgar had browsed through the book himself before wrapping it, and tried to imagine what it would be like to live that way. But who had the money to sail around the world, eat fancy dinners every night and shop where a pair of shoes cost more than his monthly Social Security check? They would have to sell their house just to afford a vacation like that, only to return homeless. As Wilma looked at the pictures, Edgar dreamed for just a moment, however unrealistically, of giving his dear Wilma—the woman he had loved for most of his life—such an extravagant gift.

§

By ten they were both tired and ready for bed. The evening had turned out better than either of them could have imagined just a few days earlier; a brief blessing of peace within a time of uncertainty. With everything shut down, turned off and put away, they made their way toward bed. Wilma waited as Edgar removed a pill from the bottle he kept in his pocket, quickly popped it into his mouth and slid the bottle under his pillow. She kissed him goodnight, closed his door and crossed the hall to her room. They had been sleeping apart now since around the time Edgar retired. That's when his recurring dreams and tossing and turning had become unbearable. He was never able to remember much from the dreams, other than he always seemed to be running—trying to get home. One particularly bad night, he got up and went to sleep in the spare room, his old childhood bedroom, to allow her to get some sleep. And somehow, sleeping there in his childhood bed, his nightmares disappeared.

She imagined that he felt some sense of comfort or safety there. He continued to sleep in that room whenever his dreams turned bad, until eventually he moved across the hall for good. With their intimate life all but over by that point, the arrangement worked out fine for both of them.

Wilma laid her robe over the end of the bed, stepped out of her winter slippers and crawled under the chilly covers. Pulling the blanket and comforter up close to her chin, she gave thanks for the evening and prayed for a magical day to come. As she began to relax, her attention shifted unexpectedly to thoughts of herself, something she rarely did, as that always made her uncomfortable. She considered her role to be that of caretaker for her small family—for Edgar—and that was what made her happy. In her mind, it was never a wife's place to dream outside of what had been given to her; that felt selfish and unappreciative. But it was Christmastime, a time when anything seemed possible. And what better time to dream—just a little—for herself. She closed her eyes and set her limiting thoughts aside. As she did, a tingling sensation, like a low-voltage electrical current, began to wash gently across her body. It was not concerning at all, but rather profoundly comforting and welcoming, and she willingly allowed it to sink in. As her mind left the outer world, and she welcomed in the mysterious sensation, Wilma fell into the first of two very powerful visions that appeared in the house that night.

§

She is on the deck of a luxurious ocean liner, floating across a vast sea of turquoise water, surrounded by all of her closest friends. They are sitting around a large and elegant table while waiters in spotless white uniforms deliver delicacies on the finest china, and colorful drinks in large crystal goblets. She looks up toward the sky, which is the richest blue she has ever seen, and feels the warmth of a tropical breeze, carrying with it the subtle aroma of saltwater. Gazing down, she notices herself wearing a glorious silk dress painted in colorful flowers. On her head is a large sun hat tied with a matching silk ribbon. Around her neck is a stunning silver necklace embedded with the finest imaginable sapphires, which gradate from small to large, ending at a magnificent center stone that appears too enormous to be real. Glancing around at her friends, she notices that they are also exquisitely dressed—in a way that most people could only dream of. Without knowing why or how, she feels somehow responsible for everything going on around her. She allows herself to feel it even deeper, and the sensation is glorious.

She is suddenly distracted, and her attention shifts to Edgar. She looks around again, to check for him. He is not here—but she already knows that. He is in his own dream—in his own special place and time. She feels a momentary weight of sadness, an emptiness beside her, but also a warmth in her heart—a deep sense of gratitude for the time they had together, and for what he had left her. His things had been well cared for, and now they were taking care of her.

The sensation of Edgar lingers, but for now she puts him in a loving, forever place in her heart, and looks forward to the time when they will meet again. Her attention then shifts back to her present moment. Gazing at the other women around the table, who are all smiling and laughing, she basks again in the feeling that places her as the source of this magical experience. Then, just as the vision begins to fade, they all turn toward her and raise their glasses.

24
STOLEN MONEY

Earl Howard was relaxing in his chair next to the unlit fireplace and drinking a beer when the pounding started, causing the front door to shake in its frame. The surprise caused him to spill beer down his front as he fumbled out of his chair. "What the hell!" he shouted at the door. There came another round of knocks. "I'm coming, damn it! You better have a good reason for pounding on my door this late at night!"

"Who is it, dear?" Grace Howard called from the kitchen.

"Probably someone trying to sell us a vacuum cleaner; I don't know; I'll get it." He thundered across the hardwood floor and instinctively twisted the switch for the porch light, grabbed the door handle and poised himself for a stern lecture on late night solicitation. "This better be important."

A rush of cold air brushed across Earl's body, and goose bumps formed on his bare arms. They were not caused by the temperature, but from the sight of two police officers standing on his dimly lit porch; their faces glowing eerily in the light. Earl took a couple of steps back. The police had never been to his house before, and he found himself uncharacteristically speechless. He didn't know whether to be scared, angry or something else. "Uh...what can I do for you, officers?"

Grace appeared in the kitchen doorway, wiping her hands on a dishtowel, a worried look on her face. "What's wrong?" she asked.

"What happened?"

The two officers stood looming just outside the metal screen door, peering into the living room. The officer on the right was a large man, about fifty years old with a gray buzz cut. He looked like an aged Marine who enjoyed a lot of post-service drinking. The other officer was much younger and thinner, and looked to be in his mid twenties. His cap was pulled down low on his head, shadowing his eyes. His freshly pressed uniform and polished shoes were an instant giveaway to his lack of hard experience. The older officer was the first to speak. "Mr. and Mrs. Howard?"

"Yes. What seems to be the problem, officers?" Earl asked as he looked from one to the other.

"I'm Officer Williams," the older officer said, "and this is Officer McCrory. May we come in for a moment?"

"Yeah, sure." Earl unlocked the screen and let them in. They brushed their shoes on the mat as he closed the door behind them.

"Thank you," Officer Williams said. "It's a bit chilly out tonight." A large caliber revolver dangled from his right side; a well-used billy club hung from the left. He reached into his back pocket and pulled out a small black notebook. Flipping through some pages, he paused at one to read some notes. The younger officer stood motionless by his side. "Ma'am, do you have a son named Edgar?" the older officer asked, looking up at Grace.

"Yes, we do," she said as her eyes darted between the two officers, and then over to her husband.

"What's he done?" Earl asked, his face beginning to flush.

Ignoring the question, Officer Williams continued, "We need to ask him some questions. Is he here?"

"What's this all about?" Earl asked again.

The officer flipped forward a few pages, found what he was looking for and said, "Carl Russell. Do either of you know this boy?"

"No," Earl replied bluntly.

"I don't know this boy either," Grace said, fiddling with the dish towel in her hands. "I think Edgar mentioned someone named Carl a few times. He said he was trading some baseball cards with this boy, but I've never seen him around the house. What has he done?"

"Mrs. Howard," Officer Williams said, "we arrested this Russell boy earlier today for breaking and entering over near *Smitty's* on Acorn Street. We've had multiple complaints over in that area from folks saying that money had been taken from their homes, stolen from purses, wallets, or just lying around the house. Not a lot of money, just small amounts, a few dollars here and there. And we believe the Russell boy never took all the money he found. He always left some, maybe to make folks think they misplaced it or lost count of how much they had, rather than thinking it had been stolen. He didn't actually break into the houses either. From what we know, he watched until the owners left and then slipped in through a window or an unlocked door. This kid was very sneaky."

Grace walked over to Earl and stood by his side. "What does this have to do with Edgar?" she asked. "Are you saying he was involved in these robberies?"

"No, ma'am. Not yet. We just need to ask him some questions. You see, when we took the Russell boy into custody, he cracked. It turns out he's been stealing for months now. There was over $100 in cash on him. We searched his grandmother's house; that's where he's been living. It was filled with merchandise that he appears to have bought with the stolen money. The grandmother is old and doesn't know where any of it came from. After interrogating the boy, he did tell us that he's been spending some of the money on pop and candy and baseball cards over at *Smitty's*. We talked with Mr. Smith, the owner of the market, and he told us that this boy had been coming into the store for a while. He would sit outside the store and open his cards, then leave the wrappers and empty bottles all over the sidewalk. Then, a couple of weeks ago, two other boys showed up. The three of them started coming into the store together, nearly every day at the same time, buying more baseball cards, pops and candy. And the Russell boy always paid—for everything. After a while, they began buying other things, too. They would look around the store for anything that caught their eye, and Russell would buy it. Not just one, mind you, he would buy three of everything, one for each of them. That is what we know so far, Mrs. Howard. The Russell boy mentioned your son, Edgar, and that's why we're here."

"Who was the other boy?" Grace asked as her husband fumed at her side.

The officer flipped a page and said, "Some kid named Jimmy. We don't know the last name, and thought that you might know who this other boy is."

"Yes, officer," Grace said. "His name is Jimmy Schmidt. He lives just three houses down on the right. He's Edgar's best friend. He's a good boy. He has asthma."

"Yes, ma'am. We'll talk to him as well. Is Edgar here now? We would like to have a word with him."

"Yes, he is. But officer, Edgar is a good boy." Tears started flowing down her cheeks as she wiped her eyes with the dish towel.

"I'll get him," Earl snapped as he pulled away from his wife and headed down the hallway.

Grace fell onto the sofa. "Oh, my. Edgar is a good boy, officers," she repeated. "He would never be involved in anything illegal. He's a good boy."

"Yes, ma'am. I'm sure you're right, but we need to do our jobs just the same. We have to gather all the facts."

Earl screamed from the hallway as he lumbered toward his son's room, "Edgar, get out here, NOW!"

§

Edgar was lying in his bed, thinking about his baseball cards and drifting toward sleep. He only needed eight more to have all the cards for 1948. It was getting harder to find ones he didn't have, but he was determined to get them all by the time his grandparents came back. And he wanted to show his grandfather how well he'd been taking care of his things. His cards were kept in neat piles, sorted by team in the top drawer of his dresser. The signed Hal Newhouser card sat on top of his *Detroit Tigers* pile. He was just starting to pass over into sleep when a loud, sudden sound shook him awake. "Huh?" he mumbled. Just as he tried to sit up, the bedroom door burst open and a figure appeared in the doorway, silhouetted against the harsh light of the hallway.

"What?" Edgar asked groggily.

"Edgar, get the hell out here, NOW!"

The booming voice was his father's, and he was definitely not happy about something. Disoriented and shaky, Edgar pushed the covers aside and sat up. His father did not wait for a response; he turned and left, mumbling something about grounding him for a year if he had anything to do with it. *Do with what?* He must have left his bike by the steps again, and his father tripped over it in the dark. Why drag him out of bed for that though? Trembling, and hesitant to go out there, Edgar stood up and moved cautiously toward the door. He heard unfamiliar voices coming from the other side of the house. *What's going on?* He shuffled into the hallway and paused at the bathroom door. He had to pee, but decided it could wait. He then noticed two police officers standing near the front door, and the shock of that sight slapped him hard across the face. Instantly, he was fully alert and awake, confused and even more frightened. His angry father was one thing, but the cops, too. He couldn't imagine what they were doing here, or what it could possibly have to do with him. He moved to the edge of the hall where it opened into the living room, searching for the comfort of his mother. She was sitting on the sofa with her hands in her lap, looking nervously at him. Her eyes were red, as if she'd been crying, or was about to. His father stood next to her, glaring at him. *What happened? What did I do?* He and Jimmy were breaking bottles on the train tracks a few days earlier, but that was nothing to send the fuzz for.

He spoke out in a trembling voice, "Ma, what's wrong? What happened?"

"The question is, young man," his father snapped back, "what did *you* do?"

Edgar had never seen him so mad. "Me? I didn't do anything."

Honest I didn't." Tears began welling up in his eyes. He desperately wanted to get to his mother, but his father was in the way. He felt the urge to run, but the cops were blocking the door. Going back to his room was an option; he could climb out the window and make a run for it. But no, they would easily catch him before he could get away, then beat him to a pulp with their billy clubs. Caught, for what he didn't know, Edgar's shoulders drooped and he began to cry.

"Okay, folks, let's take it easy now," Officer Williams said, waving his hands slowly in a calming manner. He turned toward Edgar and asked, "Are you Edgar Howard?"

His tone reminded Edgar of Mr. Pearson, the principal at school, when he was attending to troublemakers. It was that same *I'm asking you a question and you best not lie to me* voice.

"Yes, sir," Edgar said, sniffling and wiping at his eyes.

"Son, we need you to answer some questions for us. Can you do that?"

Edgar looked over at his mother again, his eyes pleading for her to come to his rescue. "Ma, I didn't do anything. I swear I didn't."

"Okay, honey, I believe you," she said. "You just go ahead and answer the officer's questions, okay?"

"Okay, but I didn't do anything." He didn't want to go to jail; he had heard stories about what happened in jail—and was terrified at the thought of being tossed in the clink with a bunch of murderers and thieves. Would he have to go to trial to prove his innocence, or was he being framed for a crime he didn't commit? He had heard about that happening on one of the murder mysteries on the radio. Standing there, waiting for the interrogation to begin, Edgar wished with all his might that his grandfather were there. He would know what to say, and how to handle the cops, to convince them of their mistake and send them on their way.

"Is there someplace where we can sit and talk to the boy?" Officer Williams asked.

"Yes, we can go into the kitchen," Grace said. "I just finished cleaning up."

She looked toward Edgar and reached out her hand, inviting him to come along. She eased him into the chair against the kitchen wall and sat down next to him, sliding her chair up close until it touched his. Officer Williams sat down across from Edgar and placed his notebook on the table. Officer McCrory positioned himself near the sink, his hands resting across his narrow chest. Edgar's father guarded the doorway to the living room, beer in hand, fuming at the idea of police entering his house to arrest his delinquent son.

"Edgar," Officer Williams said, "do you know a boy named Carl Russell?"

"Yes, sir," Edgar replied.

In his small black notebook, the officer took notes.

"When did you first meet him?"

"A few weeks ago; I don't remember exactly." Edgar glanced toward his father, certain that he was going to be yelled at for not answering the question specifically enough.

"Where did you meet him?"

"At *Smitty's Market*. Jimmy and I rode our bikes over there to get a pop. He was sitting outside the store and we started talking."

"How often did you meet him at *Smitty's*?"

"I don't know, most every day since then, I guess. Sometimes he never showed up."

The questioning continued until they reached the part where Carl started buying them gifts.

"Did he say where he got the money?" Officer Williams asked.

"He said his mother gave it to him," Edgar replied. "She gave him all the money he wanted."

While his father scoffed from the doorway, Edgar mentioned seeing the wad of money in Carl's pocket the day before, but didn't ask where it came from. He told the officers everything he knew, the complete truth, and that he never stole anything. His mother got him a drink of water from the sink while he tried to recall all the things Carl had bought: knives, pop, candy, baseball cards, lighters and even slingshots. He did omit the part where he and Jimmy shot bottles on the train tracks with them. He didn't consider that being untruthful, just wise.

Officer Williams paused, then closed his notebook. "That's enough questions for now; I think we have enough."

"Am I going to jail?" Edgar asked. It was the white elephant in the room, and he needed to know. Would it be a life sentence, or the gas chamber? Did they even do that to kids?

"No, son, you're not going to jail." At that point, Officer McCrory moved over and whispered something in the older officer's ear.

"Oh, yes, we're going to need the evidence," Officer Williams said.

"What evidence?" Edgar's mother asked.

"The baseball cards; everything that the Russell boy bought with the stolen money."

Edgar burst out, "You're going to take my baseball cards!" He surprised himself and everyone else in the room with that. But even before the words had finished passing his lips, he wished that he had kept his trap shut. He cringed in anticipation. Who would attack first, his father or the cops? He was certain to be on the floor in handcuffs any second, then dragged downtown for fingerprinting and booking.

His father didn't wait for either officer to reply before erupting, "Get up, Edgar, and get the goddamn baseball cards! All of it— NOW!"

Edgar jumped out of his chair and almost slipped on the Linoleum. He shot through the doorway and down the hall toward his room.

"Earl, relax, please." Grace walked over to him and put her hands on his chest.

Officer Williams stood and said in a deep, calming voice, "It's okay folks. Everything is fine. Let's all calm down now."

Edgar stopped cold in the middle of his room and stared around. In shock, he forgot for a moment what he was supposed to be doing; he was sobbing and trembling uncontrollably. As he yanked the top dresser drawer open, his cards, once neatly organized, scattered into a mess. There was no time to straighten up the piles. Looking around frantically for something to put them in, he noticed the pillow on his bed and grabbed for it, violently shaking the inside loose from the pillowcase. He started grabbing handfuls of cards and tossed them in as fast as he could. Once he had all of the cards out of the drawer, he stared at the emptiness left behind. His heart sank as he thought about his grandfather and how disappointed he was going to be. He moved quickly around his room and grabbed everything that Carl had bought for him, tossing it all into the pillowcase.

His father's voice boomed from the other room, "Edgar! What's taking you so long? If I have to come in there—"

"I'm coming! I've got them!" Edgar shouted.

"Make sure you bring *everything*—and turn the damn lights out when you leave your room. Who's got the money to be running the electric all day!"

Edgar flipped off the light and returned to the living room. The two officers had moved back to the front door and his father was in the middle of the room, arms crossed, glaring at him. His mother was standing at his side. She was whispering something in his ear, but her eyes were on Edgar. He walked nervously toward the officers, staying as far away from his father as he could. He held out the pillowcase and the younger officer took it. He removed his own notebook and checked to see if the items matched.

The older officer asked Edgar in a firm yet gentle tone, "Is this *everything* the Russell boy gave you?"

"Yes sir," Edgar said as he stood before the officers, his head down.

"It better be," his father grumbled.

"Thank you, folks," Officer Williams said. "Again, we're sorry for disturbing you at this late hour. If we have any more questions, we'll be in touch."

"Thank you, officers," Edgar's mother replied.

"Ma'am," they both said as they tipped their caps, and then disappeared into the night.

§

Earl Howard stood in the front doorway looking out. As the police car pulled away, he noticed several neighbors standing on their porches with their lights on, looking over toward his house. Other people were moving around in the darkness, also staring in his direction. He closed the door slowly and locked it. After turning off the porch light, he leaned over and pulled the front curtains closed. He picked up his beer from the coffee table and took a long gulp. "Damn nosy neighbors," he said. "A man goes to work every day, sweats in the factory to put a roof over his family's head and pays his taxes. He doesn't need the goddamn cops at his door." He walked toward the kitchen as Edgar moved closer to his mother. There was the sound of the icebox opening and bottles clanking; then the release of a bottle cap. After a short pause, his father shouted from the kitchen, "I better not see another baseball card in this house—EVER!"

"I didn't do anything, Ma," Edgar pleaded softly, looking up at his mother.

She pulled him closer and kissed him on the forehead. "I know, honey. Your father is just upset."

"Earl, you heard the officers," she said. "They agreed that Edgar didn't do anything." She spoke in her motherly *everything is fine* voice. "Come and sit down in your chair. I'll turn on the phonograph and we can listen to *Perry Como*, or how about *Abbott and Costello* on the radio? That will relax you. You love *Abbott and Costello*."

Edgar loved *Abbott and Costello*, too, but he felt that there would be no laughing for the rest of that night, if ever again. He thought about Carl sitting alone in the slammer and wondered if they would ever see each other again. At that moment he didn't care.

The silence from the kitchen was interrupted by the sound of the back door opening, and then slamming shut. A moment of silence followed, and then the sound of the car in the front drive-way, cranking but not starting. It stopped, then cranked again. The horn blasted, followed by more cranking. After several attempts the car rumbled to life. The headlights lit up the perimeter around the edges of the closed curtains as the car backed out of the driveway. There was some undecipherable shouting, which Edgar assumed was his father cursing at the damn nosy neighbors. Next was the roar of the engine and the sound of tires screeching on the pavement. Then the night was silent.

"I didn't do anything, Ma," Edgar said again.

"Your father will be fine, honey. I'll talk to him later. He just needs some time. You go off to bed now."

"Okay," Edgar replied, sniffling and wiping his face.

§

Edgar crawled into bed and pulled the covers up over his head. He thought about Jimmy and wondered if he was suffering a similar fate. Were the cops there now? Jimmy's father had an even worse temper than his, and the only thing that kept him from getting smacked around was his asthma. Edgar wondered if even that would be enough to save him from this. Guilty until proven innocent seemed to be how the law of parenthood worked. Glancing over at the dresser, he noticed that he'd left the top drawer open. He thought about his cards—and baseball in general—and felt a deep sadness inside. Why did it have to be so painful? He practiced and practiced, but in the end he wasn't good enough to play. So then he bought cards. Well, Carl did mostly, but he took good care of them. And now this. What did it all mean? Maybe baseball was just not meant to be. In the morning he would get his comics out of the closet and put them back in the top drawer. Comics were safe, and Jimmy liked them better, too. *Superman, Buck Rogers, Captain America* and *Flash Gordon*; they all knew how to get out of trouble. But more importantly, they never got *him* into trouble. And maybe his grandfather liked comics as well.

Just as Edgar was about to drift off, a sense of panic enveloped him. He leaped out of bed and lunged toward the light switch by the door. He twisted it and stumbled back toward the dresser. He looked into his top drawer where, up until just a short while ago, he had kept his most precious things. It was empty, of course. Why wouldn't it be? They made him bring *everything*. But some of the cards were his; the one's from his grandfather; the one's he'd bought with his own money. But that's not what caused Edgar's heart to sink. "Oh, no. No, no, no." He looked around frantically, hoping it had just fallen on the floor. But in his heart he knew where it was. Edgar pushed the drawer closed, put his head on the dresser and started crying. It was gone; his signed Hal Newhouser card was gone. He stumbled back to bed, put the coverless pillow over his head and cried himself to sleep.

§

The next morning, Edgar stayed in his room as long as he could, thinking mostly about his special card. What would he tell his grandfather? Would he be mad at him for not taking care of it, or would he get him another one—take him back to Briggs Stadium and have it signed again? Edgar didn't know exactly what his grandfather would do, but he knew that whatever it was, he would feel better afterwards. It would be something really special and unexpected, too, like inviting Hal Newhouser over to their house for a barbecue in the back yard. It would have to be on a day when his father was working, but his grandfather would take care of that; that's the kind of grandpa he was.

Around 10:00 am, Edgar finally opened his bedroom door. The house was quiet and still, a stark contrast to the hell of the night before. He moved cautiously toward the front window, checking to see if his father's car was there. Luckily, the driveway was empty. Staring out, he wondered if his father was still mad about the night before. Of course he was; his father could stay mad about something for weeks. Turning and heading into the kitchen, he looked out the back window. His mother was in the garden with her basket, picking something. On the table was a plate of dry toast and a glass of juice, but he was too sad to eat. Sitting next to his breakfast was the newspaper, with the sports section lying on top. He didn't know what to think about that. Was his mother trying to make him feel better or worse? He picked it up and without reading a word, walked it over to the garbage can and dropped it in. He left the kitchen and headed toward Jimmy's house.

Jimmy was sitting alone on his porch, leaning against the house with his head down. He didn't look up as Edgar approached. There were several comic books sitting next to him, and another one open in his lap, facing down. Edgar sat down on the porch step and stared blankly at the sidewalk in front of him. Overhead, unseen birds were singing their happy tunes. Edgar wished he had a rock.

Finally, Jimmy said, "Wanna play war?"

"Sure," Edgar replied softly. "Wanna play in my yard?"

"Yeah. I left my planes there the other day, remember?"

"Oh, yeah."

"Let me just ask my mom if I can go," Jimmy added as he headed inside the house.

Edgar couldn't remember him having to ask before. Usually, Jimmy just screamed across the house that he was going and then left without waiting for a reply. A few bird chirping minutes later he returned.

"I have to be back before—" Jimmy stopped to consider his words, and then continued. "I have to be back home before three; we're eating supper early tonight."

Edgar, who normally would have had plenty to say about such a silly thing, kept his mouth shut.

The boys played together that morning, much more reserved than usual, as if their armies had suffered a major and unexpected defeat the night before and were processing the damage, preparing a new strategy. For a while they remained lost in their own thoughts, but by early afternoon they were laughing again, running through the gates and up and down the alley, airplanes in hand, chasing each other, shooting and destroying the enemy. There were no words spoken about police interrogations or corporal punishments. There was no talk of baseball or anything related to it, and especially, neither of them mentioned the name Carl Russell. In fact, it was many years before they talked about that night. They never did find out what happened to Carl, and neither one cared.

25
THE TIME HAS COME

*S*preading out endlessly in every direction is an open field of bright green summer grass. *Above is a sky so intense that it appears almost surreal, disturbed by only a single white disc of radiating heat. A young boy stands motionless on a small mound that rises slightly from the rest of the field. In his hand he holds a bright white baseball.*

Edgar watches the scene as he descends from high above. As he gets closer, the field below comes further into focus. The boy is not alone down there, as he had seemed from the higher elevation, but rather surrounded by others. The field of green is no longer a constant hue, but a local baseball field tattered by wear. Once in viewing position, the scene comes to life; a baseball game is in progress. Edgar floats weightlessly above the field and watches.

The skinny young boy on the mound takes an uncomfortable looking windup and hurls the ball forward, where it bounces well in front of the batter. A burst of laughter and undecipherable comments come from the other players. Edgar feels a welling of sympathy for the pitcher. He wants to lower himself down to the field and console the boy, but he is unable to go any further. The boy retrieves the ball and returns to his position. Edgar can feel an uneasiness radiating up. He wants desperately to speak to the boy, and tell him something very important, but alas he has no voice.

After more distorted words from the other boys, the young pitcher continues. He winds up and throws his next pitch. This time the ball *sails perfectly through the air. But the pitcher's foot lands awkwardly on something, causing him to stumble. The ball jumps off the hitter's bat and returns back toward the pitcher, who is struggling to stay upright. Falling forward, the young boy looks up just in time to see the approaching ball. At the last instant, he raises his glove. It catches the bottom edge of the ball, which then ricochets up and hits the poor boy in the throat. As he's falling to his knees, grabbing at his throat with his bare hand, the ball, which popped straight up into the air, lands back into the boy's open glove.*

While the boy holds his throat, choking uncontrollably, the other players on the field begin jumping up and down, laughing and howling with delight. The batter tosses the bat to the ground. As the players from both sides converge upon the mound in a congratulatory manner, the oblivious boy manages to stand up. His head is hung low, seemingly unaware of what is happening around him. The batter walks forward and reaches out his hand, while the others approach with smiles and open arms. Suddenly, and without warning, the boy pushes through the crowd and takes off running. The others watch stunned as the young pitcher races across the street and into an open alley. They call after him, but the boy just keeps on running.

§

Edgar bolted upright in bed. In a cold sweat, he pushed and pulled frantically at the covers, trying to find his reality. One minute he was running very fast, or was he watching himself running very fast, and the next he was suffocating under a blanket of wet grass. His mind hovered somewhere between memories of the vivid dream and his current physical location. His mouth was mumbling, "No, no, no." He stopped when he consciously realized what he was doing. As the images and sensations began to fade, he became deeply unsettled by a feeling that he may have missed something very important.

Sliding his feet over the side of the bed, Edgar sat up and rubbed his hands over his face. He reached for the water glass on his nightstand, but found it empty. He wanted to crawl back under the covers and find a more pleasant dream, but he knew that was not possible. As he stared blankly into the darkness, a force unlike anything he had experienced before overcame him. It started as the subtlest of sensations, a tiny voice whispering to him from very far away. But even before his mind could process the signal, it was upon him like a high-powered bullet fired from a great distance. His body reacted in a seizure-like manner—shaking and twitching from his feet right up to his head. "Please, no!" he cried out, from terror more than physical pain. Inside his head, the sounds thundered and pulsated—up and down—like the volume setting was being childishly played with. He put his hands to his head and cried out again, "No. Please, no."

Across his skin, Edgar could feel his body being touched again by those invisible fingers. Even though he had instigated the return of the unknown presence, he was unprepared for the power it now seemed to possess. He thought about the pills he had flushed down the toilet, and prayed that there might be some left. *Maybe one fell on the floor, or stuck to the inside of the bottle.* While holding onto the scattered covers, in hope that they might offer some form of protection, he thought of Wilma sleeping across the hall. He selfishly hoped that she had heard him, or possibly sensed his dismay telepathically and was on her way. *What would she be able to do, except make a phone call?* The last thing he wanted on Christmas Eve was to visit the emergency room.

Scratching at his face, Edgar pleaded, "Please stop. Please stop and tell me what you want from me." Then, as if his words had rotated an invisible spigot, everything paused. The thundering beat in his head, the feeling of a thousand invisible touches—it all stopped. In that moment there was a sweet inner silence that had been missing for too long. But to Edgar's dismay, it was short-lived. Somewhere within (or without) came a distinct whooshing sound—like something turning very fast was being slowed down or adjusted. He thought of tuning his radio, adjusting it until the station came in clear. *Yes, that's what we've been trying to do all along, tune into the right frequency.*

Excited by what that might mean, Edgar tried to settle himself enough to focus in on it. As he did, yet another truth welled up from the sound, which had morphed into a gentle beat, *Bum-bum. Bum-bum.* That was not the curious part though, but rather what he sensed within it. In his mind, it seemed no crazier than what he had hypothesized already. As the buzzing had slowed down through some form of cosmic tuning, he was able to discern more clearly that it was in fact not a voice he was hearing after all, but many. From some dimension Edgar could hardly fathom, it was actually thousands of voices calling out—a whole army—marching in rhythm.

"What do you want from me?" Edgar whispered.

Bum-bum. Bum-bum

Edgar put on his robe and glasses, then stepped into his slippers. He moved across the darkness of his room and grabbed the doorknob. The vibration—*they*—were in the house somewhere, if not in some way now part of it. He spoke softly, not wanting to wake Wilma, "Tell me what you want. Please. I can't understand you." He shuffled out into the dark hallway and paused at Wilma's room. He gently pushed her door open, and felt a subtle tinge of anxiety, as if he might be taking a wrong turn.

Bum-bum, bum-bum.

You're just going to have to wait; I need to say goodbye to my wife first.

Inside Wilma's bedroom, a nightlight weakly illuminated a small spot of the floor. Edgar stepped forward and listened to the soft breathing of his sleeping wife, and wondered what she was dreaming of. He gazed lovingly at her as his mind flooded with sentimental thoughts. The voices paused again, giving him a moment of peace— perhaps an offering of respect for this final moment. He wondered if he had been a good husband. Did he provide well enough? Did she have any regrets? If she had the chance, what would she have done differently? What would he have done differently? Would their different choices still have brought them together? His mind pictured the pretty girl with the blue eyes in the flowered dress lying in the grass near the side of the road. Her hand was so soft and smooth, and he liked the way it felt in his. He hadn't thought of that in years, but the memory felt as if no time had passed. He was standing there again; a young boy with a lifetime of dreams in front of him, naïve and unaware of how each decision made along the journey had the potential to alter the overall outcome. He considered that simple moment of kindness and infatuation from so long ago, and wondered how a different choice that day could have possibly changed anything in a significant way.

Wilma's clock read 11:23 pm. Edgar had no intention of waking her for whatever was about to happen; he knew that this battle was his to face alone. They had never talked much about death, or the afterlife. Wilma was certain that Heaven was on the other side of that final doorway; her church told her that. He was not so sure. Instead, he imagined his destiny starting at the end of a very long path—a bright rectangular light—and beyond that was the beginning of something magical and new. Standing over his wife, he wondered whether the answer to that ultimate question might soon be forthcoming.

Edgar shook off the questions he had no answers to and smiled lovingly at his wife. He let the emotions of the moment overtake him, and for once he didn't try to hold back. As he leaned over and kissed his wife, a tear fell onto her cheek. He wiped it gently away and whispered softly in her ear, "I love you, hon." He then stood up and turned back toward the doorway, and what lie beyond.

After pulling the bedroom door closed, Edgar walked down the short hallway toward the front of the house. He could smell the lingering aroma of the fire and the fresh evergreen scent of the Christmas tree. He paused; his senses becoming aware of something not right, and actually had to hold back from laughing at such a ridiculous notion. It was not the voices this time, even though they were back, calling him softly in the background, as if aware of him being on his way. But this was something different, more tangible, coming from the darkness in front of him. It was the actual sound of talking, not loud enough for him to hear what was being said, but definitely coming from nearby. He took a cautious step forward, then another. *Maybe some thugs have broken into the house, or are trying to? But who would rob someone on Christmas Eve? Could it be that strange boy again, returning with his friend?*

Poking his head into the living room, Edgar could see the silhouette of the chairs and the corner lamp. In the fireplace, a few small pieces of wood glowed a dull orange, but offered no usable light. They knew the danger of leaving burning wood in the fireplace, but it helped to keep the house warm, and they wanted to get as much heat from it as possible; running the furnace was expensive. As he moved cautiously toward the front door, the voices became louder, but still unpronounced. The inner buzzing made it difficult to distinguish what was being said, or where it was coming from. Approaching the front door, he could see that the chain was off and the doorknob was not locked. His heart started racing. A hint of external light glowed from the small gap under the curtains to the left. As the muffled voices spoke, flickers of light and shadow reflected off the bottom of the windowsill. Someone was moving outside.

The burglars appeared to be inside the front porch. Edgar rarely locked the outer screen door in the winter; there was nothing out there worth stealing, and now some strangers had let themselves in. Here he was, just a tired old man trying to deal with a much bigger problem, and now some delinquents were out there looking to cause holiday mischief. Or worse yet, hardened criminals who robbed senior citizens, leaving them for dead. *Is this how I'm going to die, after all I've been through?* Hoping to cut off any pre-holiday tragedy, and get back to the business at hand, Edgar placed his slipper against the bottom edge of the door. He had seen that in a movie once; it kept the burglars from pushing the door open. With a shaking hand, he twisted the lock on the doorknob, and then reached up and grabbed the chain. On his first attempt, the chain fell from his nervous fingers and clanked against the door. Certain that he had been heard, he reacted quickly and latched the chain before the door burst open and gunfire rang through the house, damaging Wilma's nice holiday decorations.

None of that happened. In fact, there were no sounds of startled movements either, and no breaking down of the door. But the voice, or voices, were still talking. After a moment of waiting, which seemed like an eternity, Edgar had built up enough courage to get a better look. He moved over to the corner of the window and pulled back a sliver of the curtain. Up in the sky, the half moon shined through an opening in the clouds, while the wind blew the tree branches gently back and forth across its path. He noticed that as the branches swayed in front of the moon, the light and shadows broke and bounced off of the windowsill. From inside the house, it gave the impression of someone moving outside. *What a knucklehead.* Edgar then realized that even if there was nobody outside, there were still *real* voices talking. And if they weren't out there, they must be in the house.

Edgar turned and looked around the room; his night vision had become almost respectable. His eyes stopped at the coat closet and his anxiety swelled again. He moved toward it as quietly as possible and put his ear up to the door. A bead of sweat rolled off his forehead and landed on his hand, which was now resting on the doorknob. Bad ears or not, he was now certain that the voices were coming from inside the closet. *Do they not hear me moving around? Maybe they're waiting for me to go back to bed before finishing their crime.* Edgar looked for something to protect himself with. Across the room, next to the fireplace, was the poker. But he wondered what good that would do—a couple of strong men against an old man with arthritis and bad knees. With what little bit of courage he could muster, Edgar turned the knob and cautiously opened the closet door, just an inch. The voices continued, now clearer than before. *How can they not hear me? Don't they know the door is open?* Exasperated, Edgar pulled the door fully open and stood firmly and without guard, eyes closed tightly, waiting for the attack. Nothing happened.

Edgar opened his eyes and stared into the closet. It was empty, except for coats and hats and scarves and boots—and a small antique radio sitting on the top shelf. He quickly realized that the voices were not coming from the senseless scheming of teenage hoodlums or the crazed ravings of escaped criminals; it was the excited voice of an announcer broadcasting a baseball game, coming from his radio. The unexpectedness of it had Edgar a bit disoriented, but he couldn't help but enjoy the treat—a baseball game when he least expected it. He leaned his head against the doorjamb and wondered: *Are the Tigers playing? They must be. But there was no game scheduled for tonight, was there? It's Christmas Eve. Who would play baseball on Christmas Eve? Could it be a reply of an older game?*

Wherever it was coming from, the game being broadcast through Edgar's radio sounded different. There was a deep humming, an echo below the static filled voice, giving the sensation that it was coming from within a larger space, or from some unimaginable distance. Not Detroit or Cleveland or Los Angeles, but even further. He focused in on the voice, which was not the regular *Detroit Tigers* announcer, although it was curiously familiar. Unable to conjure up an explanation for the delightful distraction, Edgar decided to take a moment and just listen to the game.

"Hal Newhouser pitching to the veteran, Ted Williams. A beautiful summer night here at the corner of Michigan and Trumble."

The station faded as a burst of static momentarily distorted the broadcast. As if invisible hands readjusted the tuner, the game returned.

"Edgar Newhouser winds and pitches. Strike! Williams is currently batting .340 for the 1954 season. What we have here is the premier match-up in all of baseball; arguably the best hitter of all-time against the two-time MVP pitcher, Edgar Newhouser."

Edgar rubbed his ears, certain that he had heard that wrong.

"Ted William steps out of the box. The count is three and one. Williams battling here against the sensational rookie Edgar Howard, on the

mound for our Detroit Tigers, who at just 19 years of age is in his first full year of professional ball and showing that he certainly has what it takes to be a great pitcher."

Edgar stared up at the radio, now convinced that he had fallen into a lucid dream. He ran his hands over his face, down his chest to his thighs. It all felt real and solid. Maybe he was both in and out of the dream at the same time—a walking dream. Yes, that was it. His body was fine; he could feel it, but his mind was somewhere else. Whatever was happening though, it was not entirely unpleasant. Maybe absurd, all things considered, but he loved baseball—and this particular game of fantasy was intoxicating.

"We don't like to talk about these things so early in a young career, but I think that if young Edgar Howard here continues this type of dominating pitching, with that splendid curveball, he will one day find himself in the Hall of Fame over there in Cooperstown. Strike two!
The rookie Howard, staring down Williams. The count is full. He winds and pitches. Strike three! Struck him out! What a pitch! That was a curveball up high and at the last second dropped right out of the sky. That pitch was simply unhittable! If the great Ted Williams couldn't hit that ball, I don't think anyone could. This kid sure is something, folks.
It just makes you wonder—what it must have been like to play baseball with Edgar Howard as a youth, on the local ball field. He must have been one tough, determined kid."

"This is not possible," Edgar mumbled, unaware of the smile stretching across his face.

"The young Edgar Howard walks confidently off the mound. He glances over toward the veteran Williams and tips his cap. I can't hear what he's saying down there, with the crowd roaring, but if I could read his lips, it looks like he said, 'Take that Williams!'"

§

As the game faded back to static, Edgar's mind spun wildly. *Am I having a stroke? What year did they say it was? Who were they talking about?* He reached up into the closet, wanting to bring his radio down and listen somewhere more comfortable. In attempting to do so, he became aware of something that he had not even considered up until that point. Feeling around, he found what he was looking for and pulled it back over the top of the radio and let go. All he could do was stare at the metal prongs at the end of the power cord as it dangled from the top shelf.

Bum-bum! Bum-bum!

The force of the beat broke Edgar from his state. He moved away from the door and tried to re-calibrate his senses. He wondered if the radio, working in such a crazy, illogical way had anything to do with the voices calling him. He had no answer to that, but was beyond doubting anything. He stumbled to the kitchen and over to the sink. He picked a glass out of the drying rack and ran it under the water. With shaking hands he poured what he could into his mouth, the rest running down his face. The nightlight next to the sink was on and the curtains were open wide. Looking out the window, he saw a layer of snow covering the garage roof. It was going to be a white Christmas, according to the clock on the wall, in nineteen minutes.

Bum-bum! Bum-bum!

As captivating and unexplainable as the game was, Edgar tried to push it aside. If it meant something, and was part of the puzzle, he couldn't imagine how it might fit. Perhaps it was a distraction, a lure or a tease. But why? Such random chaos could not be part of an organized, divine plan. It hinted more at the likelihood that his mind was fragmented, possibly beyond repair. Instead of lingering in that thought, he glanced toward the basement door and, with a knowing that had been there all along, knew that the answer to everything was down below. And by the looks of the large nail sticking out of the doorframe, Wilma did as well.

Bum-bum! Bum-bum!

Moving forward, Edgar reached out and placed both hands on

the closed door. He could immediately feel the invisible force radiating through—waiting—expecting him. That familiar tingling ran up his arms and goose bumps reappeared on his flesh. The beat that first appeared as a buzzing in his ears just a few months earlier, that became a voice without words and then many, was alive and well— apparently beyond the reach of *Pfizer's* army. Edgar relaxed his tensed muscles and gave in to the feeling, letting it consume him. Inside his head, adjustments were being made, tuning into a new alignment with that of the unseen. As the frequencies merged and the signal came into focus, his mind experienced a new awareness, both shocking and profound. It was not a beat after all—not *Bum-bum, Bum-bum*, but *Ed-gar, Ed-gar*. They were not just talking—they were calling.

26
THE SADDEST DAY OF ALL

It was a Saturday in mid September and Edgar was back in school, hating every minute of it. Between classes, he avoided the kids from the park that he discovered went to his school. Most of his free time was spent alone in his room with the door closed, or at Jimmy's house reading comic books. Aside from that, and the new girl with the curly blonde hair, Edgar's life had become boring and routine.

Sitting on his bed, reading the latest Superboy comic for the second time, Edgar was startled by a sound coming from the other side of the house. It was a quick, high-shrieking howl, like a wounded animal that had been struck unexpectedly. It then softened into a deep sob that sounded like his mother crying. As Edgar's ears perked up, he could tell that it was a different kind of crying—not the angry kind. It was usually his father who made his mother cry like that, but only after a lot of yelling first, and there was none of that. That kind always worried him, like he was going to get yelled at for something. This kind was new and unexpected, and it concerned him even more.

Edgar put his comic book on the bed and tiptoed to the door. He opened it just a crack and listened for words that might explain what was happening. He could hear his father talking, but his words were undecipherable, low and calm—very unlike him. Unable to understand what was being discussed, Edgar slipped into the hallway. He took slow, cautious steps toward the front of the house, keeping close to the wall. As he got to the edge of the living room, he could see his mother sitting in her chair with her head in her hands; her body was shaking as she sobbed. His father was kneeling down beside her; one hand was on her knee while the other gently stroked her hair. He was whispering something in her ear. On his face was a look unlike any Edgar had seen before; it was not all tight and scowling, but soft and compassionate. Edgar's stomach was churning, and finally it was too much; he had to know what was going on. He stepped into the living room and asked softly, "What's wrong?"

His mother looked up at him; her eyes were bloodshot and filled with tears. "Come over here, Edgar," she said, reaching out a hand. Then she started sobbing again.

Edgar reluctantly moved forward. When he got close enough, she pulled him in and hugged him tightly, while his father's hand rested gently on his shoulder. He felt like crying, too, but still didn't know why.

"What's wrong, Ma?"

"Edgar, honey." She paused and sniffled. Trying to compose herself, she took a slow, shaking breath before continuing. "Edgar, honey, your grandpa died this morning."

Edgar stood frozen in his mother's arms; the tension in his muscles dissolved into numbness. The unexplainable tears that he had held back welled up in his eyes and started flowing down his cheeks; he did nothing to stop them. His breathing became short and jerky as his mind tried to undo his mother's words. He wanted to back up, to go back into his room and make everything return to the way it was the day before or the week before or even just five minutes before—so the whole thing could become right again. Unable to control himself, he pushed back and let it all out, "No Ma! No, no, no!" She pulled him back in while larger hands rubbed his shoulders. "No, Ma, he can't die! He told me he was coming back! We were going to have a catch, and he was going to show me—" He paused for a moment, thought about it, then continued softly through his own sobs, "He was going to show me something."

"I know, honey," his mother said. "He wanted so badly to come back and see you again."

Edgar backed out of his mother's reach. "But he can't die! It's not fair! He said he would be back! He promised! He can't just break a promise like that! People are supposed to keep their promises!" He turned and ran out the front door, letting the metal screen door slam behind him. He stopped abruptly in the front yard and looked from side to side. Jimmy was not on his porch, but he didn't want to see him anyway. Turning left, he started running down the sidewalk and then crossed the street toward the alley. As fast as his legs would take him, he ran between the houses until he reached the park. Some smaller kids were playing in the field and an older couple was walking hand in hand down the sidewalk. There were no boys playing baseball, but he didn't care either way. He continued running until he reached the far back corner of the park, where he collapsed onto the same picnic table that he shared with his grandfather earlier in the summer. Putting his head down on the table, he cried shamelessly. After a while, he moved to the swings and put his head down and cried. When some other people appeared, he moved behind one of the larger trees near the back of the park, pulled his knees up to his chest, thought about his grandfather and cried some more. By the time the sun was positioned directly overhead, Edgar was not only sad and tired, but hungry, too.

He made his way slowly back home, praying along the way that he had just imagined everything. His grandfather had not died; his mother was crying because she was so happy that her parents had called earlier with a surprise message; they were on their way and would be arriving soon—safe and healthy and alive. He just heard it wrong, and ran out of the house before they could clear things up. How silly he would feel when he got home. His mother would make lunch and they would sit and talk about how great it was going to be when the grandparents, *both* of them, pulled into the driveway again. He and his grandfather would wash the dirty blue Plymouth until it shined and then they would sit on the porch and listen to the *Tigers* game on the radio. The ladies would drink iced tea and laugh and talk about the garden. As Edgar approached the house, he struggled to keep the fragile fantasy alive and true in his mind. His stomach moaned with a gloomy unease. The house did not look alive and well; it felt cold and dead.

The living room was empty and the silence thick and depressing. Edgar shuffled into the kitchen, expecting his mother to be preparing lunch, cleaning up or cutting flowers. But it was empty, too. He peeked out the back window and saw his father working under the hood of his car. He scanned the back yard but his mother was nowhere to be seen. He headed back toward the bedrooms and noticed that his parents' bedroom door was pulled up, but not closed. He peeked in. Lying asleep on the bed was his mother; her silent sadness filled the room. He wanted desperately to go to her, needing her touch and reassuring words. But instead of going in, he just stared at her—feeling her loss—their loss. Pulling the door up, he went to his room, crawled into bed, pulled the sheet up over his head and cried himself to sleep.

When Edgar awoke later, his mother was sitting on the bed next to him. There was a tissue in her hand, but her eyes were tearless and not as red. She offered a smile that seemed to say everything was going to be all right, and then leaned down and kissed him on the cheek.

"I miss him, Ma,"

"Me too, honey," she said. "But we will never forget him, will we?"

§

Edgar's mother took the train to North Carolina for the funeral and to help her mother pack and move into a smaller apartment. Edgar asked to go, but his mother told him he had school, and they couldn't afford two tickets anyway. A part of him was relieved; he had never been to a funeral before and was not sure he could handle seeing his grandfather that way. But still, there was something missing in all of it, and that was the chance to say goodbye. Yes, he had said goodbye before they left the last time, there in the driveway. But that was a different kind of farewell. It was the temporary, not forever kind. That one left him with only a brief period of sadness— that eventually turned into excitement, and a yearning for the next time. Knowing there would never be a next time was the saddest thing Edgar could ever imagine.

27
GOING DOWN FOR THE LAST TIME

d-gar, Ed-gar

Excited and curious about his new realization, that the voices were actually calling him, Edgar grabbed the warm doorknob, turned and pulled. Nothing happened. He pulled again with both hands, harder and harder, but the basement door refused to open—only rattled mockingly in the frame. Directly in front of him, obscured by the darkness, was the nail. Once he noticed it, the futility of his efforts became obvious. *Now what?* Backing up and looking around, he noticed that the toolbox, which had been on the floor earlier, was gone. Wilma must have put it somewhere while she was cleaning up. He thought to go and ask her, but under the circumstances, he knew that was not his best idea. He pulled a fork from the silverware drawer and tried to grab the nail with it, but it was useless. Wilma, bless her heart, had really pounded it in. He searched quietly through the other drawers, hoping for another hammer, one with one of those claw things at the end. But no luck.

Ed-gar, Ed-gar

"I know, I know, I'm trying." He suspected that there might be another hammer in the garage, in the workbench. Without thinking of the consequences, or dressing for the harsh winter conditions outside, he unlatched the back door chain. As he reached for the knob, something startled him from behind. In a way, it was like the vibration in his ears—a high-pitched buzzing, but definitely outside of his head this time. He turned around but there was nothing to see but the empty kitchen, dimly lit by the lone nightlight. In the drawer at the end of the counter he found a flashlight and switched it on. It squeaked out a fraction of the illumination he had anticipated, but there was no time to search for fresh batteries.

Ed-gar, Ed-gar

The buzzing continued, emanating from somewhere near the basement door. Edgar shined the light that way but saw nothing—until the beam reached the nail. Even with his glasses on, Edgar's eyes were too old and tired to be certain of what he was seeing. Or maybe his mind was just refusing to believe. He moved in closer, then reached up with his index finger and touched the nail. The heat of it caused him to quickly pull away. But that was not what surprised him the most. He then used the end of the flashlight to touch it, and as he made contact, the nail buzzed louder against the plastic housing. At first he couldn't comprehend what was happening, or why, but as he watched it became clear. The nail was not just vibrating; it was trying to pull itself out of the doorframe. As it worked its way out, it began to twist and shake back and forth. By the time it landed on the floor, the rusty metal nail was spinning like a propeller.

Ed-gar, Ed-gar

Edgar stared at the now unsecured door, and then down at the nail, which was slowly coming to a stop. Under other circumstances, the alarm of seeing a nail remove itself from a doorframe would easily segue him into some form of institutionalization. But in this case, it wasn't even the strangest thing he had witnessed that night. Kicking the nail aside, he reached for the door handle, grasped it firmly and turned. He was too tired, and possibly deep in shock at that point, to be scared of anything leaping out. If they wanted him, they could have him. But the door opened with ease, revealing only the eerie darkness of an empty staircase. There was no red-eyed demon waiting for his soul; only that familiar breeze. Closing his eyes and allowing it to pass through him, Edgar noticed a slight variation. It was not as warm and humid as he had remembered—a bit cooler and crisper—but not like a winter cold either. To Edgar, it felt less like a muggy summer afternoon and more like a pleasant spring evening.

Edgar pulled the light string. The dim bulb barely illuminated the stairs and, for the first time in his life, he wished that he had filled every light socket in the house with high wattage bulbs and said to hell with the electric bill. He held the flashlight in one hand and grabbed hold of the handrail with the other. His body ached everywhere as he worked his way down. His head was throbbing, too, probably from the rum. There were all sorts of pills he could use right now, but the urgency of the voices told him there was no time for that. As he descended, he had no doubt of reaching the bottom of the stairs, one way or another. It was the return journey that should have caused him concern, yet going back up that night felt like something he need not worry about.

Ed-gar, Ed-gar

The house, all the way down to the foundation, was vibrating with each call of his name. Edgar wondered if Wilma could feel it as well. He prayed not, and hoped that the rum she had might assist him with that wish.

Ed-gar, Ed-gar

The descent seemed to take forever, and Edgar's hands ached from holding so hard onto the handrail. Finally at the bottom, he reached for the light switch and felt the entire wall shaking. He flipped the switch and the lone light bulb popped with a dull flash. *Just perfect.* The beam of the flashlight barely made it across the room, but enough that he could see his mother's old dishes rattling on the metal shelves. Staring around, he was no clearer on where to go than the last time he was down here. Nothing seemed certain, except for the sense of urgency. Moving to his left, being careful not to fall over anything, he kicked softly at some of the empty boxes, hoping for a reaction. The curtains on the left wall had been pulled open and a yellowish colored material glowed in the light. *That must be Tommy's work.*

Ed-gar, Ed-gar

"I'm here," Edgar cried out. "Just tell me what to do!" He worried again that he was making too much noise. If Wilma woke up and found him missing from his bed in the middle of the night, she would probably be upset with him. If she couldn't find him after searching the upstairs, she would be scared and most likely call 911. If she found him in the dark basement early on Christmas morning, wandering around in his slippers and talking about a whole army of voices, she would be furious, and everything they had enjoyed together the last couple of days would be ruined. After glancing at the doorway to the pantry under the stairs, still closed after his previous visit, Edgar turned and moved back toward the old laundry area. He pushed the door open and flipped the light switch. But the bulb there also failed to respond. *If you want me to find you, how about giving me a little light!* Continuing into the darkness with only the dim light of the flashlight, he noticed more evidence of yellow foam.

Ed-gar, Ed-gar

"Where are you?" Beads of sweat dripped from Edgar's face as he looked toward the furnace. At one time he had thought that the blower motor was the cause of everything, but now he knew better. As long as he could remember, the old furnace never spoke to him.

Ed-gar, Ed-gar

Nothing in the room moved or caught his attention. Moving forward and shining the flashlight around the furnace, he did notice something different. Sitting in the back corner was a large rattrap. Relieved to see it empty, he thought of Tommy, who was kindly determined to rid their house of its infestations. If only he knew. Edgar wondered if Wilma knew about the trap, but suspected that Tommy had made a wise decision and kept it to himself. Edgar shuddered at the thought of something like a rat in his house, then chuckled. All things considered, a rat would be a welcomed relief.

Ed-gar, Ed-gar

Noticing the door to his father's old workshop, he moved toward it, passing the old laundry cart that Wilma used long ago to hang the laundry on. Two of his dress shirts hung from the bar. He made a mental note to take them back upstairs when he went; they looked perfectly good, and there was no sense spending good money on new clothes when—

Ed-gar, Ed-gar

"Where are you?"

Edgar stared at the closed door, trying to remember the last time he had been in there. Maybe not since he was a kid, or possibly once or twice since then. There were no fond memories there— of father and son working together to build a soapbox racer or an elaborate train set with mountains and tunnels. It was as if that back corner never really existed, an even darker void within the base- ment that he disliked so much. Still, he stared at the door and felt the need to open it, to at least check. Maybe it was curiosity, or perhaps the voices had guided him back here. Either way, it was the only part of the basement he had not yet checked, and probably the most unlikely of places to find what he was searching for. With a deep sigh and an overwhelming desire to end the madness, Edgar grabbed the knob and tried to turn it. It was locked.

Ed-gar, Ed-gar

I know, but it's locked!

The exhausted part of him felt an enormous sense of relief. He had done enough; it was time to grab his shirts, go back to bed and forget about all this craziness. He had checked the basement the best he could, without going through each and every box and piece of junk, and everything was as it should be. A handful of pills, a good night's sleep and a Merry Christmas with Wilma sounded like all the medicine he needed. As he savored his reasons for calling it a night, the door before him began to speak. Unlike the buzzing nail upstairs, the new sound appeared to be coming from multiple sources. Edgar took several steps back and raised the flashlight, shin- ing it around the perimeter of the door. He watched unfazed as the screws holding the barn style door hinges unthreaded themselves. One by one they fell to the concrete floor, each with a soft *tink*.

After the last screw fell, the door jerked in the opening as the hinged side dropped to the floor. Fearful that it might tumble forward, Edgar moved quickly and put a hand on it. He held it there while considering his next move, then slid the flashlight into his pajama bottom's pocket. With both hands now on the door, he maneuvered it out of the opening. It was surprisingly light, and as he managed to slide it rather easily to the side, he couldn't help but wonder what invisible force might be assisting him.

Ed-gar, Ed-gar

With the flashlight back in hand, Edgar poked his head into the room and looked around. It was even smaller than he remembered, at most eight by ten feet. His father's workbench ran across the back wall, with boxes stacked above and below. The small window up above the workbench had the same dark green curtains as the others in the basement. Piled along both sidewalls were more boxes and various household items placed here and there. With all the boxes and junk, there was certainly no room for anything of significance to hide.

Ed-gar, Ed-gar

Starting on the left side of the room, Edgar grabbed the cardboard box closest to him and picked at the taped lid until it opened, revealing old rag dolls and dusty fabrics. With the invisible clock ticking, and no sense of what he was looking for, the delicate search became a full-blown discovery. He tossed the box aside and tore into the next one, which contained old flowerpots and gardening tools that seemed distantly familiar. He then ripped into another one.

"Ed-gar? Ed-gar?"

"Not now, hon," he whispered.

The pressure in the air changed; it felt denser. Whatever *they* were, or *it* was, it had to be somewhere nearby. Frustrated with the boxes along the side, Edgar changed his focus to the ones under the workbench. His knees creaked as he squatted down to get a better look. His back chimed in with a pain all its own; he hated being old. Putting the flashlight on the edge of the workbench, he pulled out one of the smaller boxes, noticing that the others were stacked two deep back to the wall. Holding the box in his hands, it felt lifeless and cold. Without opening it, he tossed it on the floor to his right. As it hit the concrete, something inside broke.

"Ed-gar? Ed-gar?"

"I don't know if I can do this, hon."

Sweating from his escalated metabolism, Edgar took off his robe and tossed it on top of the recently discarded box. He put his hands over his eyes and cried out softly, "I don't know what to do; please show me; this is all too much." With that request, the entire workbench began to rattle. Edgar stumbled backwards until he bumped against the wall near the doorway. Even with the unexplainable, yet harmless happenings of that evening, he still feared the possibility of things escalating and become dangerous. He listened again for the sound of footsteps above.

The rattling continued until the entire room seemed to be experiencing a moderate earthquake. Boxes move this way and that. A gap appeared between some of the ones below the workbench, drawing Edgar's attention. He shined the flashlight in that direction and noticed something else back there, in the far right corner of the room, buried behind the boxes under the workbench. He couldn't get a good view, with the poor lighting and everything moving like it was, but it seemed large. Laying the flashlight off to the side, he started grabbing at the boxes stacked in front. One by one he moved them carelessly aside. With each movement, another joint or muscle responded—crying for the madness to stop. After the clearing work was done, Edgar retrieved the flashlight and stepped back to get a better look.

Sitting in the far back corner was a huge wooden chest. Thick bands of black metal, each secured by rows of heavy rivets, wrapped around the chest and separated at the lid. On each corner were decorative pieces of metal, with more rivets securing them onto the body. On the front, attached to a thick metal clasp, hung a large metal padlock; a small tombstone shaped plate covered the keyhole. On the left side was a thick leather handle, and Edgar assumed a matching one to be adorning the right.

Ed-gar, Ed-gar

Searching his memory, Edgar found no recollection of such a chest—but he remembered nothing else in the room either. It was definitely not something that belonged to him; it must have belonged to his parents—just more of the junk they had left behind. Edgar crouched down to get a better look. With one hand securely grasping the workbench, he blindly waved his arm around until he managed to locate the strap. Wrapping his aching fingers around it, he pulled gently. There was no movement at all, not even a creak. He pulled harder, but the chest did not even budge. But at least his effort was rewarded with a piercing pain that started in his shoulder and shot down his right side. Resting his head against the edge of the workbench, letting his arm hang loosely, he waited for the pain to subside—hoping that he had not pulled his arm out of its socket. Completely unsure if the chest was even what he was looking for, Edgar remained curious enough to at least try for a closer look.

28
THE GREATEST GIFT

The next to the last day of September in the year of 1948 began pleasantly enough, with temperatures in the upper sixties. The school year was well underway and Edgar's teachers were worse than ever. But it didn't really matter, because today was his birthday, and he was finally a teenager, almost old enough to drive a car. As he lay in bed, staring at the ceiling and thinking about the day to come, another thought entered his head and shifted his mood. It had been almost a month since his grandfather had died, but the sadness refused to stay away. He found himself crying at times without warning, and would retreat to his room so nobody would see him. He pushed it away the only way he knew how—by remembering their special day at the ballpark.

He got up and made his way into the kitchen. On the table was a handwritten note from his mother saying: *Happy Birthday, Edgar!* He poked his head into the open doorway leading down into the basement. His mother was whistling over the sound of the washing machine below. He hated the basement, and would not go down there unless he had to. Not only was he afraid of spiders and other insects crawling on him, he knew that the basement was his father's domain. It stunk of cigars and reminded him of fetching beers when he was a kid. Looking out the back window, he could see the garage door open and his father moving in and out, arranging things in the driveway. It looked like he was cleaning out the garage, which meant one thing—work—birthday or not. His best option was to go to Jimmy's and hang out there, but he didn't want to miss out on breakfast. Most every day of the year it was his usual dry toast and juice, but on his birthday and special occasions his mother made him chocolate chip pancakes. And there might be presents hidden somewhere close by. He didn't want to miss out on either one, even if that meant having his father yell at him for a while for not moving fast enough or for picking something up the wrong way.

The footsteps coming up the basement stairs told him that breakfast might happen before work. His mother appeared in the kitchen with a laundry basket full of clean clothes. She put them down on the floor and gave him a happy birthday hug. Even though he was too old for such things, he still secretly liked his mother's hugs. Since his grandfather had died, he had developed a closer bond with her—as if they finally had something in common. In her kind and motherly *special day* voice, she asked him what he wanted for breakfast, like the ingredients spread out on the counter were not obvious enough. As she prepared his special meal, Edgar sat at the table and listened to her talk about the weather, the fall flowers and what was still growing in the garden. After breakfast together, she moved the dishes toward the sink and encouraged him to go out and enjoy his day. "Edgar, we'll celebrate your birthday later," she said. "I'm going to make your cake now—chocolate with chocolate fudge frosting. That's still your favorite, right?"

"Yeah!" Edgar replied.

§

Filled with more pancakes than he thought possible, Edgar headed toward the front door, anticipating Jimmy waiting for him on his own porch, probably with a present—his first of the day. Stepping out the doorway, he noticed his father standing at the corner of the house, looking toward the back yard. Frozen in his tracks, Edgar hoped he wouldn't be seen. But before he could catch it, the screen door he let go of without thinking slammed shut, alerting his father to his presence. *Crud.* They stood staring at each other, neither saying a word. His father did not look angry or upset, but there was always the chance of his mood changing at any moment, with yelling soon to follow. *Maybe he's trying to think of something I did wrong.* As his father cleared his throat and began to speak, Edgar braced himself.

"Good morning, son," he said. "And happy birthday."

Edgar's mouth fell open. He fumbled for words to use in reply to something so shocking and unexpected. All he could think to say was, "thanks, Dad."

"Hey," his father said, "I know you probably want to go play with your friends, but could you give me a hand here for a few minutes?"

Edgar couldn't remember his father ever *asking* him to do something. It was always *telling* him to do something, do it now and do it without any talking back, or else. This time it felt completely different, like the past had crumbled away at the stroke of midnight and they had moved on to some higher ground. No longer father and son, but man to man. In that moment, for the first time in ages, Edgar actually *wanted* to help his father.

"Sure, Dad, what do you need?" He hopped off the porch and followed his father around the side of the house and through the open gate. The garage door was open and most of the stuff from inside was piled in the driveway. Along the side of the house was a row of more things, including a dozen or more cardboard boxes, lamps, folding chairs and a large wooden crate with a metal padlock on the front. Each item had a small orange sticker attached to it. He didn't remember any of it, but he disliked the inside of the garage as much as the basement, and never paid much attention to what was in there.

"I decided to clean out the garage today, and try to get the car in there. I've got this stuff here by the side of the house, too, that I need to find room for. I could use a strong set of hands to help me move a few of the heavier things, and now that you're a man—"

Edgar smiled with embarrassment. "Sure," he said.

The two men worked together, carrying larger pieces of wood, old doors and car parts from the garage to the alley, where the garbage men would pick it up on Wednesday morning. They moved boxes and other smaller items down into the basement. A long piece of heavy rope was tied to one of the handles on the chest and together they lowered it down the stairs.

"That's good, Edgar," his father said as they untied the rope. "I'll take it from here. It's your birthday; you've done enough."

"Are you sure, Dad?" Edgar asked.

"Yes, you go off and play now. I can put the rest of this stuff away myself."

"Okay."

As Edgar headed back up the stairs, his father called out, "Edgar?"

"Yeah, Dad?"

"Thank you."

§

Edgar was in the best mood ever when he ran up Jimmy's front steps.

"Happy birthday!" Jimmy shouted out.

"Thanks," Edgar said as he sat down.

"What are you so buzzed about?"

"It's my birthday," Edgar replied. "Shouldn't I be happy on my birthday?"

"I guess," Jimmy said. "Here, I got you this." He picked up a poorly wrapped package and tossed it indifferently at Edgar.

"Thanks," Edgar said, turning the gift over in his hands. "I guess you're not as bad as people say you are."

"You're a real wise guy, aren't you?" Jimmy replied, and they both laughed.

After feeling the surface of the thin package, Edgar tore the wrapping paper aside, revealing copies of all the latest comics: Lone Ranger, Superman, Flash Gordon and Red Ryder.

"Whoa! I don't have any of these! Thanks, Jimmy!"

"Sure, what are friends for?"

The two boys sat on the porch all morning and read Edgar's new comics. Jimmy's mother came out with drinks and a plate of chocolate chip cookies, and wished Edgar a happy birthday. He thought of the big pancake breakfast his mother had made, but quickly decided that you could never have enough chocolate. He grabbed two cookies and said, "Thanks, Mrs. Schmidt."

"You're welcome, Edgar."

§

As noon approached, Edgar heard his name being called. He turned to see his mother walking across the lawns.

"Edgar, why don't you come home and open one of your presents? Jimmy can come, too. I made some lunch and even baked some sugar cookies."

The boys looked at each other and smiled.

Back at Edgar's house, they sat at the kitchen table and ate grilled cheese sandwiches and sugar cookies with colorful frosting. After their stomachs were full and bloated, and their heads buzzing from the sugar, Edgar's mother led them into the living room.

"Edgar, your father and I have some presents for you for later, after supper and your birthday cake, but I wanted to give you this one now."

Edgar noted a hint of sadness casting a shadow over his mother's previously cheerful face. She pulled a wrapped gift from behind the recliner and laid it in his lap. She sat in her chair, pulled a tissue from her apron and dabbed at her eyes.

"That one is from your grandfather," she said. "He really wanted to be here, to give it to you in person. You believe that, right?" She forced a smile while wiping away a tear.

"Yeah, Ma, I know." Edgar looked at the package, which was a little larger than a loaf of bread. He ran his hand across the top, feeling the texture of the paper and the weight and firmness of the box inside.

"Open the damn—" Jimmy caught himself, then tried again. "Why don't you open it, Edgar?"

Edgar nodded and proceeded to tear the wrapping paper away, revealing a brown cardboard box. Printed in large black letters was *PHILCO*, followed by *Transitone*. Underneath was *Model 48-200*. He turned the box around in his lap, to get a better look at the front, which was decorated with a black line illustration of a small radio.

"Whoa, that's a radio!" Jimmy added for confirmation. "Your very own radio!"

Edgar stared at the box; he had never received such an adult gift before.

"Your grandfather looked all over for that radio before he—" His mother paused before continuing, "He was so proud of you." She got up and hurried into the kitchen, as if something was burning on the stove.

Edgar felt her sadness, and had to resist crying himself.

Oblivious, Jimmy blurted out, "Open it already, will ya?"

"Okay, okay."

Edgar knelt down on the floor and placed the box in front of him. He slid his finger under the folded top, pried up both flaps and pulled the radio out. His mother returned to the doorway; the smile was back on her face. After removing the paper covering, Edgar laid the radio on the hardwood floor and then sat back against the sofa to get an overall look.

The radio was dark brown with a shiny finish; it looked like the frosting his mother used on his birthday cakes. The shape was rectangular, but soft and rounded at the edges. The dial was a copper color, with a bright red circle in the center, with a long point coming off the top of it and a smaller one at the bottom. To Edgar, it looked like the rings of Saturn, if you were looking at it from a slight side angle. At the bottom of the dial were the words: *PHILCO TRANSITONE*, and surrounding that were boldly printed station markers. Finishing off the front, in each lower corner, were round control knobs, one for the power and volume control and the other for tuning.

From the doorway his mother said, "Edgar, I gave you this present early because I thought you might want to listen to the *Tigers* game on it; it will be starting soon."

"I don't know," Edgar replied. It was the first time that baseball had been mentioned in the house since that night, and he felt uncomfortable talking about it. Baseball had been nothing but trouble for him, and he wasn't sure he wanted any part of it. He turned toward Jimmy and asked, "Do you want to listen to the game?"

"Naw, baseball is boring," Jimmy replied as he breathed uncomfortably. "I need to go home anyway and take my asthma medicine." He got up and headed out the door, shouting as he went, "I'll see you later…birthday boy!"

"Edgar," his mother continued. "I saw in the paper this morning that Hal Newhouser is pitching today." Then she asked again, almost urging him along, "Don't you want to listen to him pitch?"

"Maybe. I don't know." He did know though—that Hal Newhouser was pitching. He had been checking the paper when nobody was looking. The *Tigers'* record was 74-75, and with only five games left, they had no chance of playing for the championship. Regardless, Edgar was covertly excited about Hal Newhouser pitching, most likely for the last time that season.

"Why don't you set your new radio up in your room," his mother added, "and listen to the game there, where *nobody* will bother you?"

It was a good idea. An even better one would be to listen to the game on his new radio *with* his grandfather, but that was never going to happen. He picked the radio up and wondered—if this final gift represented the only connection to the game, and to his grandfather, that was meant to be. And that baseball for him was only going to be enjoyed from a distance—as words radiating safely from a small speaker.

With great care, Edgar sat the radio on his dresser and plugged the cord into the nearby outlet. He ran his hand over the smooth surface and re-examined all of the fine details. With eager anticipation, he twisted the power knob. The dial illuminated and soft static came from the lone speaker. At first he thought there was something wrong with the radio, then realized his mistake. He twisted the tuning dial, stopping each time clear sounds broke the static. Once the bright red pointer reached the 120 mark, he found what he was looking for. He kicked off his shoes and laid down on the bed. Turning onto his side, he stared at his new radio as Harry Heilmann announced Hal Newhouser's first pitch of the game. Happier than he had been in a while, Edgar closed his eyes and listened.

§

Between the third and fourth innings, Edgar wandered to the kitchen for a drink; the smell of baking chocolate filled the air. His father was off somewhere and his mother was in her sewing room. Before turning into the kitchen, he caught a glimpse of something out of the corner of his eye; a cardboard box sitting next to the front door. It was overflowing with clothes, all neatly stacked and folded—and something else. Curious, but not enough to keep him from some milk and chocolate frosting, Edgar moved into the kitchen. From the icebox he grabbed the milk bottle and proceeded to pour himself a glass. He scooped a large finger full of frosting from the mixing bowl, licked it clean and finished the milk with a single gulp. On his way back to the game, he stopped outside the sewing room door. "Hey, Ma, what's in the box by the front door?"

Without turning she said, "Oh, honey, those are just some old clothes and things we don't need. I'm giving them to the church for their rummage sale. They're coming by today to pick them up. You stay out of there."

"Okay," Edgar replied. From the opening to the living room he took one last look at the box and the spot of brown material poking out from the corner. Some unknown force kept him from moving closer, but he wasn't sure he wanted to know anyway. It didn't matter; all that stuff was safely stored in the past—where it would stay forever. Edgar turned and headed back to his room.

§

On Sunday, October 3, 1948, Edgar wandered through the quiet house. His father was working a rare Sunday shift and his mother was taking a nap. Jimmy and his parents had gone to church and then probably off to some cousin's house for the rest of the day. Edgar ended up on the front porch, sitting on the bench, leaning against the wall of the house and enjoying the cool fall breeze. It was the last day of the *Tigers* 1948 season. Sitting there, a pleasant idea floated down from wherever such things came from, inspiring him to retrieve the radio from his room. Returning to the porch, he sat it down on the bench and looked around for an electrical outlet. With nowhere to plug it in, he went inside and located an open outlet next to the big family radio. Raising the window, he reached out to grab his radio's power cord, but was quick to realize it wasn't long enough.

The need for an extension cord took Edgar to the garage. He found one in the workbench next to the window. Through the now clean glass he noticed the top edge of the wooden crate poking above the back fence. He had not been back there in some time, and was surprised that the garbage men had not taken it. Even though all that foolishness was behind him, there was something about it that remained special, and it gave him an idea. Leaving the garage with the extension cord, Edgar grabbed the crate and returned to the front porch. He sat the crate up next to the bench and placed his radio on it, then connected the electrical cords together and fed the end through the open window. He went inside to complete the connection. With the game back on, he settled himself on the porch bench, leaned back against the wall of the house and looked up and down Hawthorne Street. It really was a perfect day for listening to a baseball game. The only thing missing was the big burly figure sitting next to him. He closed his eyes as his mind returned to Briggs Stadium—the sights, the sounds, the smells. There was the game and the pitcher who stood tall in the center of everything; his hero; the card. There was the dream of that other place; the long tunnel leading to a dark sky surrounded by giant stars. There was a lingering feeling of significance to it, more than just a memory or a silly dream. He couldn't quite grasp what it meant, but perhaps one day he would.

"Edgar, are you asleep?"

Edgar opened his eyes and turned to see his mother standing in the doorway. He sat himself up straight. "Uh, no, Ma. I was just resting my eyes for a minute; that's all."

"Okay, just checking on you." She looked at the radio sitting on the crate and then to Edgar. She smiled and went back inside.

With his eyes closed again and listening to the game, Edgar heard an approaching sound. He looked out and saw Stupid Sally Morgan, laughing as she rode by on her bike, unaware of his presence. A few bike lengths behind her was that new girl from down the block, wearing a blue dress and a white sweater and laughing at something Stupid Sally had said. As she passed, the girl turned her head just slightly, like she wanted to look, but didn't want him to know she was looking. Her hair blew across her face, and through the strands Edgar could see a blue eye glancing his way. Without taking her hand off the handlebars, she wriggled her fingers and smiled. Then, as if embarrassed by what she had done, she turned away and began pedaling faster. Edgar's gaze followed her down the street until she was gone from sight. He thought for a moment about that cute girl; he thought about that other place and he thought about his *Detroit Tigers*. And for a moment all was good. Edgar closed his eyes and smiled.

29
THE CHEST

Edgar lowered himself down to the floor and, surprisingly, it was the first thing he had done that did not introduce a new pain—or perhaps there was just nothing left on his body to hurt any more than it already did. Reaching up, he grabbed the flashlight from the workbench and brought it down; the beam was weakening by the minute. Fortunately, his eyesight had adjusted to the darkness, and a bit of moonlight was coming in through the slightly open curtains above. He was not going to be reading down here, but at least he could generally see what he was doing. Reaching again for the leather strap, with his left hand this time, he took a deep breath and pulled. But the damn thing refused to budge. He stopped pulling and shined the flickering flashlight at the floor around the base of the chest. There was nothing blocking it that he could see, but something else did catch his attention. Back behind it, running up the wall was a thin green vine no thicker than a straw. *That must be a wandering root from a tree or bush near the house. Somehow it made its way through a crack in the foundation.* It was a curious thing to see, although not really worthy of Edgar's attention, all things considered. That was until it changed. Moving down the wall, *inside* the vine itself, was a bulbous protrusion. It looked like a tiny snake trying to swallow something of a larger diameter. The thing inside was pulsating, as if it were a beating heart, or had one. Edgar watched as it disappeared down behind the chest. Before he had a chance to fully absorb the phenomenon, it reappeared, only this time ascending back up the wall.

The *swallowing* appeared to be only part of it. Edgar had sensed something else as well, but thought it was just a light reflection. He aimed the flashlight away from the vine, just to be sure. That's when it became clear that his senses were right. Whatever it was, there inside the vine, it was not only beating like a heart, it was illuminating from within—with a soft greenish glow.

Ed-gar, Ed-gar

Edgar then suspected something else. Eager to confirm his suspicion, he put the flashlight down, laid his hands firmly on the floor and waited. When the next bulbous thing came down, he carefully noted the pulsations—two of them—*bum-bum, bum-bum. Ed-gar, Ed-gar.* Not only did he see it with his eyes and hear it in his head, he could also *feel* it vibrating through the concrete floor. It was all in sync—the beat, the voices, the vibration in the floor, the thing in the vine—they were somehow one in the same. Whatever it was that had been calling him these past several months, he had finally found it, and it was right there behind the chest.

"Ed-gar? Ed-gar?"

Possibilities swarmed through Edgar's mind. Whatever was back there, it was somehow connected to the vine running up the wall. The problem was, that in order to get at it, he had to get the chest out of the way first. As a younger man, he would have had the strength to pull it out, but not now. He thought to wake up Wilma and ask her to come downstairs in the middle of the night on Christmas Eve and help him pull out from underneath his father's old workbench a nearly unmovable chest, so that together they could witness the miracle that had been haunting him, and frustrating her, for months. That was not going to work; he needed another plan. But at least he now had real proof—of something tangible happening there in the house. *Look, hon, I'm not crazy. If you get down real low and look underneath, there on the wall, that little ball of light. See it moving up and down through the green vine? What other proof do I need?* Maybe he could call Tommy. But still, it was

Christmas Eve—that might be too much to ask. Aside from waiting until morning for help, or more likely after the holidays, moving the chest himself was the only solution. *If I could just twist it a little at a time, I might be able to wriggle it out. It may take some time, maybe all night, and I may not be able to stand or walk afterwards, but I have to try.*

Edgar reached forward again and grabbed the strap. Just as his fingers touched the aged leather, the chest began to buzz—much like the nail pulling itself out of the wood—but deeper and heavier. He released his hand and the vibration intensified. The metal corner pieces of the chest began to scratch against the concrete floor. Mesmerized, he watched as the chest began to rattle against the back wall. Then, as if realizing the error of its direction, it began to move itself forward, slowly, like a vibrating palm sander inadvertently left on. It crept out toward Edgar until the foremost corner was just beyond the leading edge of the workbench. There it stopped moving, yet continued to shake, like a dog reaching the end of its leash—but still trying. Sensing its need for help, Edgar grabbed the leather strap and pulled as hard as his exhausted old body would allow. His effort actually seemed to be helping, as inch by inch the rumbling chest moved until it was nearly half way out. Anxious to get a better view of the mystery behind it, he pulled himself up onto his knees and rested both forearms on the curved top of the chest, still vibrating under his weight. It was then that he finally understood what he had not even considered previously; the pulsating vine with the phosphorescent green light moving through its center was attached to the back of the chest.

Edgar pulled again. The chest, seeming to sense his enthusiasm, began vibrating more violently. As it moved further out, the vine began to break free of the wall; its tiny finger-like tentacles breaking loose of the concrete with subtle popping sounds. The pulsating light, which had been running up and down and glowing with its gentle heartbeat-like rhythm, increased to a frantic pace. Edgar felt the energy of it coming through the chest—running through his hands and up into his body. In his head, the beat increased to match. Then, with every bit of strength his tired old body had left, Edgar pulled one last time.

The chest broke free of the vine with a screeching snap. With the release of pent up energy, Edgar and the chest lunged outward a good two feet and stopped. Except for his own heavy breathing, the room had become silent and still. Picking up the flashlight, he shined it over the chest and toward the back wall. The vine, once alive with whatever unknown energy it carried, had lost its color and was shriveling up like some time-lapse photography set on fast-forward. The tentacles turned to powder and fell to the floor.

Edgar turned his attention to the chest, which was now completely out from under the workbench. Aiming the flashlight along the front of it, he saw something that caused his heart to sink once again. Hanging from a locking clasp, attached securely to both the lid and base of the chest, was that very large padlock. "Now what?" With a finger, he slid open the metal cover to reveal the keyhole. *Where could the key be?* He couldn't remember even seeing the chest before, let alone the kind of antique key the lock required.

Other ways of getting into the chest began to run through Edgar's mind. There was the unknown key, of course, wherever that might be. The hammer that Wilma used on the nail was somewhere; maybe he could find that and pound it off. There was the poker from the fireplace, and if he remembered correctly, there was an electric saw of some kind in the garage. The problem was, none of those things were nearby or reasonably easy to get to. Edgar stared at the old lock; his tired mind at a loss for any reasonable solution. As he wondered what to do, one of the many voices in his head returned and whispered a silent message—that he didn't need a key. Without even realizing what he was doing, as if controlled by something other than his own internal systems, Edgar dropped the flashlight to the floor and wrapped both of his hands lightly around the lock. As his skin made contact with the metal, the lock began to vibrate. But this time it was a distinctly different sensation—like he himself was now a conduit through which this mysterious and powerful cosmic energy flowed. A tingling sensation, like a Fourth of July sparkler, jumped from his skin to the metal lock. The energy pulled his hands in tighter until they were squeezing with great intensity—yet his muscles were making no effort of their own. As the lock pulsated within his hands, particles of dust began to fall out from the spaces between his fingers. Within his grasp he could feel the surface of the lock developing a rougher texture. More grains of metal poured out as its shape changed, becoming smaller and less distinct in form. It was getting hot, too, until eventually it felt like a handful of scorching sand. When the pain became too intense, Edgar pulled his hands free with all his might. A handful of hot metallic gravel fell to the concrete, with a piece no larger than a quarter glowing orange from the center of the pile. After blowing on his hands to cool them down, he looked up to see that the lock was gone; only the shackle was left hanging from the latch on the chest. Edgar twisted the semicircular piece of metal rod out and let it fall to the floor.

Standing up was just as hard as Edgar imagined it would be. Even though his old body was still somewhat functional, he was certain to need a hospital visit just to recuperate. The rusty hinges of the chest creaked in pain as he lifted the lid. *Now you know how I feel.* He opened it until the heavy top came to rest, held in place by two leather straps attached to the inside of the chest. Once the lid was resting securely, he shined the meager light inside. The contents were covered by a piece of heavy black fabric. He grabbed the nearest corner, pulled it impetuously aside and let it fall to the floor. The chest was packed full—and arranged in what looked like organized sections. In the front corner closest to him was a pile of old newspaper clippings, tightly wrapped in clear plastic. On the very top was a Detroit News article; the date in the upper corner was August 31, 1905. The article was about the *Detroit Tigers* rookie, *Ty Cobb*. Edgar could read the headline, but the rest of the copy was too small for his eyes to see.

Where did this come from?

Taking up almost half of the space within the chest were stacks of narrow, wooden boxes. Dozens of them. To the right, sitting on top of more different sized cardboard boxes and smaller, wrapped, odd-shaped items was a clear plastic bag. Inside was what looked like a black, leather-bound photo album. He picked it up, unwrapped the bag and removed the album. On the cover, embossed in black letters over a silver metallic plate was the name: *American Tobacco Company*. Underneath was printed: *T206* and below that: *1909-1911*. Although he could not remember such a company, there was something distantly familiar about it. He opened the album to the middle, revealing what looked like roughly 30 thick pages, each covered with a thin piece of black paper attached at the top. Edgar pulled up the cover, revealing a page of tiny baseball cards, neatly mounted into individual cutouts. Over the page was a protective layer of clear acetate. Even though they appeared very old in style, the cards themselves looked brand new, as if they had just been printed. On the front of each card was a vintage color illustration of a player. Edgar carefully folded down the black protective sheet and turned the page. The next page was the same, but he noticed that he could also see the reverse side of each card on the back of the previous page, also protected by acetate. He flipped through until he reached the last page. He paused there to read the names of the players—some of which he had never heard of before. But there was one player who caught his attention. He moved his head in until his eyes found their best focus. Printed on the front of the card was: *Wagner, Pittsburg*h. He didn't know why, but the card was trying to remind him of something. He turned the page over, hoping for a clue to jog his memory. But all that was on the back, written down several lines, was:

Sweet Caporal Cigarettes
The Standard for Years
Base Ball Series
150
Subjects

It was in that very moment that a light went on in Edgar's tired head. He whispered, "Grandpa, these must be your baseball cards." His eyes began to water as distant memories flooded into his mind. "How did these get here?" He had long forgotten about the cards his grandfather spoke of so many years before. That was a time in his life when baseball cards were sternly frowned upon, and he had long since moved on from such childish things.

He turned back to the front inside of the album. There he found a letter typed on *American Tobacco Company* stationary, dated December 18, 1911. It was from the president of the company to his grandfather, congratulating him on the outstanding work he had done on the baseball card project. He was promised a great future with the company if he could come up with more ideas like putting baseball cards into cigarette packages.

Edgar was overwhelmed, but still unclear as to what any of it meant, including this latest discovery. He closed the cover, put the album back inside the plastic bag and then sat it gently back into the chest. He shifted his attention to the wooden boxes. He grabbed one, lifted it out and shined the flashlight on it. Even with minimal light, he could tell that the box was exquisitely crafted, out of a reddish brown wood that had aged to an elegant patina. The corners were marked with zigzag looking joints. *What is that called?* After struggling with what seemed like such an irrelevant question, he remembered—dovetail joints. Edgar only knew that because Harold Watson, one of county's bus drivers from back in his working days, did woodworking on the weekends, and would sometimes bring in his projects to show around. He made a nice little jewelry box one year that Edgar bought for Wilma as a Christmas present; she still kept her knitting needles in it. Harold bragged about his dovetail joints, while Edgar wondered why he couldn't have foregone all that extra work and just glued the corners together.

On the lid of the box, printed in black over a silver colored metal plate, and perfectly centered was: *1860-1869*. Edgar flipped the tiny brass latch and opened the box. It was nearly full with more cards of different shapes and sizes. With one hand holding the box, and the flashlight tucked under his armpit, he reached in and instinctively, with the greatest possible care, pulled out a small handful of cards. He then set the box down to get a better look. They were even older looking than the ones in the album, although each one was also perfectly preserved. The cards in his hand showed unfamiliar players wearing shield-shaped adornments with stars and stripes across the front of their uniforms. Edgar went from card to card, noticing that they were arranged by player name in alphabetical order.

With the maximum care his shaking hands could manage, Edgar placed the cards back into the box and closed the cover. He returned the box to the chest and grabbed another one. It was labeled: *Extras: 1910-1920.* Like the previous box, this one was also nearly full. He pulled out a few cards and looked slowly through them, immediately recognizing several of a very young Harry Heilmann, well before his days as the *Detroit Tigers* radio broadcaster. Harry was posed with his glove outstretched, as if he were catching a ball. Further down the pile, Edgar found some cards of another player he knew very well: Babe Ruth. He stared at the card, not because of the player, but because of the unusual coloring. The card showed a young baseball player standing with his glove and looking off to the right. It was printed with a red monochromatic ink, bordered by a thick matching band. Down near the player's feet was printed: *Ruth Pitcher,* and some other words that Edgar could not read. He noticed that the corners were rounded, and like every other card he had seen, it looked as if it were brand new. Edgar turned it over to see what was printed on the back, but all he could make out was: BALTIMORE INTERNATIONAL LEAGUE and the year, *1914.* He returned the cards to the box and looked through another stack, noticing more familiar names: Ty Cobb, Eddie Plank, Joe Jackson, as well as some other players he had never heard of. In many cases, there were multiple copies of each card.

As Edgar looked through the cards, more forgotten memories began to drift forward in his mind. He remembered his small world of so long ago, holding his own cards, and the time he spent with his grandfather that one summer. He remembered the baseball game at Briggs Stadium; the only time he had ever gone to Detroit for a game—a sacred experience that could never be replicated. There were the walks to the park and his grandfather showing him the proper way to hold a baseball glove, and how to throw a curveball. Not much good that did him. He wondered again what any of it could possibly mean at this point in his life. Was he just meant to find a bunch of old baseball cards? Was this his past coming back to haunt him one last time?

Dozens more boxes filled the left half of the chest, and if each was filled like the one's he had already opened, Edgar estimated there must be close to 10,000 in total. Then, a different voice altogether whispered faintly—*9,442 and counting.* Edgar turned abruptly, but nobody was there. It spoke again—*Take good care of your things, and they will take good care of you.* It was coming back to him. Yes, he remembered that now. He did always try to take good care of his things. But there was something else, too, that his grandfather had told him. It was right at the tip of his tongue, but wouldn't come out. Unable to extract it from his memory, he chose to focus instead on what was before him. He put the cards back into the box, closed the lid and put the box back in the chest. He then noticed something else, a piece of paper sticking up at the very back. He leaned forward and pulled it out. It was not a piece of paper though, but an envelope. Written on the front in a very shaky handwriting was simply: *Edgar.* His hand trembled as he opened it. Inside was a letter, and with the fading beam of the flashlight, he read:

August 21, 1948
Dear Edgar,
*   This chest contains all of my baseball things, including my cards, all 9,547 of them. I bought some more on the drive home from Michigan! There are many very special cards here, and other baseball things I've collected over the past 60 years, and everything my father gave me. Many are things that only I have. Now, nobody else will ever care, but I hope that you might enjoy all of this as much as I have. Collecting these little baseball treasures has been one of the great joys in my life, and I*

hope you will cherish them as I have.

The doctors told me this week that my body will not last much longer. They believe that I may not make it until Christmas. But I will try, for you. I was going to give you these cards in person, and if God wills it, I will. In case I can't, I've decided to write you this letter.

How many cards do you have now? With these, you will have quite a collection! Don't forget to take good care of them. Keep them someplace safe and special, and remember that if you take good care of your things, they will take good care of you. Also remember that there is no substitute for the real deal. You are going to be a great pitcher, Edgar. I can see it in you. I only wish that I could be there to see you grow up—and pitch in the big leagues. If there is some magic to make that happen, I hope that together we find it.

So never give up on your dreams, Edgar, and they will never give up on you.

Love, Grandpa

P.S. Here is a little something I thought you might like to have back!

Looking in the envelope again, Edgar saw something else; a small item that he had overlooked before. He reached in and pulled it out, then stared with awe—his mind struggling to grasp the magnitude of it—what it might mean—both now and long ago. *How is this possible?* It was his card—his Hal Newhouser baseball card. On the top surface were scribbled lines made by a stubby yellow pencil many years before. *Is this what I was meant to find? But why? I'm just an old man. I've missed my chance to enjoy it, and my only dream now is to make it back up the stairs.*

Holding the card in his hand, Edgar looked around. He was exhausted, and couldn't possibly go through another box. There would be time for that later, after Christmas, if he made it that long. Then he could spend all the time in the world browsing through old baseball cards and newspaper clippings. But still, there were unanswered questions burning in his mind. *Why was I drawn here? Just to look at a bunch of old stuff that had been left and forgotten long ago? Why now?* As he contemplated that, an even bigger question surfaced—*who* or *what* had been calling him? The most illogical answer seemed to be his grandfather, but Edgar was incapable at that point of even contemplating such an egregious theory.

The flashlight was nearly depleted, but Edgar knew that he could at least feel his way back to the stairs. Getting up them was another issue. He slid the baseball card gently into his pajama top pocket and shuffled himself toward the doorway, keeping his arms outstretched in front of him, hoping desperately not to fall. If he did, then only the paramedics could save him. Even though he was glad to be on his way out, there was still something missing; this adventure felt incomplete. He noticed that the voices were still around, too, like fans waiting restlessly on the edge of their seats, for the big hit that wins the game and changes the teams destiny. *What do you want?* At that moment, the beat returned so forcefully that it seemed to shake the entire house.

Ed-Gar! Ed-gar!

Edgar exhaled in frustration. Behind him came the additional sound of something moving, like the rustling of paper in the wind. "What the hell?" he pleaded, before deciding on a more divine approach. "Dear Lord, give me the strength to finish this once and for all. I beg of you. Please. I don't know why this is happening, and I'm very tired. Let this be over with."

"Ed-Gar? Ed-gar?"

Ignoring the call, Edgar turned back to face the chest, resting his back against the doorframe. The rustling sound returned. Pressing himself away from the doorway, he moved with sliding feet that he no longer had the strength to lift. With the trickling light he noticed an item in the chest, something he had missed before. It was tucked in the back right corner, a small bundle wrapped in newspaper. It expanded in and out softly, as if the something within were alive and breathing. Bending his knees with great care, his flashlight hand holding onto the open lid, Edgar retrieved the bundle. Pieces of dried out vine, mixed within the layers of paper, began falling to the floor. He tore the layers away until the object became visible.

"What the—"

Edgar struggled to comprehend what he was witnessing. *How could this be?* But there was no answer, no hint or even a clue. *It's not possible.* Yet there it was. *I thought this was gone, too, like the card.* But it was not gone; it was right there. In his trembling hands was his old baseball glove and just slightly used baseball, the one he had not seen in over sixty years. *Where did this come from? How did it get here?* The astonishment of the moment was overwhelming. Here he was, an old man, alone in his basement on Christmas Eve, holding what was once, so briefly, his most cherished possessions. *What does this mean? The past is the past. It's gone, so why torture me with this now?*

There were no answers to any of Edgar's pleas for clarity, at least not in words he could understand. Instead, the ball and glove began vibrating, sending a tingling sensation into his hands, up his arms and over the surface of his entire body. It felt like a low-voltage electrical current, familiar yet still disconcerting. He stabilized himself, with one hand grasping firmly onto the top edge of the open trunk, and lowered his eyelids. A barrage of images began to fire in rapid succession across his inner vision: his childhood friend Jimmy, his mother's flowers, his father's words, the park, the rocky mound where he once stood, his baseball cards, his grandfather, standing there at the edge of the dirt and the grass, looking up into the illuminated sky—

The images stopped abruptly, leaving Edgar's mind and the world around him in a peaceful, quiet calm. Even the ringing in his ears was gone. He opened his eyes cautiously and looked around. His awareness shifted to the old chest sitting before him, and then to the baseball glove and ball still held in his hand. He looked long-ingly at the glove and got an idea. He took his right hand and tried to press it into the opening, but his hand was too big—and he remembered—it was a child's glove. Instead of frustration, Edgar sunk deeper into the calmness. His mind began to expand into a greater awareness. The glove was more than simply a precious gift. It once represented a dream, a possibility that he himself could never quite comprehend, yet his grandfather did. His grandfather did not see the 12-year old boy as unextraordinary, but rather quite the opposite. He saw him not from where he was at the time, but from a place and time far in the future, where even the most inconceivable of possibilities exist as pure truths.

Looking from the glove in his hand to the chest and then back, Edgar began to feel his own truth coming forward. He heard his grandfather's words, and felt his warm, loving presence beside him. The answers he needed were gathering, moving closer together like particles forming into matter. He remembered the promises he had made so long ago—both of them—to take good care of his things and to never give up. He did take good care of his things, but it was actually the other one he thought about more deeply. And the truth was, he had never given up on that one either. Even as circumstances took away his hope and time stole his youth, he held on. The countless times he sat on his porch, "resting his eyes" as he had so often claimed, he was in fact standing there at the edge of the dirt and the grass, under the giant stars, waiting for the magic to arrive—to allow him to take that next step toward his mound—and his dream.

As these newfound thoughts swirled around in his consciousness, Edgar began to see the answers—those that somehow existed as possibilities all along, at least since that night on the porch. He realized that this whole experience was not a curse after all, but some form of divine intervention—a gift. As he looked at his childhood baseball glove and ball, and then to the chest before him, filled with his grandfather's things, he finally understood. Somewhere within those innumerable voices was a sacred offering—a choice—not between life and death, but something far more unimaginable.

§

It was not from his mind that the choice came, but from deep within his soul—where it had been waiting all along. Edgar reached forward and grabbed the lid of the chest, and very gently he closed it. As he let his hand rest on the warm surface of the wood, he said softly, "Take good care of your things, and they will take good care of you." He thought of Wilma as fresh tears rolled down his cheeks— not from pain or sadness or even regret, but of love and eternal gratitude. Edgar then took his right hand and pressed it gently and without resistance—all the way into the opening of the glove.

"Never give up on your dream," he said, "and it will never give up on you."

§

"Ed-gar? Ed-gar?"

Edgar heard his name being called back up into a world he was not quite done with, and he was eager to return there and tell her about his dream. He turned away from the old wooden chest and the 9,547 baseball cards and took a few slow, deliberate steps. A feeling of renewal and strength surged through his body. He accelerated through the doorway, into the laundry area and past the washing machine and dryer. Something on the floor was in his way and he leaped over it. Through the next doorway he found the stairs and, in nearly a full run, leaped forward in the darkness and landed on the first thread. He continued up the stairs two at a time, not bothering with the handrail. He could see the faint outline of the door above, and knew that there was not one but many bright lights just beyond. Pushing his way upward, with a smile on his face, Edgar reached for the doorknob.

30
A NEW BEGINNING

Edgar burst out through the basement door, causing it to slam hard against the kitchen wall. His momentum carried him dangerously forward toward the back door, and within a split second his shoes were squealing on the checkered *Linoleum*. With the window directly in front of him, he closed his eyes, raised his hands and braced for impact. He came to an abrupt stop with his gloved hand firmly planted on the doorframe and his forehead thumping gently on the glass. After pausing for a moment of relief, to ensure that he was generally unharmed, Edgar opened his eyes.

As he stared out through the open curtains and to the backyard beyond, he was overcome by a sudden inner knowing that something was different. He looked down at his glove and the clean white baseball, then back out the window. The brightness of the day was overwhelming, and his squinting eyes struggled to adjust. Even that, the daylight itself, seemed somehow unexpected. He gazed around the back yard, hoping to identify what was out of place. The tops of the foliating trees swayed gently while the blue sky overhead showed not a sign of clouds. Scattered throughout the small back yard were patches of flowers blooming with new life, and as far as Edgar could tell, everything looked as it should—only covered with an unexplainable layer of newness.

Lowering his arms from the door and taking a step back, Edgar rubbed his forehead, feeling for a bruise. He noticed a mild tingling sensation starting in his head, moving down his arms and spiraling around his body. *That must be from hitting my head on the window.* Convinced that he was not seriously harmed, he turned and looked into the kitchen. Not sure exactly what he had expected to see, the scene before him also felt surprisingly out of place. *Is there something missing, or something new here?* The kitchen was filled with daylight from the open window over the sink, and a humid breeze caused the curtains to breathe with a gentle in and out motion. The sun poked through the trees out back, causing long abstract forms of light to sweep across the floor and rise up the opposite wall in a vibrant yellow glow. The warmth of the day and the smell of flowers and summer grass delighted his senses more than he would have expected. As crazy as it seemed, everything was right and wrong— all mixed together.

On the small kitchen table was the daily newspaper with the sports section placed on top. The headline read: *TIGERS CON-TINUE TO STRUGGLE.* A box of *Wheaties*, an empty cereal bowl, a banana and a glass of milk sat next to it. Standing at the sink, arranging a bouquet of brightly colored flowers in a tall glass vase, was his mother. She was wearing her favorite apron—the white one with ruffled trim and printed with a pattern of yellow daisies. The tops of her flowers were poking up from the planter box just outside the window. She turned and looked at him with a face that was stern yet loving and said, "Edgar, I've been calling you for ten minutes. Did you not hear me? Your breakfast is there, so please sit down and eat." Without waiting for a reply, as if *she* felt nothing unusual at all, his mother turned away and proceeded to trim the stem of a flower. Edgar stared at her silently. It was not just the outdoors and the kitchen that were different; it was his mother, too. It was like the summer he went away to camp for a week. When he returned home, everything looked the same, yet it felt different, as if he were gone too long and the house and his family were no longer his. It had something to do with time, and it came to him that eventually it all felt right again. He wanted to ask her about what he was feeling, but something told him not to, that she might explain it in a way that he wouldn't understand. Or worse yet, her explanation might cause the wonder of it to fade into a truth that was somehow less special.

Edgar's gaze drifted back toward his mother. *Is she wearing something new today? Did she change her hair?* His father taught him to always notice what was different about a woman, and compliment her on that. But he couldn't find the answer. It was like an amazing dream that had slipped away, and the good part you really wanted to remember was forever out of reach.

Within the strangeness was also a feeling of loss, like something important was missing. Edgar thought harder, but that something failed to present itself. He shook his head and replied to his mother in barely a whisper, "I can't right now, Wil...um...Ma." *What was that?* She didn't respond. He continued to stare as a contemplative frown distorted his face. *Maybe I'm just hungry. Should I eat something?* He wasn't sure why, but it felt like there just wasn't enough time; there was something else he had to do that was infinitely more important. With that Edgar added softly, more to himself than to her, "I've gotta go, Ma. I really gotta go."

While his mother remained absorbed in her work, and humming to the piano music coming from the other room, Edgar's legs started moving. He took a few cautious steps while watching her curiously, and then turned and shot across the kitchen, through the living room and toward the front door. The family radio was sitting next to the front window and, as if he had remembered something from long ago rather than what he should have just known, he recalled his mother's love of the piano. It felt like just moments before he would not have known that, but the next instant he did. His baseball cap was hanging on one of the hooks next to the front door. He grabbed it and slid it onto his head. As he glanced around the living room, his mother's voice called out again, "Edgar, you really should eat before you go out to play. You'll get hungry."

Edgar pushed open the metal screen door, causing its spring to extend to full tension. As he stepped through the doorway and onto the porch, a fleeting glimpse of something appeared out of the corner of his eye—a shadow by the front window. Startled, he stopped at the edge of the steps and turned to look. But the porch was empty—except for the wooden bench warming in the morning sun. *Just my imagination.* He shook it off, turned and hopped down the front steps. He continued out toward the street, stopping again near the end of their sidewalk. The strangeness was there, too, like the exhaust from his father's car when there was no wind to blow it away. The car was not in the driveway though; his father must have been at work. He thought about that. Was his father at work? Yes, of course he was; he was always working during the day—wasn't he?

Looking up and down Hawthorne Street, it seemed to Edgar that everything outside was also inexplicably different, newer than he might have expected. Painted with colors that were bright and vivid, the scene before him appeared more intensely alive than he had the words to describe. It felt as if he were stepping into *Oz* for the first time. The small trees lining the street blew gently in the wind; their limbs young and strong. Lying in the grass near the street was his blue *Schwinn*. It was the same bike he had been riding for years, but at the same time he wondered if he remembered how to ride it. It seemed to have a story as well. He waited for it to be told, but unsure who would narrate it.

Turning and looking back at the house, a small part of him hoped that his mother would be there in the doorway, and she would tell him what was going on, that it was just a harmless prank. All that stood before him though was the house. It was not something he had paid much attention to before, but like everything else that morning, he felt like it was trying to show him something. The dark green paint and beige trim looked like it was new. But why would he even think that? The house was not old, was it? The bushes along the front were neatly trimmed and some of his mother's spring flowers were coming up. The bench there on the porch was where the family listened to the *Detroit Tigers* games, with the radio sitting just inside the house, blaring out through the open window. He wondered if his team was playing that afternoon. Would Hal Newhouser be pitching? It seemed so unlike him to forget, but if so, that's where he would be—sitting under the sun, taking in every pitch.

Without warning, a windless chill came over him; the warmth of the summer sun pulling away like a comfortable blanket on a chilly fall night. Edgar shivered as goose bumps appeared on his arms and down his spine. Along with the unexpected rush of cold, his vision blurred and strangely separated before him—like two movies playing on the screen at the same time. The colorful scene he was watching began to fade, corrupted by something unknown in the background. As the sky above began to darken into night, he wanted to move back toward the safety of the house, but his body refused. The image of the house began to change before his very eyes. The forest green paint started to lose its hue, fading into a chalky gray. Spots of paint bubbled and peeled away from the wood. It looked like when his father used something called a heat gun to strip paint from the running boards on the old Model A. Other parts curled into small slivers, revealing layers of age underneath. Pieces dried and fell to the ground while his mother's flowers shrived away. The bushes twisted into a homogeneous mess as weeds crept out of the freshly cut lawn.

Shifting forward into view, the porch became covered with something—a screen with a door—and a roof overhead that looked like metal. When Edgar focused on it, it was mostly there and solid, but when he relaxed his eyes it appeared translucent. As he observed the house with nervous fascination, something even more shocking appeared, causing him to rub his eyes in disbelief. Sitting in the soft glow of the now lit porch was an old man—looking out at him. Unable to comprehend exactly what he was witnessing, Edgar called out, "Grandpa?" But no, it wasn't his grandfather; he was certain of that. They were not scheduled to arrive for another week. He did seem vaguely familiar though, perhaps part of the family in some mysterious way. As Edgar looked toward the old man, a sense of uneasiness grew within him. In his mind there appeared the image of a prison, but one without bars. The cell was not a cinder block rectangle with a bed and a cold metal toilet; it was a lonely porch.

As quickly as it all appeared, the world around Edgar began to transform back into what it was before. Daylight reappeared as the neglected weeds and overgrown shrubs morphed back into a lush spring landscape. The deep green hues of the house began to reappear, permeating out through the lifeless gray. The decrepit porch with the strangely familiar, yet unsettling old man, faded. Edgar rubbed his eyes again, wondering how he could imagine such a thing. Except for a lingering sensation that the old man was still present in some way, everything else had returned to normal—except for one other thing. He held his arms out and looked curiously from one to the other. There were fine drops of water covering them both, as well as his glove and shirt. Not soaking wet, like he had just gotten out of a bath, but as if he were playing in a light rain. *Am I sweating? Did it rain while I was standing here?* He looked up, but the sky was clear as day. On the sidewalk around him, a small wet spot had formed. He moved a foot aside; it was dry underneath. "Huh." Edgar shook his arms and then wiped them one by one across his shirt. *This should dry up quickly.*

Considering the strangeness of the morning, Edgar thought again of going back inside and telling his mother. But what would she say? "Oh, you're just daydreaming, Edgar. That's what boys do." Maybe she was right. But even with everything that had happened that morning, the day still seemed indescribably special, like the first day of summer break after a school year that went on forever. And whatever was happening, it felt important, and he didn't want to waste a minute of it.

Edgar dropped his glove and ball into the grass and patted down his front, hoping to find some bubble gum. He located two sticks in a pocket of his shorts and fed them into his mouth. As he began to chew, that other thing he had felt piqued his curiosity. He reached into his shirt pocket and pulled out something else—a baseball card. He stared at the front, and then turned it over and observed the back. *Where did this come from?* According to the markings on the back, it was the most current 1948 Hal Newhouser card, and on the front it looked like someone had scribbled something in pencil. But strangely, the card was not bold and colorful like a new card should be, but dull and faded, like the way the house looked just moments before. Unlike the house though, which seemed to change from new to old and then back again, the card looked old and new at the same time. And even though he had no idea where it came from, there was something vaguely familiar about the card. It felt like it had been his for a very long time—but that was not possible.

With game-time approaching, Edgar lost interest in the card and slid it gently back into his pocket. It was not the one he wanted anyway; there was only one card that mattered, the one he had always dreamed about, the one with his own picture on it. But that one was going to take some time to get. He looked down at his bike, lying motionless in the grass, and the baseball card stuck to the clothespin attached to the rear frame, one of the old ones that Jimmy had given him. He knelt down for a closer look. The old black and white card was tattered from slapping against his wheel spokes. Gazing at it, a curious feeling came over him, a sensation that seemed both foreign and new. For some unimaginable reason, he felt bad about the card. He questioned why it was there, being damaged that way, instead of properly cared for. He felt ashamed for not taking better care of it, but didn't know why. He squeezed the end of the clothespin and removed the card. Holding it gently by the edges, he slid it into his shirt pocket next to the mysterious Hal Newhouser card. He then gave the wheel a spin and, hearing only the sound of greased bearings, he thought that sounded just right.

Edgar gathered his glove and ball and stood up, then took one last look at his bike. Later, after the game, he would take it out for a ride, maybe over to *Jake's* for a *7-UP*. But first he had a game to pitch, and there was no more time to waste. He preferred to run to the park; it made him feel alive as the blood moved through his body, down into his legs, making them stronger. It was important for pitchers to have a strong foundation. He looked across the yards and noticed Jimmy sitting on his porch by himself, no doubt reading one of his comic books. There was a feeling about his friend sitting there alone that made him sad, like something familiar and comfortable was about to change. A part of him wanted to walk over there and sit with his friend, read comics and laugh together, but he felt as if he had done that already. He looked the other way, toward the alley leading to the ball field, and then back toward his house. The sensation of the old man was fading, and he didn't know whether to feel happy or sad. He took a few slow, hesitant steps, as if there were still a choice to be made—or maybe it was just a final pause before letting go and accepting what now was.

Edgar then took off across Hawthorne Street and turned left in the direction of the alley. His feet felt light, like he could fly. As he ran, he tossed the ball into his glove and listened to it pop. Up ahead was Stupid Sally Morgan walking with that new girl from down the street. *What's her name?* He heard Stupid Sally calling after her one day when they were riding their bikes by the house, but he couldn't remember. Martha maybe. He forced his attention back to the big game that had already started in his mind. "Edgar Howard pitching to Ted Williams. Howard winds and pitches; the curveball comes in high and then drops out of the air and across the plate. Strike three! That ball was unhittable! The rookie Howard has just struck out the great Ted Williams! Take that Williams! The crowd goes wild! Rah, rah, rah!"

A translucent pink bubble appeared from Edgar's mouth. It grew to an enormous size before disappearing with a pop and a slurp. He was starting to feel good again, great in fact. It was turning into the most perfect day. The temperature was rising and the bright sun would soon be giving his outfielders fits. The water had already burned off his arms and would return later as sweat. Coming up quickly to Stupid Sally and the new girl, who were walking slowly away from him and fiddling with their hair and giggling like silly girls do, Edgar found himself distracted from his inner game, his eyes wandering toward the new girl's dress. He had never seen a girl in a dress like that, just walking down the street. That was something they wore on Sundays at church. It was pale yellow with a pattern of green vines intertwined with pink and violet flowers. She had a matching ribbon tied in her hair and there was something about the way she walked—the way her arms moved at her sides.

As Edgar came upon the opening to the alley, the girl in the flowered dress, who was laughing and didn't hear him coming, stepped abruptly to her left and directly into his path. He jumped sideways to avoid her, and almost made it. Instead, he caught her shoulder with his, spinning her around and knocking her into the grass by the road. She let out a faint, squealing moan as she went down and a dull thump as she landed. His own legs got twisted around and he almost fell as well. Before he could stop it, the baseball fell out of his glove and rolled next to her in the grass.

Stupid Sally was already screaming before Edgar was able to turn back toward the new girl; call her a stupid fathead for not watching where she was going. But he stopped himself before the words crossed his lips. It was the first time he had seen her up close like that, and he was caught off guard by how pretty she was. He immediately noticed her eyes—vibrant blue—as if they were mirrors reflecting the cloudless sky. And there was something unmistakably familiar about them, as if he had met her before. *Maybe she just looks like someone I used to know.* Whatever it was, Edgar figured that if it were important enough it would come to him later, maybe after the game.

A far off sound caught Edgar's attention. In the distance, beyond the reaches of the alley, the baseball field was coming to life. The boys were warming up for a new game, like they always did at that time of the day. He could see the empty pitcher's mound, and a smile came over his face. He looked down at the ball lying in the grass and then to the pretty girl in the yellow flowered dress and wondered what he should do. Silent suggestions filled his head. His mother's voice appeared, telling him that the proper thing to do would be to help her up and make sure she was not hurt, maybe even walk her home; that's what a gentleman would do. Another voice appeared, deep and eternally wise. It seemed to be coming from a different place, much further away. But that was not right either. It felt like it was from some time away. In that moment Edgar sensed that the urgency he'd been feeling all morning might be coming from that very same place. The voice told him that she would be fine, that he had other things to do that day.

Between the new girl in the flowered dress and the bright white baseball stood Edgar. His eyes shifted from the girl to the ball. It was a decision so simple—yet also filled with feelings and consequences too complex for his young mind to comprehend. With an unexplainable sense of melancholy, he bent down and scooped up his ball, then stood up straight. Turning toward the alley and the baseball field in the distance, he rolled his thumb across the stitching of the ball and thought of how much he loved the feel; how he loved everything about baseball: the smells, the sounds, the laughter, the close plays and even the arguments. There was pain and intensity and competition as well, and it was all really good. He was not great—yet. Still, he was only 12 going on 13—but certain beyond a doubt that nothing could keep his dream from coming true.

Edgar looked back across his shoulder and over that strangely familiar face. Stupid Sally was still grumbling, but her voice was in another world. Edgar wasn't hearing it, and neither was the pretty girl lying in the summer grass. As their eyes met again and held softly in a tender moment that was far beyond their years, he whispered that he was sorry. She responded with a kind look of knowing, but didn't say a word; she didn't have to. Within that sweet smile and sparkling blue eyes was a simple message that said he had done right by her, and with that it was now okay for him to go.

Edgar took off his cap. With the inside of his elbow he brushed his mangy hair back over his head, turned toward the alley and the field in the distance and started walking. After a few steps he broke into a slow jog—his strides becoming longer and faster. Under his tattered shorts the muscles in his legs flexed as he ran. They were still thin, but lean and beginning to show signs of muscularity, and anyone who noticed might say he had the look of a budding young athlete. A couple of the boys at the park saw him coming down the alley and started waving. It was Charlie Moore who first began shouting, "Ed-gar! Ed-gar!" More boys turned to look, and they joined in, too. "Ed-gar! Ed-gar!" Pretty soon they were all doing it. And then, like an answer to a question that he no longer remembered, Edgar realized something. They were never just talking to him, or even calling. No, they were *chanting for* him. That was different than being called—better in almost every way. It was being called, but also wanted and validated and acknowledged all at once; it hinted at the potential for greatness.

Approaching quickly, Edgar thought about them waiting for him out there in the field. *How long have they been there?* That was a silly question, of course, but it made him feel deeper. He didn't know the answer, and even though it was the morning of a new day, he was somehow certain that they had been waiting for him since long before the sun rose above the horizon and wiped the dew from each blade of grass. It made no sense, yet Edgar had somehow entered a mysterious new world when he stepped through that doorway earlier, where the ways of the old were now powerless against the magic of this new place. He thought again of his friends, but no longer concerning himself with how long they had waited—only grateful that they had.

In his ears their words called, but on that particularly odd morning it was more than that. He felt something deeper than mere voices coming from out there in the vast field of green, that wonderful place where dreams blossom into life like his mother's flowers in the spring. Lowering his eyes, Edgar felt the rhythm of his strides and the sound of their voices—and that other thing. It was more of a deep, rhythmic beat—a vibration—moving through his body, up and down like it was searching within—for something he couldn't quite grasp. He realized that it had been with him all morning, at least since coming up from the basement. *What was I doing down there anyway?* He couldn't say for certain, but there was a knowing that it had been with him even longer than that, and maybe he would remember in time. But perhaps in time it would no longer matter. In a way it had a life of its own, and was somehow beyond that kind of measure. His heart was beating faster, too. Not from running, but as if it were trying to reach out and match the frequency of the other. In that moment the strange vibration dropped down through Edgar's throat, causing him to gasp and almost swallow his gum. He raised his empty hand to his chest and felt both vibrations there at once—two dancers coming together and merging into the synchronistic rhythm of a single heartbeat. And then they were one.

"Ed-gar! Ed-gar!"

Edgar gleaned an innocent, child-like smile, the way boys do when they are playing baseball with their friends during the heat of summer, and the future is but an eternity away and hardly a thought, yet all things remain possible through dreams that refuse to die. He continued across the street and leaped over the curb, pausing unexpectedly at the edge of the grass. Just ahead was his pitcher's mound, that magical spot where destiny had lovingly placed him. The sounds from all around swelled in intensity, escalating from the voices of a few good friends to the chants of many thousands—commanding a singularly powerful beat that vibrated to his very core. It felt right, like it was always meant to be. He gazed at the line between the dirt and the grass, and then up. He saw not a blue summer day, but imagined a deep indigo sky, surrounded by hundreds of giant stars beaming down upon him. With a fresh heart filled with joy, and a young mind overflowing with intensity and purpose, Edgar stepped onto the grass and continued toward his mound. With each stride he was forgetting the strangeness of the day, and very soon that other part of him would be no more than a faded memory, gone forever, and he would simply become lost in his love of the game.

EPILOGUE

The auction took place that following spring in New York City, amongst the blossoming flowers and a brand new season of hope. During the months leading up to the event, word had spread rapidly, making it the talk of the sports collectibles world. For two weeks prior, thousands of visitors waited in endlessly long lines and paid eagerly, simply to view the collection defined by the media and experts in the field as utterly incomprehensible.

Two grand ballrooms were required at one of the city's most luxurious hotels, one to stage the enormous collection, and another for the auction itself. More than 3,000 bidders from 28 countries registered and attended, while hundreds bid via phone. *ESPN* was on-hand to broadcast, giving millions more around the globe the opportunity to witness the unprecedented and historic event.

The auction consisted of exactly 9,547 baseball cards, and hundreds of other never before seen artifacts dating back to the earliest days of the sport. Bidding was frantic as professional athletes, celebrities, and the top collectors and investors from around the world competed for a chance to own the rarest and most exotic baseball treasures known to exist; every item in the most exquisite condition.

It took four days to complete the auction. When the final gavel struck on that Sunday evening, every item pulled from the basement of the small house on Hawthorne Street, including the now legendary chest, had found new homes. The centerpiece of the auction was a black leather album, and a letter demonstrating its uniqueness and authenticity. Among the hundreds of cards mounted within, it included the finest ever example of the world's rarest and most famous of all baseball cards, featuring the image of Pittsburgh Pirates shortstop Honus Wagner, produced by the American Tobacco Company of Durham, North Carolina. The album commanded a final bid well into seven figures, making it the single most valuable sports collectible ever recorded.

Once the lights were dimmed and the chairs stacked and put away, and all of the proud new owners returning to their homes, the receipts were tallied. In total, the proceeds from the auction came in at just shy of two hundred and fifty million dollars.

Take good care of your things, and they will take good care of you.

Discovering the Chest

The chest as it was discovered in the Howard's basement

Shown here is the leather album containing the *American Tobacco Company* T206 collection, and the letter from J.B. Duke to Edgar Howard's grandfather.

This photo shows the contents of one of the dozens of boxes containing baseball cards. Also shown is the score book for the game between the *Detroit Tigers* and *Cleveland Indians*, held on July 1, 1948.

For more photos and videos, go to:

rogerhardnock.com/love-of-the-game

Acknowledgments

To my dear friends and family. I am grateful for your endless stream of support and encouragement, and for all the times you had to listen to me say "It's almost done." And never once was there an eye roll—at least not to my face. To Tom and Ruth Banasiak, for letting a stranger into your home that day, and for your patience and good humor as he made a mess of everything.

To my beta readers: Raffi Minasian, Susan Young, Michael Smith, Tom Schuler, Cat Skinner and Tom Wilkes. I am grateful for the precious time you gave, and for your perceptive observations and honest, thoughtful comments. This work is infinitely better for it.

A Note to the Reader

I sincerely hope that you enjoyed reading *Love of the Game*. Writing this book was a labor of love, and nothing would please me more than knowing it was enjoyed by you—the reader. And if you did enjoy *Love of the Game*, please share the story with others and consider posting a reader review online. For there is no better way to acknowledge and support a debut author, and encourage future work. Thank you in advance.

Please visit me online at:
rogerhardnock.com/love-of-the-game
on Facebook as **RogerHardnock-Author**
on Twitter **@rogerhardnock**

Photo by Emilie Hardnock

About the Author

Roger Hardnock was born in sunny Southern California, but lived most of his childhood in the small town of Wayne, Michigan. There he spent his summers listening to the Detroit Tigers games on his radio, riding his bike, collecting baseball cards and playing baseball in a tattered old field. When not writing or editing, he spends his time taking good care of his things, pursuing his many creative endeavors, or simply contemplating the ongoing existence of life.